Happiness

dhtreichler

Dedication:

To all those who risked or gave their lives to keep as many of us save
and healthy as possible during the COVID-19 Global Pandemic. And to
the researchers developing a vaccine to keep us that way.

Chapter One: Jazmin Braveheart

Phoebe gives me a look. I've seen it a hundred times, if not more. Her big green eyes squint just a little. Her long lashes slowly move up and down, to accommodate her blinks. She seems to be trying to guess why I would make such an absurd comment. Her dimple becomes more pronounced and her lips part, but barely. I can tell she wants to say something; probably thinks I'll not be happy if she does. Phoebe wraps strands of her long auburn hair around her left index finger. *I've seen it before. Seems to be an unconscious habit she resorts to when nervous about something.* I'm just about to ask when she frowns. She slightly turns to glance over her shoulder, apparently hearing something. I can't see what she's looking at. *Why not? I should be able to.*

The frown is gone as she looks back toward me, and now I have to ask, "What?"

"Thought I heard someone," she answers with a slight sing song lilt she gives to every conversation. I don't know if it's because she lives in Scotland, but that's just how she talks. It may also explain why she seems to dress in dark hues. Frequently a white blouse, but never anything bright or complex. Her long hair always stands out and looks good against the white backdrop. I wish my mousy brown hair looked as good.

"You expecting someone?" I realize I might be keeping her from someone else she wants to talk with. "I can come back on later."

Phoebe shakes her head. I watch her long hair shimmering with a sheen I've never achieved. Phoebe's hair is the natural color. But my mother, Ophelia, has told me over and over no two people are alike. What's good for one may not be appropriate for the other. So I decide to test the theory.

"Do you think I should change my hair color?"

1

Phoebe puzzles on my question for only a moment, "Why would you want to?"

"Thinking I might need a change," I respond with the only explanation I can give, not wanting her to think I might be jealous of her hair.

Phoebe looks at me, studies my shoulder length stringy brown mop, my pale complexion and thin frame. I've had all the surgeries to change my appearance and now I've moved into the attractive category. At least the doctors have told me I have. They should know since they do the surgeries for everyone. Those who have the most money get into the top category and the rest of us… well, we move up. Kind of like going to college. Those with the most money or power or influence get into the elite schools. And everyone else? Well, they get into a school somewhere.

"Have you tried the alternatives app?" Phoebe finally responds.

"The one displaying me with any hair style or color I want?" I think I know what she's talking about.

"Here, let's try it." Phoebe responds and in only a moment the wall screen before me changes so I'm looking at me. Phoebe has moved up into the right-hand corner. I still see her fine because the screen covers the whole wall before me. I'm actually larger than real life just as she has been until now. Phoebe gestures at her screen. In only a moment I'm looking at myself as a blonde. Same hair style, just different color.

"Not sure I look good as a blonde, my skin color's too pale, I think," I respond without really giving it much thought.

The next thing I know Phoebe has given me a facial tan. I have to admit I do look a whole lot better. "More than one way to approach your appearance."

"What about black? I've always wondered about being 'raven-haired', it seems to be a favorite of some of the top actresses."

2

"With a deep sheen?" Phoebe asks as my hair color changes and skin color returns to natural.

"I like that," I admit, turning so the image before does as well. I want to see what it looks like in the back. I can't see by turning. But Phoebe must be reading my mind as the image of me spins slowly around so I get the whole 360-degree effect.

"You need to fill out a bit to really look your best," Phoebe notes.

I shake my head, "I'm cocooned."

Phoebe knows what I'm talking about since we've talked about it before. In a cocoon, I have a prescribed diet maximizing health benefits and maintaining a weight theoretically increasing my lifespan. I spend an hour every day with my virtual trainer, Gloria. She makes sure I exercise for strength and stamina, even though I only participate in virtual sports in the cocoon gym. Gloria assures me if I ever ran a race or participated in an actual game or match I'd perform just as I do virtually, but I've never been able to reconcile how in my own mind. Somehow I just don't think virtual sports are as taxing on the body as the real things appear to be.

"You need to talk to someone," Phoebe responds. "You're too thin. Do something about your boobs, at least."

Phoebe is the perfect shape. No wonder she has more boyfriends than girlfriends. Most of her girlfriends live somewhere other than Scotland, from what I can tell. "Ophelia said no to an implant, so I don't see a change until I'm on my own."

"What's your mother's concern?" Phoebe seems truly surprised. "Implants have been regarded as a safe procedure forever."

"She doesn't like the idea of an inert substance in my body. All the surgeries I went through just basically rearranged existing tissue. She points out a breast implant is not natural. I understand her argument but I don't agree with it."

"You telecommuting to MIT when you graduate, or are your

3

parents actually letting you go there?" Phoebe is telegraphing what she sees as a possible solution.

I feel the slight smile I know I'm exhibiting in response to her question, "I'm still working on them."

"Meaning you're telecommuting, at least for the first year," Phoebe correctly guesses.

"Don't think Ophelia is sympathetic to my plight. Jason realizes I'll probably learn more if I'm actually there working with the people and building things in the labs. But even he's not given me any hope," I reflect on the many discussions with my parents on this topic and know they're not over yet.

"Do you always call your parents by their first names?" Phoebe inquires.

"Everyone I know does," I reflect and answer at the same time.

I watch as Phoebe frowns again and glances over her shoulder. I try to see what she's looking at, but whatever it is must be outside my field of view. This time she turns to look further around and shakes her head as she returns her gaze to me. "I must be hearing ghosts. There's no one there. But I'm sure someone…"

Phoebe doesn't finish her sentence, glances around in the other direction and then back to me again.

"Are you home alone?" I suddenly wonder.

"Everyone went to my brother's match," she responds. "They're playing Edinburgh South, our big rivals for the championship."

"What sport does he play?" I ask not remembering.

"What you call soccer," Phoebe reflects for a moment. "The rest of the world calls it futball, but you have your own version no one else in the world plays. Something much more like rugby. It's too bad you just didn't adopt Rugby instead."

HAPPINESS

"Did they come home early?"

Phoebe looks up, probably at a clock and shakes her head. "They're still in the first half. Might be the cat, although he's usually napping this time of day."

"Do you want to investigate?" I ask to be helpful.

Phoebe looks at something on her wall screen. I guess she's consulting the security system. She then shakes her head. "Nothing. Must be the cat." Phoebe changes my hair color to a chestnut brown. Then she makes it shorter, waits a moment and then makes it longer. I have to admit it looks a lot better longer with my pale complexion. She increases the sheen. I turn my head to see it move. I very much like what I see.

"Nice," I volunteer.

Then Phoebe changes something else. I don't realize at first what she did but know I look even better. Then it dawns on me, she's increased my bust size and made them firmer. "Didn't know the app could change anything other than hair," I remark.

Phoebe puts me into a bikini bathing suit, followed by an evening gown and finally a tennis dress, all with the augmented shape and long chestnut hair. I have to admit I hardly recognize myself. "This is you."

I know it will be a long discussion with Ophelia if I want to do either of these changes, but then I get an idea, "Can you save this and send it to me?"

Phoebe apparently does, looks up and smiles at me. "I expect to see you transformed in our next discussion."

"I'll make a run at Ophelia, but I'm not optimistic," I reflect on our past conversations on this topic.

Suddenly the wall screens go blank and the lights go out. With no windows in the room I'm standing in total darkness. This has never happened before. I'm not quite sure what I need to do to bring it back on. The automation should take care of it. As the moments grow in number I become more uneasy wondering why. I hear the door to my room squeak as if someone is opening it, "Jason?" I call out still not able to see a thing in the total blackness enveloping me.

No response, but someone else is definitely in the room. I hear someone's breathing, labored as if he or she had been walking a long way or running maybe? I reach out expecting to make contact since only Jason and Ophelia are home with me, "Ophelia? Why are the lights out?" I don't feel anything even though the sound of breathing is getting louder, closer… in this direction? I turn to my right where I think the breathing is coming from. I cautiously step forward hoping to either find whichever one is playing this horrible game on me, or the wall. But something has to be wrong. Whichever one is in here should at least respond to me, tell me what's going on. Then I feel something coming down over my head.

I instantly try to pull it back up, and off, but now I feel hands trying to stop me. "What are you doing to me?" Still no response. I begin to fight desperately against the bag, the hands, but now another set of hands try to restrain my arms. I try even harder to pull it off, push the hands away, "Stop! I don't want you to do this to me."

I feel a prick in my neck. Try to swat it away but the many hands stop me. I try to fight even harder. Then I feel the pain of something injecting into my neck… slowly warming under my skin. Then the breathing fades. Silence envelops me in my sightless world.

Chapter Two: Ophelia Braveheart

I walk down the hallway to Jazmin's room. She's usually up by this time. I see the door is open, continue on down to look in. She's not here. Curious. I wonder where she could have gone. There are only so many places to hide in the cocoon.

She may be in the gym, even though it's early for her session. Sometimes she likes to go in and warm up if it's going to be a strenuous workout. But she's not here either. I wander toward the kitchen, tour through it and proceed into the lab where Jason does most of his work. No Jaz. She wouldn't be in the entertainment pod this time of day. "Jason!" I call my husband who is getting dressed after showering.

"What?" he calls back.

"Have you seen Jaz?"

"Not this morning. She should be getting ready for her work out," he notes apparently trying to help me find her without doing anything.

"She's not there or anywhere I can find her," I explain as I walk towards the bedroom door. He looks up at me as I enter the room.

"Must be here somewhere," Jason responds with a puzzled look as he buttons his shirt.

"You look," I suggest since he apparently doesn't believe me.

I follow him through the cocoon. By the time we get to his lab he goes directly to the security monitor. "Jazmin Braveheart," he calls to MC, our system master controller.

"Yes, Jason," MC responds in the confident synthesized voice I've never liked.

7

"Find her for me, please."

I keep telling Jason he doesn't have to be polite with MC, as I never am, but he does out of habit, I think. The large master wall display goes to the last image of Jaz. She's entering her room.

"What time was that?" I ask. No please.

"Eleven-thirteen last night, Ophelia." MC responds in the same voice so I clearly didn't hurt its software feelings by not being polite.

"Nothing since then?" Jason asks.

"Bio sensors indicate she was in her room until five-forty-eight this morning." MC responds.

"And then?" Jason pursues, clearly not understanding what is happening.

"It appears the power was off from five-forty-eight until six-twenty-two am when it was restored by the power company. The message traffic indicates the service line to the cocoon failed. The utility company was forced to dispatch a robot line mender to re-attach."

"The power never goes off," I respond trying to understand what MC has described.

"The robotic inspection of the failed line indicates something apparently fell on the line and ripped it from the meter." MC responds to my comment.

"What fell on the line?" Jason isn't buying this explanation.

"The inspection report notes while the line was ripped from the meter, there was no indication of what caused the fault to occur."

Jason shakes his head at me. I see the frustration in his eyes, "Where's the meter?"

The outside surveillance camera zeros in on the meter. We see the service line to the house attached to it. Jason approaches the wall screen, points to the ground below the electrical attachment point. "Magnify here."

The image zeros in on the ground just below the meter. I can't tell what Jason is looking for, but he then calls out, "Magnify here," and Jason touches the screen at the image he wants to see better.

The image changes. Jason is looking at what appears to be footprints. "MC, tell me if there is anything distinctive about these."

A moment later MC responds, "The tread matches the pattern used by Wilderness Boot Company style Klondike. They first came on the market seven years ago. They are sold through a number of retail providers globally. This particular image would indicate the person wearing the hiking boot is a size ten and a half and weighs approximately two hundred and seven pounds. Jason, you have a pair of those hiking boots size ten and a half in your closet in the back row of shoes. My conclusion would be the imprints in the ground were caused by you when you did the inspection with the contractor last week."

Jason shakes his head again, only this time he's looking more closely at the ground for some sign of what brought down our power line. "I'm going out there."

"Wait," I stop him. "MC, you said Jazmin's bio sensors indicated she was in her room until the power went off. What happened when the power came back on?"

"Her bio sensors were no longer operational."

"What do you mean, no longer operational?" Jason yells before I can respond, my heart in my throat now.

"There were no inputs to the data collection system from her sensors after the power was restored," MC responds in the same neutral voice I know is supposed to be calming, but this is a damn emergency and I'm not at all calm.

"So either the sensors were turned off, or somehow rendered inoperable." Jason is the one who's trying to back down on the anxiety level. He's trying to be logical in figuring out what happened to Jaz.

"Your conclusion would be supported by the evidence," MC responds.

I am about to freak out since none of this discussion is telling me anything about where Jaz might be now. "I don't give a damn about conclusions and evidence, MC. Tell me where my daughter is."

"I am sorry, Ophelia. Without sensor data or imagery from the security system, I am unable to provide you with the information you have requested."

Jason comes over and puts his arm around me. I'm sure he just wants to calm me down so he can ask his questions.

"Bring my daughter back home," I push away from him and put my hand over my face, shaking my head and simply not believing this could be happening.

"MC, could Jazmin have turned off her bio sensors and still be in the house somewhere?" Jason asks.

"As you know, Jason, the bio sensors are implanted just below the skin in the upper middle back where she could not reach them. So the answer to your question is, Jazmin could not have turned off the sensors by herself."

"Could the sensors have been shorted somehow?" Jason continues his questioning, trying to eliminate what might have happened.

"If Jazmin had somehow been subjected to a strong electrical shock it could have shorted out her sensors."

"Like touching a live electrical line detached from the meter?" Jason pursues.

"The sensors indicate Jazmin was in her room at the point in time when the sensors stopped operating. Suggests the bio sensors went off line not because the sensors stopped transmitting, but because the receiver was without power."

"But why wasn't her bio sensor data picked up again when the power was restored," Jason is trying to remain calm, but I hear the frustration rising again.

"Since the sensor data stream should have restored when the power came on, the only logical conclusion is there was a failure of the sensors during the time of the power outage."

"A failure at that time would have to be more than a coincidence," Jason continues to think through what we know and what we don't.

"Your conclusion best fits the facts as we know them," MC affirms.

"Was she awake when the power went off?" I think to ask.

MC responds immediately, "She was on with Phoebe in Scotland when the power went out."

"She was awake," I look at Jason. "So she may have just gone out… for a walk or something."

"She wouldn't," Jason responds without evidencing any doubt.

"You may not think so, but I'll take it and hope for the best," I cling to the one possibility this may all turn out to be nothing to worry about. But somehow I have a deep gnawing fear this explanation is not the right one.

Jason still puzzles, "MC show us the surveillance footage at the meter just before it went off."

"The image is blank for approximately fifteen seconds before the outage began."

"Blank?" I almost shout back at MC. "How could it be blank?"

MC plays the last images before the black out. It appears something comes down over the camera lens, as it is not totally black until the power apparently goes out. Browner like a bag or something.

"Take us to the first seconds after the power was restored," Jason asks. No more pleases from him.

The image shows the meter and the area around it. Like nothing had happened. Like no bag or whatever it was had been placed over it.

"Whoever put a hood over the camera took it off before the power was restored," Jason concludes, looking at my increasingly fearful expression. "This was no accident of nature pulling the service line down. Someone deliberately cut off our power. Made sure the surveillance system couldn't pick up anything useful. Whoever cut our power knew exactly what he or she was doing and did it expertly."

"You have arrived at a logical conclusion," MC responds.

"MC, send a copy of this discussion to the police with a 9-1-1 missing persons request. I'm going out to the meter." Jason hugs me before going down the hall to the bedroom to put on his size ten and a half Klondike style Wilderness Boot Company hiking boots.

Chapter Three: Amare Stebbins

I try to put pieces together in my mind about this case. *Unusual circumstances.* The door opens to the large monolithic structure where Jazmin and her family live. *Nice home, but then anyone who lives in a cocoon has money.* I recognize the man. Late 30s, average build, athletic, brown hair. He had the better surgery as he is more rugged in appearance than most. "I'm Detective Stebbins, Napa Valley Police."

Jason Braveheart checks the infrared and bio monitors next to the door to determine if I'm carrying a virus or sick in any way. He nods the usual greeting nod and gestures, "Come in."

I do, as I adjust my hospital air filtration mask and look about. The home is even nicer inside than the exterior would indicate. *Clearly one percenter.*

"What would you like to do first? Ask questions?"

"Actually, I'd like to see the house if you don't mind," I respond in a friendly fashion, not wanting to upset him further. "I like to put things into context. Then I can ask better questions."

"Certainly," Jason nods once, but then turns as the woman I recognize as Ophelia Braveheart comes up behind him.

"Detective Stebbins," I give her the usual greeting nod. "Napa Valley Police."

She seems uncertain for a moment, but then returns the nod waiting for me to say something.

"Your husband was going to show me through the house… so I can visualize events," I hope to put her at ease as well, but I know it's not going to be an easy task. She steps back as I follow her husband.

Jason leads me back to the girl's bedroom, "This is where she was last seen."

"Eleven-thirteen last evening," I recite so he knows I've reviewed the tape sent over. I enter the room. Standard girl's bedroom. Video screens covering all walls, a massive walk-in closet full of the latest styles, a bathroom with a makeup table and mirror. Three walls of video screens are a continuous pastoral scene. The fourth is the working screen which at the moment shows more of the same pastoral scene. I think it must be somewhere in Wisconsin as there are green grass, grazing cows and a water pond with a large weathered red barn and shake shingle white farm house in the distance. "This a stock image, or does this have some significance for your family?"

"Stock image," Jason responds. *No elaboration. Means he's either not yet tuned into this being an investigation, or he's deliberately giving me only what I ask for. Seems he doesn't want me to know much about his family or the events.* I wonder which.

"Do you mind if I look at the last conversation she had?" I gesture towards the screen, letting them know they can say no.

"She was talking with a friend when the power went off. Usual girl stuff," Jason responds. *He's letting me know there's nothing helpful there, but also not letting me see the recording. It's his right. Just might cause a resolution to take longer if the conversation has any clues. But privacy laws being what they are, I don't really have the right to view it if he doesn't agree. I'm getting negative vibes from him.* I wonder why.

"Mrs. Braveheart, is there anything you might be able to recall leading you to believe your daughter had become a target?" I'm still trying to be circumspect in how I ask my questions to keep her calm.

"For what?" she nearly blurts out revealing the emotional turmoil she is in.

"I would assume since you're cocooned, you don't go out much."

"No need," Jason responds for his wife.

"Might indicate an on-line predator. Someone who became not only aware of your daughter but also had enough information to know where she lives," I give my standard summary as those who cocoon seldom are targets other than from on line crimes. I've not investigated an abduction from one before. These houses are usually almost impossible to break into. *But this time was different.* I wonder if it's the start of something. *Has someone figured out a way to get past the security systems? Will this be the new norm?*

"Jaz is very popular…" Ophelia Braveheart begins but does not finish.

"She talks with people all over the world," Jason clarifies for me. I can't tell if he is correcting his wife or simply putting a different spin on it for me.

"Do you monitor her communications?" I ask without trying to sound accusatory.

"Only in the aggregate," Jason informs me although I'm not quite sure what he's trying to say.

"I assume you're telling me you look at her metadata, but don't monitor the calls themselves," I suggest to see if he will clarify.

"Correct." *Again, no elaboration.*

"I would suggest one or both of you go back through her communications," I decide to move on. "Go back as far as you need to. Look for anything indicating someone's unusual interest in her."

"What do you mean unusual?" Ophelia Braveheart asks.

"You said she was very popular."

Ophelia nods.

"Are there any communications with someone who seems out of place? An older man, for instance, who is not a teacher or parent of a friend. Someone who just seems like he's not expected given who she's communicating with."

"You think she was abducted by an older man?" Ophelia comes right back at me.

"Not necessarily. Could be a woman who's not a parent or teacher. Could be someone who has sold her something on line, but seems to communicate with her when it doesn't seem necessary. Could be a classmate she never seems to communicate with but suddenly seems to be around. Lot of potential people who just don't seem to fit into her daily routine."

"What if it was a stakeout?" *Jason is going to a place I had considered when I first watched the file.*

"A program running behind the scenes and monitoring her?" *I clarify so he can confirm we are talking about the same thing.*

"We'd never see it or even know it was there," Jason points out probably for his wife's benefit.

"You could do a scan," I suggest. I would do it but he seems not to want me to have access to her system. Again, it's his right, but I'm always suspicious of people who seem to want to protect something in an investigation.

"MC. Scan stalkerbot," he responds to my suggestion, which surprises me since he's not been willing to do anything with the system in my presence.

"I have commenced the scan, Jason. Is there anything else you would like me to look for?" the system responds in a neutral male voice new to me. *Must be a custom system. Might mean Jason Braveheart built this system himself. Would explain why he doesn't want me to have access to it.*

"Scan for any other cling-on programs not specifically authorized," Jason responds and glances at me, studies my reaction. *I notice a slight grimace. I suspect he's realized I know this is a custom system.* I wonder what it does.

16

"Yes, Jason," the system responds, "The scan for stalkerbots indicates JWGacey.bot entered the system thirteen days ago in disaggregated code attached to a series of images Jazmin scrolled over from Philippe, who lives in Puerto Princesa, in the Republic of the Philippines. This code reassembled itself into a silent monitoring and reporting program once downloaded. The communications path would indicate the information captured about her communications have been going through at least fifteen relays in twelve different countries with the last detected and only domestic hub being in League City, Texas."

"The end of the line?" Jason asks as if he's been down this path before.

"The premise appears to transfer to land lines which then switch to internet protocol phone systems which once again transfer to cellular carriers with a wide range of final numbers, at least fifteen of which appear to be throw-away phones."

"Are any of the final IP or cellular addresses California numbers?" Jason asks hopefully.

"No. All South American final numbers with the predominance being Colombia and Paraguay."

"Can we trace the location where the phones were when the messaging took place?" Jason asks.

"Technology for geolocation is still in development." The system responds in the same neutral voice.

Jason looks at Ophelia and shakes his head.

I instantly leap to the next possibility, "Is there someone who would abduct your daughter for a reason having nothing to do with her, but everything to do with you?" I gaze directly at Jason.

"Me?" Jason responds as if not expecting the question this soon.

I don't answer, waiting for him to do so.

Jason looks at his wife and some form of communication takes place, but it is non-verbal. Unfortunately I can't decipher what it is.

"I can't answer your question," Jason finally responds to my constant glare.

"Why not?"

"I'm a technologist." Another glance at Ophelia. "I develop technologies doing a wide variety of things. Would one of those technologies cause someone to come after me through my daughter? I can't imagine who would or why. But there may be someone out there who wants something from me, but simply hasn't asked… at least not yet."

"If someone were to want something from you, who would you guess?" I put out there.

Jason continues to look at his wife. *There's something there, but will he tell me?* She finally shakes her head and Jason looks at me, "I really…"

I interrupt, "Mr. Braveheart, I can assure you if we don't find your daughter today, the probability decreases by fifty percent each day thereafter. So if you know something, please tell me now."

Chapter Four: Jazmin Braveheart

As I open my eyes, I instantly know something's not right. *This pillow smells wrong.* As my eyes focus I don't see things I expect to see in my room. *Where am I? This must be a dream. Not a particularly pleasant dream.* But then I feel something crawling on my face, slap it and look at my hand. *A spider! Euwww!* I flick the spider away with my other hand and realize, this is no dream.

How did I get here? I look around slowly. This room is small, dark, foul smelling. *Doesn't anyone clean this place?* The lights are low, but somehow they seem normal here. As if whoever lives here never intends to make it brighter. I continue looking around. I finally see a desk with three tiny monitors on it in a corner across the room. I raise myself up a little. *Can I see anyone? No.* No one there, but whoever it is has a small spotlight on the desk for some reason. *Why would they need a light?* Then I look more carefully and realize the walls are not monitors. *No wall monitors? Who lives here?*

I raise myself up on one elbow. *Nothing on the walls. No furniture except the desk with the monitors and light and this... what is this? It's like a mattress on the floor.* A pillow and blanket. No sheets. *Maybe why it smells foul. Whoever sleeps here doesn't sleep on sheets. Their sweat must have stained the mattress. Ugh! I need to get up and off of this...*

Standing up is harder than I expect since my bed is a good two feet or more off the floor but this sits on it. I have to actually stand up rather than roll out of the bed. Now I'm up on my feet taking another look around. The room is small, at least small in comparison to what I'm used to. At the cocoon the rooms are large and airy. Tall ceilings and light floors with monitor walls changing with whatever image I select. Here the floor seems to be this gray hard substance. Not wood. No cushion when you walk on it like I'm used to. No carpet. No design to it. Just plain gray. The walls aren't active and seem to be this dull beige color. No art, no pictures, nothing to look at. Just a dull plain surface to stop me from going any further in a direction. *Why do you need a wall if there's no active screen to display an image? I don't understand.*

Since the only other thing in the room is the small desk with three tiny monitors I approach it, quietly, not wanting to make any sounds attracting attention. I look at the tiny monitors. Each displays a different image. The first is a program, I recognize the logic and realize it's a python algorithm. It's an ancient programming language seldom used anymore. From the small segment on the screen I can't tell what it is intended to analyze. The center screen is a security camera. It shows a building nestled in a small grove of trees. I wonder if it is the security for this place. Again I can't tell as I have no idea where I am. And the third screen is social media posts from a variety of sources. I start to read them.

A picture of three men, two wearing hospital filtration facemasks and the third a ski mask, all hoisting a beverage in a salute to whoever is taking the picture. Two look happy. The third with the ski mask, I can't tell. *Why?* The picture tag reads, 'Stick it in your ear, mate.' Certainly not very friendly. *Must have come from the one with the ski mask.*

"Scroll," I command the screen, but nothing happens. I touch the screen to see if it scrolls down like my phone. It does and the next picture is of an electrical meter with a cable disconnected. *No tag. No identification of any kind.* I scroll down and find a real shocker, a picture of me asleep. But I'm not in my bed. I don't know where I am, but I'm not here either, wherever here is. It looks like I'm in the back seat of a vehicle. Asleep. *Who took this picture? Why did they take it?*

A noise startles me. Sounds like someone coming in a door somewhere. Not far away. I scroll back up to the top of the page and head over to the mattress to wait. It doesn't take long for someone to come storming into the room. It's the guy wearing a ski mask and a baseball cap with a stylized M in front. Don't know what team that is since I don't follow baseball. From his build and swagger I'd suspect he's late twenties or early thirties. Hard to tell from here. Might be brown hair as a little sticks out in the back of the ski mask. Medium height. Not muscular, but I wouldn't want to give him a chance to hurt me because he probably could. Rough looking. Dark color outdoor clothes like a flannel shirt and jeans. Hiking boots. Someone out of the back woods like a lumberjack.

He sees me staring at him which causes him to hesitate for just a moment, but he sits down at the desk and is instantly absorbed in the screens, paying no attention to me.

"Hey," I call to him. "You need to take me home. This has to be some mistake."

The guy pays no attention. Seems to have gotten absorbed in something on his screens. I'm not sure if I should approach him or stay as far away as possible. I'm wary of anyone who doesn't talk to me.

I wait a few more moments to see if he responds, but he doesn't. *Guess I need to move closer so he can't ignore me.* I cautiously cross about half the distance to the desk. The guy is still absorbed in his screen and paying no attention to me. I take another step closer. Still no reaction from him. I wonder if I go to the door he came through if I could just walk on out, but somehow I don't think it's likely.

"Excuse me," I try politeness since my demand went nowhere. "Could tell me how I can go home?"

No reaction. *Maybe the guy's deaf.* I wave my hand to get his attention, but no response either. So I come to the edge of the desk.

In an instant he is on his feet right hand jammed up under my throat. With one arm he lifts me up, carries me across the room with my feet dangling and slams my back against a wall.

I'm dazed… and choking… and so startled and afraid I have stopped even trying to breathe. I don't know how long he continues holding me up this way, but suddenly I gasp for air and find it hard to fill my lungs.

I open my eyes. Try to tell him to let me go, but all I can do is look into his eyes. I instantly know he would have no compunction keeping me like this until I've passed out. At the moment it seems imminent.

And just as quickly he releases me.

I fall to the floor, trying to fill my lungs with air. Trying to slow my racing heart.

The guy returns to his desk without saying a word. *What did I do?* I lay there looking at the guy as my breathing slowly comes back under control. I have to consciously try to slow my heart rate. I'm afraid to move, afraid to say anything to him. *I don't know what to do.*

I sit up against the wall, draw my legs into me to protect myself as much as possible. But the guy seems to have forgotten I'm even here, having retreated back into his screens. *I think I can dismiss any notion this is all a mistake. The violent response. The picture of me sleeping or maybe unconscious, I'm not really sure. I'm here for some reason, although at the moment I have no idea what. I'm not going to ask this guy any more questions. So how do I figure out what's going on?*

I put my forehead down on my knees and hold my legs to me. Closing my eyes I can pretend to be somewhere else. I do that all the time in my room, but there I have the wall screens immersing me in any place I care to go. Now I have to rely on my memory of those images to be transported to those places. But at the moment it seems I have no choice but to rely on my memory to go anywhere.

Chapter Five: Ophelia Braveheart

This man. This detective. He makes me very uncomfortable. There's something wrong about him. I need to say something to Jason. Does he get the same feeling? A feeling of what? I don't know what it is, but I don't want him in my house. Jason doesn't seem as antsy as I feel, usually meaning he's not feeling the same thing. He'll probably tell me it's all in my head. I'm imagining things. Over reacting is what he usually tells me. But I'm not overreacting when Jaz isn't here with us as she should be.

"Jason, can I talk with you for a moment?"

"Would you excuse us?" Jason asks the detective.

He follows me to our bedroom where I close the door. "You need to get him out of here."

Jason looks at me curiously. "What's the matter? He's just doing his job."

"How do you know?" I demand loudly and watch him pull away from my near shout. *I need to get my emotions under control or Jason will just dismiss me. He's done so before.*

"Settle down," Jason puts his arm around me. He pulls me into him to reassure me, but I pull back almost instantly. *He's not going to put me off.*

"No. You get him out of here or I'll do it. Where's your gun?"

Jason crosses his arms across his chest, basically telling me he's not going to cooperate. "What's got you spooked?"

"How do you know he's a cop? He could be the one who took Jaz from us. How do you know?"

"Let's go ask for an authentication," Jason responds, catching me off guard. He's basically acceded to my request. "Right now. Let's do it. Maybe then you'll settle down and let him do what he has to so Jaz can come home."

"How can you be so calm about it?" I push back with another surge of emotions spilling over. "Are you in on whatever's going on? Did you arrange for this guy to take Jaz from us for a ransom or something?"

"Did you hear what you just said?" Jason asks me as if I've lost it, *which I probably have.*

"What kind of bullshit question…?" I step away from him. He's trying to make me feel bad about my behavior like I'm Jaz. I've seen him do this all too many times and know the game.

"I'm serious," Jason unfolds his arms. He's letting me know I can come in for a hug if I need one. But I'm not ready yet. "You're being totally unreasonable. You made a good point, we should authenticate him. Guess I'm getting sloppy since no one ever comes to visit us. But once we confirm him you need to answer his questions and let him do his job."

Jason holds out his hand for me to take and follow him out to the living room. There we find the detective appearing to review the file we sent him from when we discovered Jaz was missing.

The detective looks up, "We good?"

"I'd like to do a verification… with your office," Jason explains.

The detective seems surprised, but after a moment of reflection nods, "Makes sense."

Jason turns to the active wall, "Call the Napa Valley Police Department."

In only a moment the screen changes images to a fit looking brunette-haired woman in a blue police uniform and hospital mask. She sits in an office area with other uniformed and non-uniformed officers walking down rows of desks behind her. I've never seen something like this, where people are working at desks all day. Staring at tiny monitors on their desks rather than on the wall. "Napa Valley PD," the woman answers.

"Hello. I'm Jason Braveheart. I'd like to do a verification on a detective."

"Oh, hi, Amare," she nods to the detective. "Just a moment Mr. Braveheart. My records indicate Detective Amare Stebbins was dispatched to handle your 9-1-1 call. Missing person according to our records."

"Is this person next to me Detective Stebbins?" Jason asks.

"Sure looks like him," the officer responds. "Do you have a print reader?"

"I do," Jason offers and points to the print pad on the security desk running our surveillance systems.

The detective walks the few steps and gives impressions of both index fingers. It only takes a moment for the uniformed officer to nod, "Detective Stebbins is verified," she hesitates for a moment as she looks at something on her monitor, but then her gaze returns to us, "What else can I do for you today, Mr. Braveheart?"

"Find my daughter and bring her home," I yell at the monitor. The officer nods, "Detective Stebbins is one of our best. He will find your daughter. For now... "and the officer's image is gone.

"I'm glad you verified," Detective Stebbins, I think is his name, sounds contrite. "I forget sometimes wanting to get right to it. But while you were talking something occurred to me, I've not asked why you think she was abducted."

"You're not sure?" I have to ask.

"At this point, Mrs. Braveheart, I'm not sure of anything," the detective responds in a tone of voice making me understand he thinks I need to think through my questions before I just ask them.

I must look chastened or something as he turns to Jason, "Any idea?"

"You hear about things like this in the media, but you never think they could happen to you or your family. You know what I mean? It's all disorienting. Crazy it could actually happen. I'm just beginning to think it through. So forgive me if my answers are half-baked. You see, Jaz is popular and all, but it's virtual. She doesn't go out..." Jason begins to explain, but seems to have difficulty finishing the thought.

"You're telling me she doesn't hang out with a bunch of other girls I need to go talk with," the detective seeks to clarify.

"Not in person," Jason answers as if he's not happy with his response. "It's like with the systems we have here, there's really no need. She can see them, hear them, joke around or whatever. But she's not in danger when she's here."

"Is that what this may be all about?" the detective asks in a funny way, although I'm not sure I'm following.

"What? That she's cocooned?" Jason picks up on his question faster than I do.

"Wouldn't be the first time a young woman rebels at being locked away from her friends," the detective informs us, although I can see he's testing our reaction.

"Jaz wouldn't run away," I dismiss his assertion.

"How would she cut the power if she was in her room?" Jason asks. "The power went off and the sensors said she was still in there."

"Accomplice? Someone she knows from her virtual relationships?" The detective is persistent on this point.

"You mean does she have a boyfriend?" I throw back at him. "No, she doesn't."

"Not even a virtual boyfriend, who might actually be an avatar for someone else?"

I see Jason is considering his question. Does he know something about Jaz I don't?

"Let's look," Jason turns to the active wall monitor. "MC. List the male contacts Jaz has had in the last year with the number of contacts and the frequency of such contacts in the past month."

"Dimitri Shashkavilli, seven conversations, none in the last six months. Zalid Malik, six conversations, none in the last eight months, Patrick O'Henry, five conversations, once in the past month, Matty Bain, four conversations none in the past month, Sergio Valenta, three conversations, none in the past month…"

"MC. Enough. I think we get the picture," Jason stops the report for some reason.

"What about postings? Has she had anyone show particular interest in what she's posted?" the detective asks next, apparently satisfied she hasn't been conspiring with someone over the phone.

"MC?" Jason asks.

"Phoebe has been her most constant correspondent. They react to each other's postings an average of fifteen times each day."

"Phoebe?" the detective asks.

"She lives in Scotland and was the person she was on with when the power went out," Jason confirms. We both watched the recording. "There was nothing indicating she was conspiring with Jaz to do anything except maybe change the color of her hair."

"Any males respond to her more than others?" the detective asks next.

"Reinhold Timmerman. In the past ninety days has liked or

commented on nearly a third of her postings."

"Where does he live?" the detective has taken over the inquiry of MC.

"Wiesbaden, Germany," MC responds.

"Where is he now?" the detective follows up.

"Berlin, Germany. He is enrolled as a freshman at the Berlin Technological Institute studying advanced analytics and data science."

"Has Jaz ever met him?" again the detective is pursuing some theory, or eliminating suspects, I can't tell which.

"No. Their media interactions have only been in the past fifty-seven days." MC clarifies.

"Does the scan erase your suspicions of my daughter?" I throw at him.

"No, but it lowers the probability of a jailbreak."

Jason holds me back as I'm about to rip his throat out.

Chapter Six: Jazmin Braveheart

The mattress is too foul smelling. I can't lay back down on it. So I continue to sit on the floor with my back to the wall and my legs pulled up in front of me. My arms circle my legs to hold them tight. The guy just works away at his terminal. I have no idea what he's doing, but it's clear he's not going to explain it to me or point out the way to go home, either. I'm still having trouble swallowing after being held up in the air by my neck with my feet dangling off the ground.

I hear someone open a door and come into the house. Not quite sure if it's a door inside or the door to freedom. I keep my head down and watch to see who else is here now. Someone who has come to take me home, I hope. But somehow I'm not counting on it.

Then the door opens and closes again. The guy at the computer seems to be ignoring the sound, as if it happens every day at this time or something. After his last reaction to my questions I'm reluctant to ask any more, but I can't help myself. "You going to see who's there?"

The guy at the computer ignores my question, although I get the distinct impression he's no longer ignoring me. He seems to be keeping an eye on me while he's working. *Probably wondering if he permanently scarred my psyche.* But then he gets up and leaves the room. I wonder if I have enough time to go look at his monitor and see what he's been working on. Before I can move he comes back with a plate of food and utensils so I can eat. *Big of him to make sure I don't waste away.* But then I realize he or someone must be planning on keeping me here for a while. The fact he's feeding me would indicate he recognizes I'm going to need food but also probably means he's not planning on sending me home today. *Not what I want to hear.*

He hands me the plate and instantly turns away. "Excuse me," is my instant reaction.

The guy glances back at me almost like I must be ungrateful or something.

"None of this is on my diet," I respond without thinking. "I have a strict eighteen hundred calories a day. Mostly vegetables and legumes. This is a hamburger. Don't even know how many calories. And the fat content? No way can I eat this. "

The guy shrugs and returns to his workstation.

I inhale the odor of the burger and am almost nauseated. I've never had one, although I've heard about them forever. Used to be the dish of choice for many Americans. Guess it still is. I set the plate down next to me and resume my near fetal position to ward off whatever is coming next.

The guy looks over at me repeatedly for a few minutes. He soon approaches. I lower my head to ensure he can't pick me up by my throat again. But I didn't need to worry as he scoops up the dish with the burger and returns to his workstation. To my amazement he picks up the burger, raises the ski mask covering his mouth and stuffs nearly a third of the burger into it. I see he's not clean shaven, but doesn't have a beard either. He's probably lazy. He doesn't shave every day, but neither is he trying to make a statement with a beard. But then, three bites and the burger has disappeared. *I can't believe it. The hamburger would be at least a dozen bites for me. What am I realizing about me and him?*

Guess he doesn't care about what I can eat as I don't see him calling anyone to inform them of my dietary restrictions. Guess I'm going to bed hungry tonight, although I refuse to sleep on the stinky mattress again. Starting to look a lot like sleeping on the floor. But then I've only been awake a short amount of time. And I have no idea what time it is. The lights went out, about what time? Six am? Maybe. I was on with Phoebe and she's in Scotland. I think her country is eight or nine hours ahead of California. But then I realize I have no idea if I'm even in California anymore. I could be anywhere in the world, depending on how long I was out. Nothing tells me how long.

Then I start wondering. *There's something else on the plate. Something I could eat and would fit into my calorie restrictions? What is that?* But then I see the guy stuffing short brown sticks into his mouth with something red on one end. *Something else I never eat?* I watch in amazement, but by the time I realize what's been going on, the sticks are all gone. I'm starting to get hungry.

I get up and look at the plate on his desk. There's a slice of tomato and a leaf of lettuce still there. I hesitate going anywhere near this guy, but my stomach is sending out signals. *It's not happy. How long can I go without eating?* I don't know since I don't remember ever going more than a day. I slowly get up as I'm afraid a sudden move may cause a response from the guy. I approach cautiously. The guy looks up at me but I hold my hands up so he knows I'm not here to do anything stupid. I reach for the tomato and lettuce, stopping before I pick them up so he knows what I'm trying to do, He just continues to watch me like I'm from another planet or something. I pick up the tomato first and take six bites of it, chewing each thoroughly before swallowing. Then I pick up the lettuce. The guy watches me curiously like he's never seen anyone eat the lettuce and tomato. The way he inhaled the burger, maybe he hasn't. The lettuce tears. I chew each piece slowly. As I always do, given the restricted amount of calories. Not eighteen hundred but looks like it's all I'm going to see this night. I nod my thanks and go back to the wall. I sit down next to it and resume my prior fetal position.

Again I hear the door open. *Did someone bring dessert? Did someone call in my diet so they can provide a proper meal?* I wait. Suddenly a short guy, same baseball cap with the stylized M and the usual hospital face mask, comes in. *Similar rough clothes. Hiking boots.* He carries a knapsack which he drops next to the work station and looks over the shoulder of the guy at it. "Have you tried a different algorithm? Looks like the one I see you using for just about everything."

The guy at the desk glances up at him but still doesn't say anything. "Aces, there's got to be a better algorithm."

Aces. Now I know his name. So who is the new guy?

At this point the new guy sees me sitting there. "Ho! You her?"

"Her?" I ask happy someone is at least willing to talk with me. *Maybe I can convince him to take me home.*

"The rich bitch who's been cocooned her whole life," *sounds like he's already formed an opinion of me.*

Not the description I wanted to hear. Tells me I have to dig out of a hole. I have no idea how. "Why am I here?" my own voice sounds different to me.

"Where do you think you should be?"

"Home," I want to shout at him, but I'm sure it comes out as a whisper from my sore throat. I'm afraid and can hardly talk at this point, not knowing who he is or what he might do to me.

The new guy cocks his head, studies me from afar, "You might go home, but it all depends."

"On what?" I absolutely need to have this answer.

He laughs. "That's up to Grendele's Modor."

"What?" I have no idea what he just said.

"Look," he begins. "You're talking to the wrong guy if you're looking for answers. I'm just an engineer. An integration engineer at that. Do you know what the difference is between an engineer and an integration engineer?"

I shrug.

"An integration engineer is the guy who fixes all the mistakes the software and hardware engineers make when you try to drive hardware one guy builds with the software someone else designed."

Again I shrug to make him think I'm not following, although I understand exactly what he said.

"What I'm saying is someone else makes those decisions."

Not sure where this conversation is going, but then something else occurs to me, "What's the story with your friend?"

The new guy glances over his shoulder. "Did he eat your hamburger and fries?"

"I take it he does that a lot?"

"Usually just to me, but I saw the plate on his workstation desk and took a wild guess. He must have been really hungry tonight. He even ate the garnish. He never does."

"Who are you?" I dare to ask since he seems to be willing to talk with me, unlike Aces.

"People call me Stash," he offers as he looks back at me. "I have no idea why. It's just what people have called me since I was a kid."

"Jazmin," I nod to him as the customary greeting in the age of pandemics.

He returns the gesture, "Jazmin? Pretty name. I'll take a wild guess and say it's your real name."

I nod. "Can you take me home?"

Stash laughs. "Not in my job description."

"Then how do I get home?" I hear myself almost pleading.

Stash smiles at me, but I see in his eyes he won't or maybe can't help me get home.

"Tell me about Grendele's Modor," I ask since he didn't respond.

Stash shakes his head and glances at Aces. "You don't want to know."

"I absolutely do if it's my ticket home."

"Grendele's Modor is not someone you want to go up against. She will eat you or me alive."

I've not heard of anyone described quite this way. "What does she want with me?"

"She doesn't consult me, so I can't help you."

I deflate again, seeing another door to going home close in my face. "Then what good are you?" I ask.

"I'm a really good integration engineer," he offers as a consolation.

"What do you integrate?" I ask although not really curious at the moment.

"All the systems keeping things up and running," Stash tosses off as if it's no big deal, but is secretly hoping I'll realize it is.

"What things?" I push as he's not really telling me anything helpful.

"Cocoons mostly, but also smaller cities here and there," Stash responds as if I should be grateful.

"Cocoons? Like where I live? You could take me home." Suddenly I'm becoming hopeful again.

Stash glances at me as if he's revealed something better kept from me. He then looks at Aces. Apparently decides something, "You need to just chill while things play out," he says, deliberately not confirming.

Chapter Seven: Amare Stebbins

"I understand, Mrs. Braveheart, but you must understand this is an unusual circumstance," I see the near panic in her eyes. *She's in transmit mode only. No matter what I say now she's not going to remember it in thirty seconds.* "You husband has pointed out how sophisticated your security systems are. From what I've seen, most of the cocoons have similar systems. People don't break into homes like yours..."

"Are you saying someone found a vulnerability we haven't anticipated?" Jason Braveheart attracts my attention.

"I am." I see the confusion in Jason's expression. *As if something monumental had just been revealed to him.* I ask, "Do you build security systems?"

"My company does among other things..." Jason is somewhat distracted considering the insight he just gained.

"Apparently no one found a way to cut the power and disguise it as a weather-related outage in the past?" I ask Jason, but he's barely listening already deep into solving some engineering design flaw. *So here I am trying to get basic information I need to proceed and neither of the witnesses are paying any attention to me. This has to be one of my better investigations, or maybe not.*

"Mrs. Braveheart, what can you tell me about your daughter?" I hope to get something from her. "Just general information. Things like age, interests, and things like that."

Jason answers for her, "She did an admissions video. For MIT."

"Was she accepted?"

Mrs. Braveheart has now engaged seemingly slighted, "Of course she was accepted."

"Could I see the video?" which is what I thought Jason was suggesting.

Mrs. Braveheart nods and calls to the active wall, "MC. MIT application video."

In only a moment I see a seemingly frail young woman, resembling her mother, but with her father's bright eyes and smile. Dark hair and complimentary high cheek bones completes the picture of someone who had more than the usual surgeries to make her attractive. Yes, it may be an assumption on my part, but from what I've seen, when someone looks this good, it was extensive and expensive.

"Hi. I'm Jazmin Braveheart. That's Jazmin with a Z because I'm no shrinking violet and someone you will remember. I'm a typical sixteen-year-old. Family, friends and teachers shape my understandings of the world, but I don't stop there. I consume information at an accelerated rate. I create my own perceptions of today and what the future can be from the good, the bad and the irrelevant. I seek to find the heart of the matter and characterize it in a way permitting insights into the world not everyone has."

Self-assured, but what would you expect from someone trying to get into a prestigious university?

"A key influence in my life is my father, Jason, who is the owner of Braveheart Systems, a high-tech manufacturer of consumer, industrial and governmental decision support and other systems. What makes his systems unique is they aren't just software running on someone else's hardware. He builds integrated capability maximizing the delivered insights. Now what I just described may sound like marketing speak, but I have worked extensively with my father for the past five years. I have seen first-hand how to push frontiers, how to combine emerging hardware with advanced software scripting. I am expert in fifteen software languages and my code is resident in hundreds of delivered systems providing unique insights daily."

I have to stop to reconsider here. *I was going down the path someone wanted something from the father. Whether money or some technology his company builds. I had no idea a sixteen-year-old girl could have this kind of skills. Maybe someone kidnapped her because of what she could give them.*

The video continues, "While I like to think I'm proficient in technology, I realize I'm just beginning to tap my potential. I expect my years at MIT will help me realize not only potential but insights needed to build a new future. It should be noted I have completed three years of undergraduate studies through advanced placement. So the first year is the capstone year. Defining and delivering a new integrated solution with the help of the MIT faculty." She flashes a winning smile, one sealing the deal as far as I'm concerned. *If I was on the admissions committee... well what can I say? She seems a prime candidate.* Then something else occurs to me, she's a prime candidate for kidnapping. Although who and why is still not evident at the moment.

I turn to Mrs. Braveheart, "Your daughter is impressive."

"My daughter is missing. You're sitting here watching videos rather than finding her and bringing her home," *the tone is not hysterical... yet.*

"The video has been incredibly helpful to me in understanding who your daughter is. Without this insight I would be searching in the dark for someone because there currently is no clear motive. But this video has let me see there may be motives I would not normally consider."

"Then who do you think has my daughter?"

"Mrs. Braveheart. I have only just begun the investigation," I respond.

She turns to her husband, "I think you need to hire someone. This guy is clueless."

I have to admit she catches me off guard, "Who do you think has your daughter then?" I challenge her.

She glances at me as if I'm a bee buzzing around. She's not quite sure if she should swat or just ignore me. "What?"

"If I'm clueless, you must think you know who has your daughter," I explain a little testy although I'm trying to keep my emotions in check.

"I have no idea who has my daughter," she fires back. "Why would I be sitting here helplessly talking with you if I did?"

"Because I can arrest that person and you can't," I suggest as a reason.

Ophelia Braveheart looks at me as if I'm not really here, but I can see her perceptions are changing as she continues to consider something. She glances over at her husband, but is not willing to share her thoughts. I know I have to wait patiently and hope she finally decides it appropriate to discuss her thoughts with me.

"Jason, what about Albert?"

"Truex?" Jason responds as if he is attempting to connect a line of dots on a page.

Ophelia Braveheart does not respond, but rather lets her husband consider what she has just suggested to see his reaction.

Jason frowns, "He may be a lot of things you don't like, but I don't see him…"

I write down Albert Truex in my cell notes. "Who is Albert Truex?"

"My business partner," Jason responds shaking his head, apparently still dismissing the idea.

"Tell me more," I ask of either or both.

"Ophelia has been telling me for years I need to sever my ties to Albert," Jason offers. "She thinks he's unethical. But he's on the sales side. I'm the technical guy. He deals in shades of gray all day. I deal in absolutes all day. He promises to meet a spec. I have to figure out how. There are often a lot of sleepless nights for me trying to figure out the how of what he's promised. Doesn't make him a bad guy. What he does is essential as I probably couldn't sell refrigeration in the Sahara."

"He's made comments," Ophelia Braveheart responds to her husband.

"Innocent comments," Jason looks at me apparently wanting to gauge my reaction to this discussion. "He's a sales guy. Once he's made the sale he wants to move on. You know what I'm saying?"

"No," I react honestly.

"He's been married... what?"

"Six times," Ophelia Braveheart responds instantly.

"Like I said, he closes the deal and moves on to the next. Unfortunately he's the same way when it comes to relationships. Personally, I think he gets bored once he's gotten his new lady to the alter..."

"You mean into bed," Ophelia Braveheart corrects her husband's choice of words.

Jason nods reluctantly, "You can almost predict when he's going to be out screwing around again. Always less than a year."

"What does this have to do with your daughter?" I'm the one who has lost the thread.

"He's made comments about Jaz," Mrs. Braveheart responds to me, really talking to her husband.

"What kind of comments?" I have to ask now.

"Jason?" she asks her husband to tell me.

Jason Braveheart shakes his head again, "She's making something out of nothing."

"Jason. She's your daughter!" Ophelia takes head-on her husband's dismissal.

Jason clearly wrestles with what to say. "He wasn't serious," finally dismissing his wife's concerns.

"Tell him, Jason," Ophelia Braveheart pushes back. "Tell him how your partner, who you've known almost the whole time we've been married, said to you Jaz was someone he'd be willing to do."

"Meaning sleep with," I interpret her choice of words.

"He was complimenting her surgery," Jason responds to his wife. "That's all."

"You weren't happy with him at the time," Ophelia shoots back to remind him of their discussion.

"It was inappropriate at the time, but I don't see it as a smoking gun," Jason admits. "I'm sure if you asked him he's probably completely forgotten."

"How would you feel if he said the same thing about me?" Ophelia continues to put him on the spot.

"I'd say at least he has good taste," Jason responds apparently knowing it is going to send his wife into orbit.

Ophelia has had it with her husband. She stalks out of the room, although I'm not sure where she is going. I look at Jason and wonder aloud, "So who do you think may have her?"

Jason continues to look introspective and shakes his head slowly.

Chapter Eight: Jazmin Braveheart

Stash has settled in on the other side of the table where Aces is working. His laptop is up and he's plugged in his earbuds. Seems to be in another world now, only it's probably my world, just from the other side I've never seen and frankly never even thought about. I wonder what the problem is he's trying to solve. Only I doubt he would want to talk about it. Least of all to me. But then maybe he's as curious about who lives in the cocoons as I am now about who is keeping them up and running behind the scenes.

Aces is also apparently deep in thought. He sits staring at his screen. I'm curious why they're using such old technology. Everything in the cocoon is voice activated. Don't know as I've ever even seen a keyboard other than in old movies and histories I've watched. I decide if Stash doesn't want me looking at what he's doing he can tell me to sit back down, so I approach him quietly, but make my presence known in a non-threatening way.

"Oh. Wasn't expecting you," Stash pulls out one earbud. "What do you want?"

"I don't have any idea what it takes to keep a cocoon operating," *I try to sound helpless, although Ophelia would never think of me that way.* "Would you show me what you're doing?"

Stash hesitates, "I've got to fix this comms link," he looks at me, then reconsiders, "Restore the communications between a server and a sensor because the air conditioning is running hot."

"Is that my cocoon?" I ask wondering if he would tell me if it was.

Stash shakes his head as he goes back to the issue he was trying to address. He seems to trace down the problem, re-establishes an IP address and watches as the comms apparently relink. "There." A self–satisfied grin and he looks at me again. "I usually don't get involved in things this simple, but the tech who was working it quit and there was no one available."

"What did you do?" again sounding like I have no idea.

"Do you know anything about how an IT system works?" Stash is trying to decide what he needs to tell me to answer my question.

My turn to shake my head.

"Hmmm. Well, it's like this. The cocoon is full of sensors gathering data about how the cocoon is operating. We set a range of possible readings representing the normal situation. In this case it's the temperature. The cocoon should be operating at approximately 72 degrees Fahrenheit or 25 degrees Celsius. The sensors are set so if it is within two degrees either way nothing happens. But if it goes beyond that in either direction the system will send a message to the HVAC…" Stash looks at me apparently wondering if I'm following him. I give him a blank look to see what he will do. "That's heating, ventilating and air conditioning. The system maintaining the desired temperature range. Anyway, in this case the sensor couldn't send the messages to the controller indicating the temperature was rising above the range."

"Why?" I ask to let him know I'm listening but make him think I'm not following.

"Well, the IP address was corrupted for some reason."

"IP?"

"Internet protocol. It's code identifying the sensor sending the information to the controller, so it will know what to do with the information."

"Kind of like an address? Like where I live?"

Stash gives me a funny look, but then apparently dismisses whatever he was thinking. "Yeah, like an address. So I updated the IP address. The controller was then able to identify the sensor and get the readings. Here…" Stash points to his screen. "You can see the HVAC has switched over to cooling and the temperature is dropping back into the range."

"So you reset things and it's working properly again," I want him to think I'm seeing him as good at his job. *Positive thoughts so he'll think positively about me.*

"Back at 72 degrees, so yeah. It's fixed."

"Is your job to fix things? You said you were an integration engineer. Someone who fixes things doesn't sound like an integration engineer to me."

Stash rolls his eyes as apparently he thinks so too.

Stash glances at Aces before he continues, "Something's always being upgraded or there's a software patch, or one thing or another. When you're dealing with software intensive systems things are always changing. That's where I come in."

"What do you mean?"

"Someone has to be able to understand the logic of the system and the software driving it," Stash sounds proud of what he does. "Someone has to be able to track down where the software is sending a command or not sending the right command to the hardware and figure out why. That's what I do."

"And then you fix it." I give him a tentative smile.

Stash nods, "Sometimes I do more than fix it. Sometimes I actually have to rewrite some of the code. When I do the company I work for sends the information back to the manufacturer so they can change the source code."

"Source code?" I try to sound clueless.

"The code copied and installed in all the other similar units."

"So you're the most important person who keeps my cocoon working," still trying to confirm he knows where I live.

"I like to think so," Stash apparently doesn't realize his admission.

"If you're the integration engineer, what is Aces doing?" I nod towards the silent person on the other side of the monitors. I notice Aces turns his head like he's listening to this one.

Stash glances towards Aces, but then back to me, "He's a technician."

"What does he do?" I try to sound confused.

"He knows how to fix simple things, but not the more involved issues like a design flaw which is where I'm more likely to get involved." Stash glances back at Aces to see if he's reacting, but he seemingly can't see him behind the monitors and turns back to look at me.

"Like resetting an IP address?"

Stash looks surprised I'd ask this, "Yes. Aces would normally fix IP address issues. But in this case he's been working on a project with higher priority so I took care of it for him."

"Are you the boss?"

"Not hardly. Aces and me... we're just cogs in the wheel. Someone else tells us what we need to do and then sets priorities if needed."

"Who?"

"Grendele's Modor," Stash sits up straighter. He's clearly thinking about what to say next. He apparently decides to say nothing more. Stash catches a flashing light from his laptop screen, turns to give it his full attention.

"What's the matter?" I try to keep the same innocent voice.

"Malfunctioning delivery van," Stash checks a few things. He then starts trying to give it instructions. I assuming the instructions are to reset something.

"Another bad IP address?" I ask to keep him talking with me.

Stash shakes his head. He tries even more things. I come around and look over his shoulder. Stash is ignoring me as he keeps checking sensors to see what's not working properly. The autonomous delivery van has come to a stop, which tells me a sensor is malfunctioning sending conflicting information to the master controller so it doesn't know which sensor is correct. I watched a video on this very problem only a few weeks ago. The controllers are programmed to stop as a safety precaution in those circumstances, but I don't say anything, letting Stash show me how he figures this out.

I notice Stash has taken an entirely different approach to solving the issue. He's checking out basic information about the vehicle, such as the state of charge on the battery and whether the sensors are working, not whether they are working properly. It's like he's going through a check list, rather than looking at the symptoms and working from the logic behind them.

It takes a while for Stash to confirm all sensors are working. Only now has he started up the higher-level logic to see if he can find conflicting data. I spotted the camera on the left front apparently has been obscured by something. It's working and sending data but the data is incomplete. Mud maybe. If Stash would do a physical inspection of the vehicle from nearby camera systems he might be able to spot the issue visually, rather than checking data feeds. But I guess he's doing what they teach integration engineers to do.

Stash still doesn't see the issue as he goes through the data feeds. Data is coming, it's just not complete. The data coming across is not providing the controller the complete picture it needs to be sure there's nothing in the path of the vehicle on that side of the road. I want to say something, but if I do, Stash will know almost instantly I've been playing him. That wouldn't be good.

I leave Stash to his problem, knowing if I continue staring at it at some point I'm going to say something. I go back to my wall, sit and pull my legs up in front of me. I lay my head down on my knees. If I do this maybe I can figure out how I'm going to get Stash to take me home. It's clear to me Aces isn't going to. I expect if Stash finally agrees Aces will likely try to stop him. So I have to hope at some point Aces will leave us.

"I found it," Stash sounds victorious. "Malfunctioning sensor. Sending erroneous data the master controller wouldn't accept. I've shut it down and instructed the master to compare data from two other sensors to fill the hole in the data stream. That way the delivery can be made. Later someone can go out and replace the defective sensor." Stash looks over at me to see if I'm listening. I've looked up at him from my fetal position and I guess it is enough for him. "Routine fix. But you'd be surprised how often things like this happen. No system can heal itself. There will always be problems. That's why people like us are out here, working behind the scenes so the owner's family can enjoy their day without having to worry about any systems issues."

Stash is trying to backtrack about working on our cocoon, but I now think he does. *So are Jason and Ophelia in danger of being kidnapped too? Is anyone safe there now?*

Chapter Nine: Jason Braveheart

Inspector Stebbins questions me although I'm only half listening to him, trying to decide if Albert might have convinced Jaz to run away so he could sleep with her. *He's been alone with her on video on more than one occasion, but I've never seen anything…*

"…footprints?" the Inspector has asked a question. *How do I answer when I didn't hear it all, and yet I don't want him to think I'm not paying attention?*

"The footprints? You mean at the meter?"

"Yes. Were you able to determine whether they were your footprints?"

"Well… as I mentioned I do have a pair of them, although I don't remember standing next to the meter when I did the walk around."

"So they could have been from whoever cut the power."

I don't want to seem flustered, but I'm not really sure how to answer his question. "Possible. But I also can't be sure they aren't mine. I really wasn't paying much attention to the contractor or what we were looking at when I was out there. It's a simple job. I was in the middle of a project when he came by. I tried to get my wife to go out. Show him what had to be done. But she said that wasn't in her job description."

"Seems to be a lot of tension between you and your wife. I would guess it's not just over your daughter's disappearance." The detective points out, looking for me to provide more detail.

"Do you live in a cocoon?" I decide to ask as a way of making a point.

Detective Stebbins shakes his head, "Out of my price range on a public servant's salary."

"You get out and about," I note for him. "Spend your days with others, whether at the police station or conducting your investigations. We spend all day, nearly every day, together in this small house."

Detective Stebbins nods apparently in understanding. "The active walls don't help? I mean you get to immerse yourselves in new places whenever you want. You have conversations with people all over the globe. Don't they expand your world in ways those of us who have to trudge the streets to get from one place to another never get to experience?"

"It's like anything," I try to answer his question, although it's hard to give an answer he will appreciate. "You quickly assume the way things are is how it is for everyone. You don't think about it as being different for you than anyone else. It's different for everyone, not because I have active walls and you don't, but because every circumstance is different. Ophelia and I come from very different backgrounds. A lot of things draw us together and other things just drive the other up a wall. The more time we spend together the more it seems the latter moments dominate. I know that doesn't answer your question, but about all I can say is we love each other. We love our daughter and will do whatever we have to in order to bring her home."

Detective Stebbins nods, although there seems to be some question in his eyes.

"What's bothering you?" I finally decide to test what I think I'm seeing.

"I get paid to ask a lot of questions, and sometimes they get to be uncomfortable," the detective responds with what I think is almost amusement in his tone of voice. *I don't like him.*

"But let me assure you my questions always have a relevance. In this case I'm trying to understand why this disappearance occurred."

"That's absurd," I protest immediately, but Detective Stebbins must have known my response was coming and has his hand up to stop me from saying more.

"You and your wife had a role in what's happened, although I'm sure you don't think so. But you did, even if it's indirect. In most cases you can only see your role after the fact."

"What do you mean?" I'm still angry with his accusation.

"It may have been encouraging her to apply to MIT. It may have been doing the admissions video. It could have been some event you took her to, where someone noticed her because of a remark you made, or something she said about working with you at your company."

I still don't like what he's accusing us of doing, but I need to let him conduct the investigation or I have no idea how we'll ever find Jaz.

"Now the question about the tension between you and your wife… that's usually an indication something happened I need to look at. One or the other of you said something or did something to make the other uncomfortable. That's a prime place to start."

"I can assure you Albert…" again the hand comes up to stop me. I grimace.

"No need for assurances. I've made a note and will investigate him as I will every other person of interest we identify. If your evaluation of the situation proves out, there's no problem. But at least we will have removed one suspect from the case and will be able to focus our energy to more promising areas to investigate."

I understand his logic, but I'm already exhausted. I know it's just getting started. Then a thought occurs, "You said I may have done something that caused this without knowing it."

Detective Stebbins nods curiously.

"I didn't think about it before, but what about the contractor?" I see Detective Stebbins react with an almost puzzled look. "We were just talking about the footprints being near the meter. I took the contractor around the house. He got a clear understanding of how to take us offline if he wanted to. Do you think maybe he had something to do with the abduction?"

Detective Stebbins makes a note in his cellphone, "I assume you have the information on the contractor?"

I nod.

"Did you get the name of the individual who came out?"

"I was just trying to remember," *it hasn't come back to me yet.* "As I said, I was all into a project when he came by so I was only half listening to him."

"What did he look like?"

"About my size, plus or minus ten or fifteen pounds," I try to picture the guy as I describe him. "Maybe an inch or so taller."

"Any distinguishing marks?"

"I really didn't see his face. He had a hospital mask on like everyone. Trying to keep from getting or spreading a virus I suppose."

"Hair color?"

"He had a ballcap on so really didn't notice. About the only thing I can say was it was most likely dark. You know, brown or black. I think if he was blonde or red, I would have noticed."

"Why?" the detective asks as he makes more notes, doesn't look up until I don't respond immediately. Then he looks at me, probably wondering why I haven't answered. "Why would you have noticed?"

"He was wearing a Giants ball cap," *I assume he knows what I'm talking about but he's giving me a blank stare.* "You know the one, black with an orange 'SF' logo. Dark hair would just blend, but red or blonde would have stood out. I don't remember anything standing out about him."

"Clothes?"

"What you'd expect. Work boots, stained jeans…"

"What kind of stains?"

"Well he's a painter so… paint stains I would guess," *I have to think about it for a moment.* "You know… splotches of different color paints. Probably painted a number of different houses with all different colors."

"If he's a painter, was he darkly tanned, like someone who works out in the sun?"

"Suntans don't mean anything with the sunscreens everyone uses now," I push back as I quickly try to decide if he was or not. "But it seems at least his hands were tanned. I remember he pointed out a couple things he was going to have to address I'd not noticed. Thought at the time he was building a case to charge me more money. But now as I think about it he was pointing out things someone may have been able to use to figure out how to bring the power down."

"What do you mean?"

"Well he asked if I wanted exposed wires painted over," I remember aloud. "He showed me where cable entrances were drilled. Showed me they probably needed to be sealed to keep insects and rodents out of the house. Told me squirrels will gnaw away at almost anything in an attempt to get inside. I hadn't thought about it before."

"So he was at least knowledgeable about how to interrupt your communications and security systems from his walk around," the detective summarizes.

I nod, "Would seem so," *I should have been paying more attention to what I was doing, but it was just a contractor. Why should I have had any concerns for our safety?*

"I didn't notice, has the contractor done the work yet?"

I should have expected this question, "No. I haven't put him under contract. I was busy on this project and just haven't gotten around to it."

"So you may have frustrated him if he was intending to put any kind of interrupt systems in place while he was painting. May be why he resorted to the power outage. I've not seen anyone take that approach to bring down a security system before. Usually they put a bypass in so those who are monitoring the house won't notice what they are doing. Gives them more time."

"I know all about bypasses," I have to admit. "My company makes them, although only for the government and law enforcement agencies."

"Then you know the kind of person this may be," Detective Stebbins fills me with dread.

Chapter Ten: Jazmin Braveheart

I wake with a start. *Where am I?* I lift my head from my knees and slowly open my eyes. I'm aching everywhere. I realize I'm sitting on the floor with my back to the wall. How long…? Then I remember I'm not in my room, nor in my bed. I'm somewhere… I don't even know where or why. As my eyes focus I see Stash and Aces sitting on opposite sides of the lone table. But then someone else comes rushing in.

He… I think it's a he. Hard to tell really. Dressed like the others, hospital mask over his face, ball cap with the same stylized M. The whole working-class uniform, I guess. He comes right up behind Aces, puts his hand on the masked techie's shoulder and says through his mask, "Time to move." He looks at Stash who glances back at me. "Bring her."

Stash grimaces as he rises. "You need to come with us," Stash says in a tone betraying his reluctance. I don't know if he doesn't want to make me come with him, or he'd rather not leave this place where he has apparently worked for at least a while.

"Where?" I ask, trying to sound groggy, which isn't hard since I am.

"Wherever Rocketman is taking us," Stash responds with a tilt of his head in the direction of the person who has just joined us.

I decide asking about Rocketman is probably not a good thing to do at present. The new guy would probably simply tell Stash to shut up. Better to wait until he leaves us in our new destination. Stash might even be able to give me clues as to where I am, if I keep being nice to him. I get up off the floor and clap my hands together to get the dust from the floor off them. Run my hands over my body to make sure there aren't spiders crawling over me. Rocketman watches my brushing off, mask still in place. I still can't tell if he's a him or a her.

Stash waits for me. Hands me a facemask as I follow Rocketman. I note Rocketman has a battery-operated soldering gun in a holster on his left side. I've never seen anything like it before. Both Aces and Stash follow me carrying computer equipment, although Aces left his monitors. *Curious.* I note Stash turns off the lights. *Also curious since lights are all automatic in the cocoon. I didn't realize you had to turn lights on or off manually anywhere.* I'm starting to understand things are very different here and probably in a lot of places I've never been. Sure, I see them on my wall monitors. But I've never noticed details like this.

The house we are in appears to be smaller than the cocoon. I've apparently been in the garage as we walk into the house to go outside to get into the car. For whatever reason, Rocketman chooses not to open the garage doors I now notice in the low light. He leads us into the small house to the front door. I can't see how big it is, but the rooms are very small with no furniture. Now outside I see it's nighttime. *Did they wait until now so fewer eyes will be on us as we leave?* I would guess it to be the reason for moving now.

I look around. I don't recognize the trees or flowers so I can't tell where I am. It's dark enough I can't tell if there are mountains in the distance or desert or maybe even an ocean, which might give me an indication of where I am. *This yard is typical of so many I've seen so I really have no idea where I am or where I'm going. Not helpful.*

I'm quickly pushed into the back seat of the auton, or autonomous vehicle. I hear the door locks click in place so I know I can't get out until we reach our destination. Someone is going to extreme measures to ensure I'm kept captive, at least for now. Rocketman and Aces take the front seats with Stash in the back with me. Rocketman apparently doesn't want me to hear an address. He leans over a touchscreen and inputs the address he wants to go to rather than just saying it for the controller to map out the trip. *Never seen that before.*

I look out the windows of the auton. Stash glances over but doesn't say anything. I suppose he could have tried to keep me from seeing where we are going. But at the moment, it probably doesn't matter since I have no idea where I've been. *Are we still in California? No idea. Nothing I've seen would help me decide whether I am or not.*

"Why are we doing this?" I ask Stash in a low voice, hoping Rocketman and Aces won't hear.

But Rocketman instantly turns to me and responds forcefully. "Not your concern."

Stash shrugs and looks out his window. I would really like to know why both Aces and Stash seem to defer to Rocketman, but there is no hope of getting answers in the auton, or likely even when we get to where we are going until Rocketman leaves. But based on my observation so far, neither Aces nor Stash have left yet so likely I'll have to wait a while.

The auton has taken us up onto a superhighway. But unfortunately the names on the buildings are those I could imagine seeing anywhere in the US. Nothing I'm seeing would cause me to say I'm definitely in Los Angeles or San Francisco. Those are the cities I know the best from the many virtual trips I've taken for school. I'm starting to wonder if being cocooned has actually been a good thing for me. Sure, I've seen the world from the limited view the monitor walls provide. But I'm not sure I really have a memory of the places I've seen. Would I recognize Buenos Aires, even though I've seen much of the city virtually? If I walked down Bourbon Street in New Orleans would the smells and sounds really tell me where I am? I don't think so having never experienced them. I'm driving in an auton in the middle of the night. The sensory perceptions normally telling me where I am are completely failing me. For all I know I could be in Saudi Arabia in the American oil producers compound and not know. What I'd see would not look significantly different.

I have to make a decision. *Do I continue looking out the window in hopes of seeing something... anything... telling me where I am? Or do I sit back and wait until Rocketman has delivered us where we need to be? As defined by someone I apparently haven't met yet. Someone who has life and death decision-making over me. Someone who could, at the wave of a hand, in essence, end me?* The thought sends a chill through me.

I look out the window to see what I can see. *Not much.* Office buildings with nationally known company signs. Apartment complexes without enough information to tell me what I need to do next. The rent per month is apparently the most important piece of information a prospective renter needs to know. Where these rental properties are? Not an issue. The renters expect you've already decided how much of an issue the morning and evening drives are going to be. Decided if you want to be right next door to where you work, or at least made a decision about how far away you want to be.

We have come into a city. *Not sure what city, but we are clearly more downtown than suburb.* I wonder if that's a part of the strategy. *Move me from suburbs to urban and then some other demographic so it will be harder to track me down. Find out what these people really want from me?*

The auton turns into the underground parking garage for what I can see in the brief moment I have to look up, an apartment high rise. I still have no idea where I am. But now I'm in the parking garage under a tall building. Will they put me into a room with windows this time? A high rise would seem to be a place where the apartment would want to have lots of windows so you can see where you are. I'm now hopeful I'll be able to see enough to decide if I'm still in California or not.

We pull into a designated parking space. The auton must have known this was the place to park. Not sure how it knew, but it did. I expect to get out of the car, but we wait. I look out my window and see a couple, probably in their late forties or early fifties, walking together from an auton to the elevator entrance to this building. We are apparently waiting for them to go up before we get out. Not taking any chances I might call out to them. Seems to be a decision Rocketman would have made. Not sure Stash would have thought of what I might do, but I could be wrong about him.

The couple has disappeared into the elevator entrance, and yet we still wait. Probably giving them time for the elevator to come pick them up. Then Rocketman is on the move. He opens his door and all the others seem to open at the same time. I sit still, but in only a moment Rocketman comes to my door, reaches in and pulls me by my arm out of the auton. He roughly pushes me ahead of him. None of them surround me as they did to get me out of the last place. Now I'm leading the pack towards the elevator.

Aces pushes the button summonsing the elevator. No words are exchanged, but apparently everyone except me knows what's in store for us. The elevator light illuminates as the door opens. A young man, probably not much older than me is in the car. I'm slammed against the wall so hard it takes my breath away. Someone steps into me so I can't say a word. I'm surprised the young man on the elevator doesn't notice. But if he does, he refrains from saying anything. I don't see him other than for one brief instant as he is gone when they pull me forward and push me into the elevator. As the doors close I realize Rocketman is the one who was so brutal to me.

We only go up to the second floor. *I'm not going to see much from here even if there are windows.* Someone has given this a lot of thought. Whoever is in charge... Gendele's Modor? Whoever... apparently... she is, planned this to ensure I'll not have much information to give anyone when or if I'm released. The only one I could recognize is Stash. What are the chances I'll ever see him again? I don't even know if Rocketman is a guy or a girl. The way I was tossed against the wall I'd have to think he's a dude. But even my perception may be stereotype. Maybe it was just so unexpected....

When we exit the elevator Rocketman is the one with the key to the apartment. Key? Really? Why doesn't it just recognize you like the cocoon recognizes me? I'm becoming even more aware of how much there is a difference between those of us who are cocooned and those who are not. Technology has enabled a lifestyle only available to those who can afford it. For everyone else, it's a very different existence. *Better or worse? I don't know yet. But clearly different.*

We enter the apartment. Appears to be just three rooms and a bath. The first thing I observe is a desk with dual monitors like the place we just left. Aces goes to it immediately and redocks his computer into the screens. The kitchen has the usual appliances. I see a bedroom beyond. When I reach the door I'm surprised there's nothing in the bedroom. *No bed, no dressers, nothing on the walls.* Whoever is behind taking me from my family and home doesn't expect anyone to stay long, nor worry about comfort. It's also clear no one lives here regularly. *This must be a 'safe house'.* A term I've heard before, but never really thought much about it. With this first move so quickly after I woke up, my guess is we are planning to stay where we were only for a day or two. Probably not much longer. *Keep moving me so I'll be harder to find. Any indication of where I am? The police will go there and find I'm already gone.*

I'm standing at the end of the kitchen countertop when the realization hits me. I collapse to the floor and sit in a lotus position. Legs tucked in and leaning forward. *Time to meditate. Get my spirit back into harmony. If they are going to threaten me, let me get back into a mental state where I'm not threatened, but in harmony with my surroundings even if they are not surroundings of my choice.*

Rocketman looks at Stash, "What's she doing?"

Stash doesn't answer. Since I'm not looking at him I imagine he simply shrugs at Rocketman.

"Put her in the bedroom. I don't want her interrupting what we need to get done.'

Chapter Eleven: Stash

She seems so frail. I don't want to hurt her, but neither Aces nor Rocketman seem to care. All they are concerned about is how much is going to be in their bank account on Friday. I get that, but there has to be some balance, you know?

I help her to her feet, although she resists. Guide her into the bedroom and close the door behind her. I don't want to know if she goes back into the same position once she's in there. At least she's out of sight. Not sure if she's safe in there as I've heard rumors about Aces. Not sure I'd want to leave her alone with him very long, although they were apparently able to avoid any encounters before I got to the Modesto house. I think I would have noticed if he'd already raped her. Maybe she's just not all that developed he'd want to screw her like nearly every other woman he's encountered. At least that's the rumor about him. Maybe he just doesn't see her as a woman… yet. Could be a good thing for her.

As I close the door to the bedroom, Rocketman nods to me from across the room. "She's not going to be with us for long. So don't get any ideas."

"About what?" I push back at him.

"She's not our problem. We're just doing what we're told. Got it?"

"Hey, I'm just here to do my job," I respond to his admonishment. "The fact we got to babysit her? That's just a short-term gig."

"Then get back to work and forget about her." Rocketman is apparently not happy I'm kind of lingering at the bedroom door. I'm sure he has no idea I'm concerned about Aces. I'm certainly not going to say anything about it. "Not your problem," he concludes.

59

"Why are you all of a sudden the one in charge?" I toss back at him as I cross the room and set up my laptop. "No one I know promoted you."

Rocketman pushes me hard, but I catch myself and get right in his face. "Last I knew you were just a technician, fixing things I assigned to you. So stop. You're not in charge here. You never have been. The fact she told you where we needed to take what's her name didn't change anything. So get back to work. There's a problem with an auton controller in your region, so get on it. Time to restoration is money, if you've forgotten."

Rocketman pulls his solder gun from his holster and points it at my face. Pulls the trigger. I just frown at him and shake my head.

"Probably software," I respond to let him know he won't likely need to fix a hardware problem even though fixing hardware was why he was hired in our group.

"Then why you giving it to me and not Aces?" Rocketman pulls the trigger on his solder gun again.

"Because he's working a higher priority issue," I respond in as determined a fashion as I know how. "That's all you need to know."

Rocketman looks at the bedroom door, shakes his head and goes to set up his computer on the kitchen countertop. There's no more room at the small desk where Aces is already back working on his software debug.

I go over to the desk and set up across from Aces as I did in the other office. I bring up my email and notice something new has come in. From Grendele's Modor. She seldom sends me email. So this has to be important. I open it and read her note telling me there has been a change in priorities. We are to work here for the next twenty-four hours. An auton will show up to take us to the next location. We are to meet it in the same stall in the garage exactly twenty-four hours from now unless she provides other instructions. *What's this all about? Why is this girl here in the first place?* Modor hasn't given us any insight into what's going on. I have to believe it's deliberate.

I send back a note acknowledging the instructions. I then ask if there are any other priorities we need to be focused on.

The response is quick, meaning she's on-line now. "You know your highest priority."

I do, but she's never given me enough information to really understand why it's important to keep this girl out of sight. Modor described it as a simple case of holding onto someone until things were worked out. Then we can release her to her parents. Never any information about why or what the real risks are we're running by doing this. She made it clear there may be police involved, but not much more. The money she offered was good for someone like me, but still not enough to want to go away because of it. But then you never think things will go wrong when you get into anything.

I decide to search the social media to see if there's anything about the girl. See if I can figure out what's really going on. Since I don't have a name or anything telling me how to search, I just use the general inquiry of 'missing persons.' A long list of names comes up, but no pictures. I modify the search for pictures of missing persons. A whole plethora of pictures come up. I start scrolling through, but soon realize this is going to take a while. I don't want Rocketman or Aces to see what I'm doing. So I shut down the images and bring up the work we've been assigned. I have a new issue to deal with. Apparently a repeater failure on the communications backbone. Causing a whole bunch of cocoons to go off line. I know the longer it takes me to bring this up the more likely I am to hear from Modor about it. She gets the first call. I get the second. But if it takes too long I get a constant barrage of queries I need to respond to. The calls make it almost impossible to fix the problem. *Learned a long time ago to avoid calls from happening as much as possible.*

I go to work on the repeater, isolating the one off-line, pinging it to see if it's receiving messages. It's not. Means it's stone cold dead. I send instructions to the robotic repair service with the specifics of the unit and its location with instructions to replace with like. I see a message come back with confirmation of a drone dispatch. I forward to Modor so she will know the problem is being addressed and can answer any questions she fields. The robotic repair service estimates thirty-eight minutes until service restoration. I know probably thirty is getting on site. The swap out is pretty straight forward. Once a new unit goes in the whole communications line will come back up.

I hear the bedroom door open and glance over. The girl is shyly looking around, notes I'm looking at her. She points to the bathroom. I nod and watch her cross the room, closing the door behind her.

When I turn back to my computer I note Rocketman is also looking at her. Don't know why she's of so much interest to him. I'm sure if I ask he won't tell me. Aces, on the other hand, seems to completely ignore her. He's probably figured out the issue with the software debug and is focused on writing the fix. I'm still trying to figure out why he was selected to work the software issue since he's not software. It's one I normally would have handled. But Modor sent the note down instructing him to work it. Something about Aces found the issue originally and she wanted him to figure out how to fix it. At the time I thought it was some kind of training exercise or something. But the more I've thought about it, I'm not so sure. I wonder if she wants to put a trap door or other malicious code into the system and wants it to be something the rest of us don't know about. Aces was a hacker for a while before he decided he needed to feed his habit and stay out of jail for a while.

The girl opens the door to the bathroom, glances around like she wants to know where everyone is before she comes out. I can understand her reluctance to engage us, she doesn't know why she's here, or what's going to happen to her. She seems real wary of Aces. Makes me think he wasn't gentle with her before I arrived. I wonder if he tried something, but looking at her, if he had, I doubt she could have done much to stop him. I'll have to keep that in mind when Aces comes up for air, particularly if we have to go out and leave him alone with her.

Chapter Twelve: Amare Stebbins

"Certainly your right," I respond to Jason Braveheart's forceful announcement as I watch his face on the video wall of my office at the Napa Valley Police Department. "I can't advise you not to hire your own detectives, but I must inform you if they interfere in any way with the investigation I am conducting I will put them in jail until I find her."

My response doesn't seem to faze Jason. I note Mrs. Braveheart is not in the room with him, so I presume she is the one who has pushed him into making this decision.

"He has already begun," Jason confirms for me.

"Would you be willing to share who you've employed so when he contacts me, and I assure you he will, I know who I can provide information to and who I should not."

Jason does a double take apparently not understanding my question. "You think whoever took Jaz might contact you?"

"They might," I respond to get him to think about his decision. "Generally they pose as a newspaper reporter who is running down a tip."

"The abductor comes to your office?" Jason is still trying to process this revelation.

"The usual approach is a call to my office. Most of them know I can't trace the call unless I'm expecting it. Even if I am, the person usually will call at an odd time. Either early in the morning or in the evening. Start out telling me they're working a deadline and just want to know if there is an investigation ongoing. I always tell them there are several investigations ongoing. Do they have any more information they can share?"

"They give you the name of the missing person?" Jason tries to follow.

"Not always at first," I continue this thread to see where he goes with it. "Sometimes they'll say they don't have a name, just a vague description which always is the person involved."

"What do they want to know?" Jason still tries to figure out why the kidnapper would call the police. "I mean, you're not going to tell them anything about an ongoing investigation."

"No, but the press knows we never confirm if there is an ongoing investigation unless we need help finding someone," I inform him. "The fact we will neither confirm nor deny is an indication we are… investigating something and don't want broad help yet."

Jason seems to consider something. He then frowns and reengages me. "Do you think the person who took Jaz might… call your office?"

"Impossible to tell," he still seems to be considering something. "Why? Does your company make phone tap devices too?"

"As a matter of fact…" Jason hardens his expression. "How would you like a report of all the people who call you? Name, address, phone number and last known employment?"

"Would depend on how you obtain the information. At the moment I can't think of a legal means of doing so without a court order," I caution him.

"Set that aside for a moment… if you were to see a list of names, would you be able to tell which ones called you on any given day?"

"As a law enforcement officer I can't set unlawful activity aside for a moment or even a nanosecond. I have to warn you if you engage in illegal activity I will be required to arrest you and see to it you are prosecuted to the full extent of the law."

"Say for a moment… I should come into possession of a list of names from a third party…"

HAPPINESS

"Who happens to use a piece of equipment your company makes?" I guess instantly.

"Also beside the point," Jason puzzles on something for a moment.

"It's not beside the point I'm making," I'm starting to get angry because he keeps pushing something he shouldn't.

"What if a law enforcement officer were to provide such a list of names to me?"

"I can only advise you not to go down that path," I respond leaving no doubt.

Jason apparently makes a decision, "I'm sure that won't be necessary. But you asked a question. What was it you wanted to know?"

"Who is your detective?" I respond still angry.

"Peter Tate."

I see the glee in Jason's eyes. Peter Tate is a former FBI agent with an impressive history of bringing in the bad guy. But Peter left the Bureau under a cloud about two years ago. The rumors were he had gone rogue, acquiring his own technology to obtain evidence without necessary court orders. It would seem Jason Braveheart may have been the supplier of the technology Tate used. *What else does Jason Braveheart make at his fantastic tech factory?*

"Does your relationship with Mr. Tate have anything to do with your daughter's disappearance?" I have to ask now wondering if a motive has been revealed. *What else is Jason not telling me?*

Jason sits back in his chair. Apparently I've made him consider something else he's not sharing. "My relationship with Mr. Tate is not what you're probably thinking. My wife called him."

"What is the relationship your wife has with Mr. Tate?" *I get the*

65

feeling this isn't going to be pretty.

"Mr. Tate was her first husband," Jason responds apparently thinking through the implications.

"Is he…" I leave hanging out there purposefully.

"No, Jazmin is mine," Jason responds too quickly. "Ophelia divorced him more than a year before I met her."

Great. Sounds like I'm going to have a disgraced rogue cop barging around my investigation, looking for what I have to believe is his daughter, even though he apparently never claimed paternity. From Jason's response it would appear he knows.

"Because of their past relationship Ophelia was able to get him cheap," Jason concludes.

"If you want me to give any information to him, you'll have to send me a written release." I shake my head so he will know I don't think it's a good idea.

"MC, provide the detective the release," Jason says to his system. A moment later I see the release arrive in my message inbox.

"I take it no one has contacted you about your daughter," I seek confirmation and make it sound like I believed him about Jazmin's paternity, although I clearly don't.

"No." For the first time Jason sounds depressed.

"Has anything else come to you about the day she disappeared? Anything giving us a direction?"

Jason shakes his head sadly.

"Anything else about the house painter?"

Jason looks at me quizzically. "I thought you said he didn't work for the painting company."

"He didn't according to the owner. Apparently he had one of your phone intercept devices and took the call himself. Ironic don't you think?"

"Other companies make similar devices," Jason deflects my accusation.

"But it would appear your painter knew who you are and what you do for a living. Seems he deliberately turned your technology against you."

Jason stares at me. I'm having trouble deciphering whether he's already come to my conclusion, or whether he has an idea of who might be behind the abduction of his daughter. Either way, he's not going to tell me.

Chapter Thirteen: Jazmin Braveheart

I sit on the floor next to the slightly open door to the bedroom. No furniture in here. At least I can see what the three guys are doing, which at the moment is working on their laptops. *I'm still amazed anyone ever worked this way.* Rocketman leaves the kitchen counter in response to a doorbell ring. I hear the door open. He doesn't say a word to whoever is there, but the door closes almost immediately. I hear the locks click in. He comes back into the kitchen carrying two large but flat boxes. I smell them although I don't recognize the odor. Aces and Stash are on their feet, crowding around him.

"That one has everything. This is just extra cheese and peperoni," Rocketman informs them. I see Stash taking bites out of thin triangles he holds, although I've never seen this before. *It must be time to eat. I've not even thought about food since the tomato slice and lettuce. Seems like a long time ago.*

Just looking at the triangles I simply assume it's not something I can eat, with my diet.

Stash looks at me, "Come have a slice."

I shake my head, "It's not on my diet. I'm strictly vegan."

"No wonder you're so thin. You could stand to gain a few pounds…."

"Not an option," I respond but don't intend to tell him why.

"You got a medical condition or religious belief thing going there?" Stash comes closer while the other two are listening.

"I've been on a plant-based diet my whole life," is all I'll offer by way of explanation.

"Pizza won't hurt you," Stash takes another bite before continuing. "You should just try it. You might find you like it."

"Food's not something you like. It's a biological necessity," I consider for a moment before continuing, "Liking it must be what leads you to look like you do."

"You saying I'm fat?" Stash seems surprised as he grasps his belly through his flannel shirt. "This is just my reserve for the next virus shut down. I was eating stale potato chips and ripe olives for like a week last time."

"Virus shutdown?" I ask having not heard the term before.

"Oh, that's right. You're a cocoon baby. You have everything delivered. Comes from special stores, ones people like us can't shop in. You get your vegan food from those same stores. Well, you'll eat whatever we have when you get hungry enough." Stash shoves the rest of the triangle into his mouth and chews with his cheeks bulging. He swallows and returns to the kitchen for another slice.

I bring my knees up to my chest and bring my forehead down to them. I need to relax. I guess I wasn't aware of how tense I am. Probably normal but somehow I haven't focused on it until now. My shoulders are where I start. I think about relaxing them. *Bring my right shoulder down, and then the left. Let my arms go limp. Just hang there.* I listen to my heart. Deliberately try to slow it down as it's beating faster than usual. *Slow. Slower*

I feel my heart rate begin to slow.

"Last slice…" Stash calls, "Oops. Aces took it. No more pizza. Guess you'll just have to continue to wait."

I look up, "You going to order something I can eat tomorrow?"

"Any of you guys vegan?" Stash asks, looking at Rocketman and then Aces who ignores him. "No vegans here."

I decide to change the subject, "When are you going to tell me why you brought me here?"

Stash looks at Rocketman, "You'd have to ask him. He's the one who got the call."

I look at Rocketman who ignores both of us, although I get the distinct impression he isn't.

"Whose apartment is this?" I push Stash.

He shrugs, "I just go where I'm told. Here today, someplace else tomorrow."

"So you don't have a permanent office you work out of?"

Stash shakes his head, "Never have. This job is for freelancers. You work for one company for a while if they have contracts. If they lose them you go someplace else. Just the way it is."

"How long have you been working here?"

"I don't know," Stash considers my question, "Been a while. Year maybe."

"That's all?"

"It's what it is. I mean I've worked other places for a month. Then they tell me they don't have any work for me even though I've been working my ass off and not even taken a day off."

"You're all right with…?" I'm surprised he would accept such working conditions.

"What's to be all right with?" Stash sits down in the chair at the desk across from Aces. "I'm the old guy here. I mean neither of them were on this job when I started. In fact, I don't think anyone on our team was. Just the nature of work. You work when you can, and when you can't you look for another job. Somebody always has a malfunctioning system and is looking for someone to come fix it. That's what we do. We just float from one dysfunctional system to another."

HAPPINESS

"You said you were fixing things at my cocoon," I'm trying to figure out how to ask this question so he will answer it. "What was wrong with it?"

"Your place?" Stash considers my question. "Somebody there's a data hog. I mean I had to continually add bandwidth, was always getting requests for more processing speed. The house wasn't wired for it so I had to add an external microwave link. Direct, line of sight system to get you what you wanted."

"I don't know anything about how it works," I want him to continue thinking I'm naive.

"Probably your old man," Stash dismisses my question.

"Why did you say 'probably my old man?'"

"Your father's some big deal, isn't he?" Stash looks at his computer screen. "He would have to be for you to live there."

"What are you saying?" I push him, sounding defensive rather than angry.

"You don't see any of us living in a cocoon," Stash shoots back. "There's a whole lot more people like us than like you."

"Like me."

"Yeah. Look at you," Stash gives me a once over. "Never seen pizza. Too good to eat a hamburger. Only vegan food. You don't even have a virus mask. Nobody goes out there without one. So you never leave your cocoon. Your clothes. Where did you get those clothes? You don't dress like anyone else here. So yeah. People like you and your rich parents and your cocooned friends. I bet you never met anyone who worked for a living before did you?"

"I have," I try not to sound too defensive so he will believe me.

"Who?"

"My father works."

71

"No. He doesn't work. He owns the company. People work for him. Have you ever met any of them?"

I nod, "I know several people who work with him. Talk to them on the video wall when they call for my father."

"Not the same. We're the first real people you've ever met."

"What do you mean, real people?"

"What are you, a parrot?" Stash flashes angrily.

"No. I'm just trying to understand what you think I need to know about you."

"You don't need to know anything about me. But you do need to know the world isn't the one you live in. You and your family might as well live on a different planet. There's nothing about our world that even resembles yours. We live in a world where we survive the best we can. We take shit jobs because they're the best we can get. Every time we go outside we risk infections that could kill us. The food we eat is synthetic because nothing's real anymore. All the media does is try to convince us to buy something we don't need. They try to tell us we aren't important if we don't wear what they tell us we should because someone we don't know does and we should want to be just like them. I mean our life sucks, but it's the best we got for now."

"Then why don't you move to a cocoon?" I ask innocently.

"You're not listening," Stash dismisses me, but then thinks again, "You got to have money to live in a cocoon. We don't have money. The three of us together don't have enough money."

"Then why don't you get a different job. One where you make enough?"

"How old are you?"

"Old enough," I respond not wanting to tell him.

"There's the one percent of all people who have the money. The rest of us don't. You're a one percent family. You should be happy, because the ninety-nine percent got nothing and you got it all."

"If you got a different job couldn't you become a one percenter?" I'm not entirely sure what I should make of his description of the world.

"If I had my own company? Maybe. But you got to have money to make money." Stash looks at what he's wearing. "I got the clothes on my back and a laptop to my name. Not exactly what it would take."

"That's your laptop?" I take a closer look. I've not seen one before.

"Old but serviceable."

"Doesn't the company give you what you need to do your job?"

Stash laughs. "Something happens to my trusty laptop I'm gonna starve because I can't get a job."

"My father would hire you."

"The only thing your father would do for me is put me in jail." Stash turns away finished with me for now.

Chapter Fourteen: Rocketman

Stash has to learn when to shut up. Nothing to be gained by talking with her. Besides she won't be here long, either way it goes. We need to just forget about her until we know what's to be done. "Aces, lock her in the bedroom."

Aces and Stash both look at me like I'm crazy. But Aces gets up and goes over to do as I ask. Stash clearly looks unhappy, but doesn't stop him.

The girl seems to steel herself as Aces approaches her, as if she is expecting something… and not something good. Do I have to say something to him? Probably not. Likely Modor will let him have her when this is all over.

When the girl is locked up Stash is up on his feet, "What's that all about? Modor didn't say anything about locking her up. We just need to keep her out of sight."

"The girl's not your problem," I remind him.

"As long as we all got to watch her, she is," Stash is thinking again. Got to put an end to that.

"You don't have to work out of here. Aces and I can handle a kid," I turn back to my computer to let him know I think the discussion is over.

"Someone has to provide adult supervision here, and neither of you morons are going to make this painless for everyone."

I shake my head, but don't look up, although I'm not really thinking about the problem I need to solve either.

"What's the plan, if you even know?" Stash walks over towards me.

"You got the instructions the same time I did," I remind him.

"You talked to her about coming here. So did she say anything more?"

"About the plan? No."

"So all we're supposed to do is wait. She'll tell us what to do next?"

"That's the plan," I confirm.

"What's in this for her?" Stash asks, although I'm not sure if he's asking me or just asking.

"She's not telling us shit about what's in it for her, so don't bother to ask," I clarify for him what our role is. "We're just the hired help. She doesn't have to explain anything. We agreed to do this because she's paying us. You could have said no. But you didn't. And here we are. So don't complain. Don't ask questions and most importantly, don't get involved with the kid."

"You're not in charge," Stash apparently decides to clarify a few things himself. "We agreed to do this together. We all get paid the same amount. So don't go telling me what I can and can't do here."

"What's your problem with leaving well enough alone, Stash?" I turn to face him now, looking over Aces who is doing his best to stay out of this whole discussion. "I mean why do you think you need to be her best friend? She's not going to do shit for you, if that's what you're thinking. Be the nice guy. When it's all over she'll tell Daddy you saved her from the rest of us. Maybe he'll give you a job like she said. Maybe you'll make enough you can own a cocoon. Wake up. That's never gonna happen. Probably too late now, but if I were you I'd start wearing your virus mask around her. You could hope she'll forget what you look like, but that's not likely. You ask me, I think you screwed yourself in this whole deal. But you did it to yourself. You could of done it right. Kept the mask on like the rest of us. Kept your distance.

Not get involved. That's the only thing that made sense given she's not paying us enough to go hide somewhere, which is what you're gonna have to do when this is all over." *Probably more than I should have said, but sometimes Stash just doesn't get it.*

"You may be right," *he begins, although I think I know where this is going.* "Probably are right. But she's just a kid, as you keep pointing out. She's probably scared shitless we're likely going to murder her. She has no idea what's going on."

"Neither do we," I remind him.

"Maybe so," Stash looks at the bedroom door. "But we both got ideas about that. Maybe you think this is all going to go to shit. I don't. Maybe she don't talk to me very often. But she wouldn't be running things behind the scenes for all those cocooned families if she didn't have sway… have insight into what's coming down. Ever since the first pandemic everything's changed. Maybe the kid's family company makes vaccine or something. Who knows? But whatever she's chasing, it's gotta be big, is all I'm saying."

"If it's big, then you and Aces and me… well, we're gonna get crushed 'cause those kind of people don't take it in stride when you go after their family."

"If you knew, then why'd you sign on? You coulda walked."

I shake my head, not about to give him insight he might use against me if this does go bad. This could easily be every man for himself if Modor screws it up somehow. But I placed my bet she has everything wired. Haven't known her long, but like Stash said, she wouldn't be where she is if she didn't have connections in some powerful places.

Stash continues staring at me, as if he thinks I'll eventually answer his question. I look at my screen, but I really can't think about a traffic problem miles away until I settle this with Stash. I stand up and look directly at him. "You got a job to do and so do I. That job has nothing to do with the kid. So I suggest you get back to your day job or she might just fire your ass and then where will you be?"

Stash doesn't react.

"What is it with you?" I push him. "She's not gonna let us screw up and have her other customers start complaining about one thing or another. She's not the only service provider out there. The cocoon owners got choices just like we do. They don't have to use her. If we're not getting the job done, you can be sure people will start walking out on her."

Stash shows a slight smile, "You got this all wrong," he begins. "She's not going to fire any of us because we got the kid. She can't afford to have us walking around unhappy. No telling who we'd talk to about what she's doing. The shoe is on the other foot. If anything she's more likely to assign our regular work to someone else since our primary job right now is to keep the kid out of sight."

Of course he's right, but I can't afford to let him know he is. "I wouldn't test your theory, if I were you." I turn to my laptop and study the traffic issue I've got to deal with. Looks like a control box is malfunctioning. Normally a single box failure's not a major issue. Can be swapped out next time we have someone out that way. But for some reason it appears a whole bank of them may be faulty. Don't think I've ever seen this situation before. I count eleven boxes to be offline. I take out my cell and call the service lead.

"Roy, it's Rocketman. From what I can tell, it looks like there's a bank of auton controllers out on the twenty-one hundred block of Wilshire."

"Let me take a look," Roy's response takes a moment. "Here it is. I count one... two... hmmm... eleven units off-line. That what you're seeing?"

"Yeah. What do you think?"

"Not seen so many before. It's usually a couple... maybe three. Makes me think maybe it's not the units, but maybe electrical. Let me send someone out to take a look."

"I'm sending it over to you," I click off and route the service notice over to him. Then I glance over to see what Stash is doing. He's still standing there, just looking at me. So I decide to get rid of him for at least a while, "Roy needs help. Twenty-One hundred block of Wilshire. Get going."

"Not my job," Stash responds.

That just does it for me. I dial the one person who can inform him of what his job happens to be.

"What?" comes across cold and annoyed.

"Stash needs instructions. I asked him to go help Roy with a block of malfunctioning auton boxes and he tells me it's not his job."

"Put him on," *simple, direct and clearly not happy.*

I hand my phone to Stash. I hear the conversation even with the phone to his ear.

"What the fuck is wrong with you?"

Stash doesn't hesitate, "I'm software. The problem is hardware."

"How do you know?"

"Limited set of boxes on an array. Those before and those after are working properly. So must be a hardware failure."

"What's really going on?" is softer but I can still hear her clearly.

"I leave you got no adult supervision." Stash looks directly at me. "Don't think you want unintended consequences…" and he looks at Aces.

She apparently thinks about his comment for a moment. "Put Rocketman back on."

I take the phone from Stash, who has a self-satisfied look. I go on offense. "I thought you had my back. You said you did."

"You go." *I have to admit I'm surprised at her response.*

"Why me?"

"Did I ask you to grow a brain? Just get the fuck out of there. If Stash wants to be responsible, let him. I just can't afford to have you two measuring dick sizes."

"You gonna pay me regardless?" I got to know what she's really thinking.

"I pay you to do what you're told. The longer this conversation goes on the less money I'm making today so haul your ass over to help Roy get those auton sensors back on line."

Stash may have won this battle, but he's not gonna win the war...

Chapter Fifteen: Jazmin Braveheart

I hear a knock on the door to the bedroom. Aces locked me in here. The door opens and Stash peeks in before entering. He sees me sitting in the corner with my knees up in front of me. Almost seems to be my default position. Huddle up so I'm as small a target as possible.

"Who is Rocketman?" I demand to know.

"He's gone for now, so don't worry about him."

"Gone where?" I'm not sure if him leaving is good or bad for me.

"Out on a job," Stash responds. "He'll be back in a few hours, most likely."

"I don't understand how this all works. You all work for the same company?"

Stash nods, but doesn't elaborate.

"But you're not a team, working together. You're all working separate issues, but all work from the same office or whatever this is?"

"Not an office. We generally work from where we live, but in this case we all have a special assignment requiring us to work from the same place."

"Am I the assignment?" I'm starting to understand why there's so much tension among them.

Stash doesn't answer, seems to be wanting to say something but is having difficulty deciding how to say it.

"What do you want to tell me?" I decide to come right out and ask.

Stash remains hesitant, "Nothing bad. Just want you to know you're going to be alright. Think of this as an adventure. Hopefully something you'll never experience again. So just be patient and everything will turn out okay."

"You just give me a pep talk?" I challenge him.

"Well… I just don't want you freaking out or anything."

"If you were the one being held against your will, wouldn't you be freaking out?" *his ask is totally unrealistic. Of course I'm freaking out, just not in the emotional way he's expecting. I'm freaking out because I can't solve this problem. I always find the answer. But not this time.*

"What can you do? Nothing. So isn't it better to just go along? I mean you can sit here and be patient. The time will just pass. Isn't that the best way to handle it?"

"Getting on-line would be the best way for me to pass the time. I could at least be getting some of my lessons done."

"Lessons?" Stash puzzles at my word choice.

"Watch lectures from professors so I could take care of a few of my prerequisites."

"Watch lectures?" Stash still seems to be wondering what I'm saying. "Don't you read up on things?"

"Read?" Now I'm the one who's confused. "We don't read anymore. We listen, watch simulations, and augment reality to superimpose alternatives we might want to consider. But read, like a textbook? No we don't read books anymore."

"What about literature? Stories. You know… if you don't read does that mean you don't have the opportunity to read a good book?"

"Like War and Peace?" I suggest. "Why would I want to read the book when I can watch the movie? See the characters for real, rather than have to conjure them in my mind from page after page of words?"

"There were a lot of pages to War and Peace," Stash reflects.

"You read it?" I have to ask since he brought it up.

"I have," Stash seems to be remembering something. "Took me a whole summer between my freshman and sophomore years."

"High school?" I ask without thinking.

"College," he corrects me.

"Where did you go?" I'm just having a conversation now.

"Pomona Poly."

A good middle-class tech school. Tells me why he's doing the job he has now. He went to the wrong school to be doing anything more. Not many entrepreneurs coming out of Pomona. "Why would a math guy be reading a novel?" I ask a little confused by this whole conversation.

"It was a challenge," he responds with a smile. "My grandmother. She was Russian and thought it was the greatest book ever written… after the Bible. Anyway, she challenged me to read both. I read the Bible when I was in high school and War and Peace in college. That summer when I was reading it, she would ask me what I was learning about the world and life and all from what Dostoevski had written. Then she would ask me about how Dostoevski's world differed from what the Bible said."

"Were you close to your grandmother? It sounds like you were."

Stash nods, "She passed a few years ago."

"She thought you should be a writer?"

Stash looks at me as if I'm a mind reader or something, "My father was the one who insisted I had to have a skill, one permitting me to get a job. Writers starve, he'd always say to her."

"From the way you've described things, you'd probably have not been much worse off," I point out. "Do you like to read... now?"

"War and Peace was the last novel I read," he admits.

"What's the story with your father?" I ask since he's seemingly willing to discuss his personal life.

"He's gone too. Succumbed to the third wave virus the year after my grandmother."

"He was an engineer too?"

Stash nods, "Civil. Built roads and bridges, and airports. Was working on the auton control system deployment when he got sick."

"What happened?" I ask.

"His whole team passed that year. Never did figure out who brought it in. Someone on his team infected everyone."

"Is that why Aces and Rocketman always wear the mask but you don't?"

"What do you mean?"

"You're expecting you're going to be infected at some point because your father was, so you don't fight it. You've just accepted the same is going to happen to you."

Stash considers my observation. "How old are you?"

"Sixteen," I admit, but instantly question whether I should have told him. *He might tell the others*.

"I've never met anyone who asks questions like you do at sixteen. Hell, most teenagers I know are all in to party time and friends."

"I have friends," comes out almost too defensively.

"Virtual friends, maybe," Stash challenges my assertion. "Living in a cocoon, you don't get out much. That much I know, because I'm keeping all your services up so you never have to leave."

"Why didn't you answer my question?" I redirect him, calling out how he sidestepped my observation, which I also noted he didn't deny.

"Never really thought about it."

"But you do this all the time, don't you," I push him to respond.

"What?"

"Take off your mask. You don't like to wear it. Makes you feel like a victim rather than someone who's in control of your situation."

"You're not sixteen. You act like someone older."

"Still not answering my question," I point out, not taking the bait he's offered on my age.

"What you're asking is whether I'm a fatalist."

"Pretty good insight for a techie," I point out he's not even who he thinks he is.

"My grandmother made sure I wasn't going to become a drone."

"Your grandmother couldn't save you from your father, but she equipped you to think for yourself. Unfortunately, you've not taken advantage of the insights she gave you since she passed on."

Stash looks like he's been struck by a two by four.

I press, sensing an opportunity. "Is your grandmother's passing why you've not read anything since War and Peace? That you couldn't stand up to your father even though it disappointed your grandmother? Who were you closer to?"

Without even thinking Stash responds, "Gram."

"You were afraid of your father, but you loved your

grandmother."

Stash looks totally disoriented. He wanders back towards the door. "I loved my father…"

"But did he love you?" I pounce on what I'm not hearing.

Stash looks at me wide-eyed. "What kind of a question is that?"

"Let me rephrase, was it clear to you from his behavior that your father loved you?"

"Of course he did," Stash looks totally befuddled.

"Not the question I asked. I'm sure your mother told you your father loved you, but did he tell you he did? Did he seek you out to do things you wanted to do? Did he do anything more than lecture you about what it was going to take to be successful?"

"Why?" Stash asks. "Is that what your father does to you? Lecture you about what it's going to take to be successful? But never showing you he loves you?"

Now I'm the one who must be staring like a deer into headlights.

Chapter Sixteen: Ophelia Braveheart

I need another pill. The medicine cabinet is in the master bath. It seems like I'm on remote control as I find myself floating through the house towards the siren song I hear, drawing me towards the oblivion one pill will afford me. *One pill to make me larger. One pill makes me small. Which is it I want to be today? Go ask Alice, when she's ten feet tall. Ten feet tall. It seems I need a pill to be to stand up to Jason when he gets into his condescending mood. Thinking I'm just a decoration and not an equal partner in this relationship. How do I get him to see how he makes me feel? How I feel the need to escape into my mind. Escape from the reality this cocoon has shrunk my world into being. Maybe I should take the small pill. Then maybe this cocooned world won't seem so small.*

The question I need to ask is whether I need a pill or just need to take a virtual journey using my active walls. *Where is it I want to go? Anywhere but here. Anywhere? Would I want to visit hell? Or heaven for that matter? Do I believe in either? No, but a lot of people believe in both. So who am I to deny their existence when they certain do exist for millions, if not billions of people?*

What I want is for Jaz to come home. She won't from me taking a pill or a virtual journey. The question is when is she coming home? I don't know why someone came into our home and took her, although I get the impression Jason has a pretty good idea who did and why. But he's not saying anything. Not even to me. I'm supposed to be an equal partner in this whole deal. But there are times when he just shuts me out. This is one of them. Why does he shut me out? I don't know and I can't get him to talk to me when something happens. When things happen he didn't see coming. It seems ever since the third wave virus infection so many things have happened we didn't see coming. When was that? Seven years ago, I think. Jaz was nine. It was also our first year in the cocoon. Probably the only reason we survived when so many didn't. Including Jason's parents. Both passed on. They conveyed the family company to Jason. The family company has been the enabler of our success and the millstone continually bringing us back to reality. Back to acknowledging we have made an outsized contribution to what the world has become since then. Both good and bad.

I reach for the tall pill. But my hand stops before I can grasp the container. For some reason my attention has been drawn to the tabs in the red box. Jason's box. He doesn't like me to put one on my tongue and watch the world melt away from me. He doesn't like to watch me morph with the fabric of time and space and color and nature and all that makes up the reality boxing in my cognition. He doesn't like me to open myself up to the possibilities of the universe he regularly visits as part of his expanded consciousness campaign. *Good for the goose but not for the gander. Why does he diminish my self-worth? I've confronted him about his behavior. He just dismisses it. Says I can do what I need to do and he will do what he needs to do to be successful. Can't innovate when you're confined by the size of your brain. Need to be able to get outside yourself. Look at the world from a perspective you can't gain just looking up. I think it's all a rationalization. Before LSD people innovated all the time. He could if he wanted to, but he likes feeling the release, likes feeling as if he's outside himself. Likes feeling as if he's walking a road no one else has travelled. With so many people in the world, that's a hard place to find. Some one of the ten billion or more people in the world has already been there.*

I open the red box. The red dragon on the top reminds me we bought the box at the weekend market in Bangkok. *When was that? Must be ten years ago now. Jaz was six then.* We followed her through the acres of winding paths between the thousands of booths selling anything I could conceive of. Amazingly we didn't buy much because Jaz was only interested in things that moved. Animals we weren't bringing home with us. But there were merchants selling interesting things like this Chinese lacquered box. Jason keeps his tabs in it. We both know what's kept there. The Bangkok trip was the first time we took LSD together. It scared the shit out of me. Jaz was with us in the hotel room. While we were tripping she was left to her own devices. When I was next coherent I discovered Jaz had opened the door to the patio, but for some reason hadn't gone out. She had emptied the contents of our suitcases and found the various medications we had brought with us. Luckily, she hadn't been able to open the containers. She had also strewn the contents of the kitchen silverware, plates and refrigerator throughout the hotel room. She was fast asleep when I awoke, but just all the opportunities she had to harm herself scared the shit out of me. I haven't tripped since. That's precisely why I'm thinking about it now. *She's not around. Not because I don't want her here, but because someone took her from us.*

I open the red box and remove a single tab. Six hours of mind expansion. Am I up for it? Jason would tell me no. Tripping when I'm distraught is not a good thing because it will send me off in a nasty direction. Make me even more unhappy about my inability to bring Jaz home.

I strip away the back of the packet and look at the tab for a long moment. Suddenly I feel strong hands on my wrists, pulling them apart so I can't put the tab into my mouth.

"Let's not do this," Jason whispers into my ear. "Not now."

I turn to him and put my arms around his neck. Hug him with all the strength I possess. Then I just hang on him, relaxing with my cheek next to his. Let the tension flow from me into the ether. Into the larger world where it dissipates.

"When's she coming home?" I ask, hoping he has an answer for me.

"Soon," is his simple response.

"Not soon enough," is all I can think of in response to his one-word answer. Jason does this to me all too often. Give me a one-word answer when I'm looking for a paragraph or more.

"Stebbins is optimistic," Jason continues.

"Spring is coming…" I respond.

Jason hugs me tighter for a moment and then moves me out to arm's length. "If you have any better ideas tell me and I'll pass them along to Peter."

Jason is telling me he knows I've already spoken to my ex about Jaz. Peter is a lot of things, but he's among the best at what he does, which is to find people. Two decades trying to find people for the CIA and later FBI gave him a skill set not many have. Peter will find Jaz. I just hope when he does, it's not too late.

"I can't close my eyes," I confess to Jason.

"I can't either," he reassures me. "But if Stebbins can't find her, Peter will."

Jason releases the hold he has on my upper arms. I instantly bring the tab up to my mouth. He reacts with a "Nooooo!" But I've already secured it on my tongue, feeling it dissolve and the world begin to melt around me. I look at Jason who says something to me, but the sound of his voice now seems to be a baroque fugue of discordant tones, not making sense, but entertaining in their own right.

As my gaze moves from right to left, the images on the video walls begin to move. Initially the images seem to vibrate. Slight movements but the images remain intact. The longer I stare at them, the more the movement increases. Now they begin to swirl as if a hurricane has superimposed itself upon the images in my view. Then the hurricane multiplies. Now there are three swirling masses of color ripped from the images on the screens of the room. Now six swirling masses of color. Now twelve. I'm afraid to close my eyes, afraid the hurricane like swirls will take over my balance and cause me to fall.

Jason apparently grabs me as I move backwards, picks me up in his strong arms and carries me somewhere. The images I see don't permit me to understand where I've gone physically as the only thing I can accurately perceive is the images in my mind. It's as if I've ripped myself from the space-time fabric and closed into my mind, where the images I brought with me have become the only source material for the cacophony of images I'm trying to make sense from.

Suddenly Jaz appears, looking at me with those big expression filled green eyes. She seems to be waiting for me to say something. To answer a question she asked of me, but I don't remember the question. How can I answer her? How can I satisfy her curiosity when I don't even know what it is she wants from me? I try to ask, "What's your question?" but the words come out as distorted tone poems. Beautiful in and of themselves, but devoid of larger meaning. The meaning with which I created those sounds.

Jaz melts away from me, absorbed into one of the dozen hurricane swirls, passed along to another and then another. I reach out wanting to bring her back to me, but am too late. The swirls have turned into a river of color and movement and chaos. I'm not quite sure what to do to bring her back, but as I step forward it seems she moves even faster away from me, sliding down the oozing turbulence of colors. Escaping my grasp. Beyond my reach. Again I try to call out to her, but the sound of my voice is more like a calliope than words. Sounds that signify movement, motion, happiness. But the words do not slow her long slide away from my grasp, her spinning squeals signifying her loss of control over her own destiny. I don't know what to do. She has moved beyond my grasp, beyond my reach, beyond my lunges to bring her back to me.

Then from one side Peter Tate, tall, rugged and deceitful enters my view. From the other is Jason Braveheart, steady, blueblood, genius. It's as if their contrasting traits have decided to do battle in the lake of perception before me. Just out of my reach, but close enough I can see everything. Peter looks at me with his piercing steel blue eyes. Those eyes hypnotized me when we first met. I couldn't stop looking into them. All I saw was what I wanted to see. I thought it was love, but it was lust. He wanted me for my body. Wanted me for the challenge I presented, because I wouldn't give up my career for him, wouldn't give up who I was. But that was my mistake. I thought he respected me for the stand I took. But he didn't. I was a conquest. Once he'd won he was on to his next victim. My mistake was taking my experience with him as a lesson learned. I thought to win and keep Jason I needed to do what Peter expected of me. Needed to be the good partner. Only I've discovered my assumption has not been working. Being what Jason wants me to be has caused me to stop being me. Caused me to give up what I believe in. Give up what was important to me other than Jaz…

Now she's moved beyond my grasp. I should have known it would come to this. She was going to leave and go off to college at some point. We knew it would happen, but I've been denying it… trying to find a way to keep her close even though she's able to think for herself. She no longer looks to me to be her north star. She has her own now. Has an internal compass she has become more and more reliant upon. So what is the use of a mother when you no longer need her approval to decide?

What's the use of a mother, indeed? My own scarred me. My experience makes it hard for me to back away when I know there are still challenges to come. Decisions to be made about what kind of person Jaz wishes to be. I can help, but I have to admit I didn't take the help my mother offered. I went my own way. Will Jaz do the same to me? I hope not, and I hope I get the chance to be there for her now when she needs me.

Chapter Seventeen: Amare Stebbins

I expected the world-famous detective and former spook Peter Tait to take longer to come see me. But here he is, sitting across from me with his hospital mask covering most of his face. Even so, I recognize the face with a significant part of it blocked out. I've been amazed how my mind is able to complete pictures of people I've seen before, even with the ever-present mask.

"Your theory is the contractor who came out to provide the estimate…" Peter is summarizing the discussion to this point. *All what I've learned. Nothing about his insights. Why is it famous people seldom do the work themselves, but take what others have done, repackage it and call it their own?*

"…was checking out the property," I finish the thought since he apparently hasn't gotten to it yet, or has made an assumption about what I am thinking. From the raised eyebrow I get the sense he wasn't thinking what I just said. Another thing about masks… it's hard to read reactions when so much of the face is covered. But I can't ask him to remove the mask since everyone is at risk in this day and age. *Multiple virus strains infecting people and you never know who has what strain, which ones you've been inoculated against and which can kill you.*

"So just a scout," Peter echoes my thought. "No evidence he may have been the one who took Jazmin from the house?"

"Whoever is behind this understands security systems. Even when the contractor was making his rounds with Jason, he kept his face away from the cameras. So we have a general description… height and weight kind of information, but with the mask, hat and clothing he wore, we really have no distinguishing marks to go on."

"Not even the color of his hair?" Peter asks apparently hoping for at least one more identifier.

I shake my head and decide it's my time. "What have the Bravehearts told you?"

Peter Tate apparently considers what he can tell me and what his clients would prefer to be kept between them. "What you want to know is if the theory they gave me is the same as they gave you."

"They haven't given me a theory... at least not a specific theory."

"Jason's partner?" Peter zeros in where I thought he would. What I'm hoping is he has already done some investigation there which may affirm what we've learned so far. "Ophelia's concerns are credible, but I've found no indication he was involved. At least no indications tie him directly."

"So you haven't dismissed him entirely," I note, which is exactly where we are.

"Don't believe him to be the prime suspect, although at the moment I'm not sure we have one. Have you zeroed in on anyone?"

"Not a specific person. We've been more focused on motive. Why would someone abduct Jazmin Braveheart? There doesn't seem to be anything she has done to attract attention. That makes us believe someone wants something from her father and is intending to use the daughter as the bargaining chip. But what's curious is the amount of time passing with no contact. What do you think about the situation?"

Peter Tate shifts uncomfortably in the chair. "What I tell most of my clients is the longer things go the less likely the missing person is to return."

I instantly skip ahead, "You think whoever abducted her may have botched the job and killed her accidently?"

"You've said the person or people involved know security systems. Tells me they're professional. Probably done something like this before. But there are always unforeseen events. Could be they injected her with something to put her out so they could remove her without Jason or Ophelia hearing. Could be whatever they injected her with put her into respiratory failure or heart failure or who knows what. We see all kinds of strange reactions people are having to the viruses in the air and bacteria in the water now. I'm not trying to be pessimistic. I still think Jazmin is likely okay… but possibly something has changed the abductor's plan. Or maybe this was the plan all along. To get Jason and Ophelia to a point they'll do anything asked to get her back. I've seen that particular tactic as well."

I nod, having seen the same. "What else do you need from me?"

"I'm hoping to get your summaries. If I can save going back over the same things you've already examined it will save a lot of time. I think all the time saved here may be important." Peter partially closes one eye. "I think we have to assume her captors know exactly what they're doing, what they're going to ask and what it will take to get what they want."

"What do you think they want?" I have to ask.

"I'm beginning to think money isn't it. At least not money from the Bravehearts. If it was just money they probably would have contacted them with a ransom request by now. What I'm just beginning to do is take a look at Jason and his business. He does a lot of things nobody knows about. That's a problem for you and me because we have to convince him to talk about what he does. He's not going to want to. But if I'm right, someone knows about something he's doing from which they've determined they could make a lot more money than Jason could pay them. Apparently they think Jason would never willingly part with whatever it is they want. So coercion is the means they chose."

"Have you worked one like this before?" I'm curious.

Peter Tate nods, more to himself than me, "When I was with the agency there was a similar case."

"How did it turn out?"

"The boy's body was found about six months later. He'd been fed rat poison and had lost about a third of his body weight, which is probably what it took for him to eat the poison."

"Did you catch those responsible?" I wonder aloud.

"We put several people in prison, two were killed in a shoot-out, but I was never convinced we put the right people in jail. That's the problem with cases like this. The people responsible, the people who benefit, are often not those who carry out the act. That's what makes it so hard to know if you got the right people in the end." Peter inches forward in his chair as if getting ready to leave.

"What did you learn that could help us now?" I'm trying to get whatever insights I can before Peter Tate walks out of my office. Likely I'll not have this kind of access to him again.

Peter sits back and considers by question. "I'm not sure I can tell you what I learned. It took place in Brazil, a country where kidnapping is almost a sport. When I was down there once, people were talking about a recent kidnapping. Daughter of a banker. Kidnappers called the father and demanded a large but not outrageous sum for her return. While they were talking, the daughter grabbed the phone and shouted at her father he needed to pay double what they were asking because she was worth the larger amount."

I nod understanding the difference, but then he continues.

"What is similar is the kidnappers wanted an untraceable cell phone a company had developed. Turns out those responsible were the drug lords in Bolivia who were trying to evade detection and capture by US Drug Enforcement Agency agents. While I'm reasonably sure we caught those responsible for starving and murdering the boy, I don't think we ever were able to arrest any of the drug lords themselves. Not only was there no evidence linking them directly, but they also reside in a different country. So not every case has a happy ending."

"Did the drug lords get the technology they wanted?" I'm still trying to fit the pieces together.

"They did," Peter seems regretful about how the whole thing turned out.

"What can we do to make sure this doesn't have the same result?"

"Find her quickly," Peter is emphatic and begins to rise again.

I put up my hand to stop him from leaving. "I need you to pursue what his company does. Since you're his employee, he is likely to tell you things he will not tell me. I've already seen his reluctance to tell me things in the conversations we've had. He goes to a point and then pulls back. It makes me wonder what he does know he's not sharing. I know if I had more of his insight it would be a lot easier to solve this case."

Peter half smiles back at me, "You are likely correct. I've not been to the house yet, simply reviewed what they sent and had a quick conversation with Ophelia."

"You've not spoken with Jason yet?"

"Ophelia hired me not Jason. I doubt he's enthusiastic about my involvement."

"I didn't get that impression when he told me you had been retained," I suggest to see how he will react.

Peter looks at me with a penetrating gaze as if he were trying to understand what I'm saying by reading my mind. "Look, detective. I know what my reputation is out there. All I can say is a reputation seldom reflects the reality of the situation."

"Your reputation is you get results," I respond flatly.

"Doing whatever it takes… legal or not."

"If you break the law I will be forced to take the appropriate actions."

"Arrest me, in other words," Peter goes right where I want him to go.

"I'm a sworn officer. You are not. Your status gives you certain latitude I don't have." I want to set the record straight.

"It also protects you from the civil liabilities I have to be concerned about," Peter stops before continuing, apparently wanting to make sure he says this clearly. "We each have the ability to do certain things the other can't. I'm hopeful we can find a way to take advantage of the situation to bring this to a rapid close." Now Peter stands. He really is leaving.

"One last thing…"

Peter stops, waits.

"I read your divorce from Ophelia was acrimonious. Accusations made about you sleeping around on her and even one report of physical threat. Why would she go back to you with the history you have?"

Peter sighs. "You're thorough. Glad to know that about you. I can't tell you why she called me. We haven't spoken in years. I took the case because she asked me to. But you'd have to ask her why she called."

Chapter Eighteen: Stash

If someone could tell me why code fragments corrupt, I would be very happy. It's never the same thing. Always something else prevents a simple cookie cutter response. Have to go in and look. Trace the logic and figure out what's different than in the other sensors doing the same thing. Once you write code it should stay the same no matter how many times the code is called on to perform whatever it's designed to do. But that doesn't happen. It's like a virus, mutating over time so it's never the same when it hits you the next year or five years from now. That's what makes a virus so dangerous and what makes code corruption such a pain in the ass. But she pays me to figure it out. So I do. I'm Mr. Code Fixer. Still better than being hardware where you have to get in a vehicle and go out, look at something in the field. Expose yourself to all the corruption in our atmosphere. Pollution. Viruses. Fouled water. Who in their right mind would want to spend all day out there? It could be dangerous to your health. But Rocketman doesn't seem to care. He hates to be kept indoors. Good for him. I don't want to catch something and die trying to do my job. I may not be cocooned like the rich people are, but I'm at least in control of my own destiny by staying away from what can kill me. Staying away from all the people who are infested with who knows what?

"What are you working on now?" the girl asks me, looking over my shoulder as I sit across from Aces at the work desk. The fact it's either work here or at the kitchen counter where Rocketman is working is enough incentive to want to stay here. I glance over my shoulder as I've been trying to ignore her since she called me out in the bedroom. I'm trying to avoid thinking about the conversation with her. Don't want to consider whether I made a mistake following my father's advice rather than Gram's. I am where I am. Can't do nothing about what went down back then. It would just make me crazy to dwell on it. I wonder… is that what she is trying to do? Drive me to distraction so I'm not keeping an eye on her? No. Not likely. She may be insightful but I don't think she's that smart. I certainly wasn't when I was sixteen, or whatever she really is.

"Nits," I finally answer.

"Could I ask a question?"

I nod.

"Why don't you go to a sensor working properly, copy the code from it and paste the properly functioning code in here rather than spending all your time trying to find what changed?"

"I could, but then I'd not know what changed or why," I respond to her suggestion, which is one I've heard before from other technicians who are always trying to find the shortest way to solving a problem.

"Does it really matter?" she asks simply.

"Part of my job is to try to figure out why the code corrupts," I explain why it matters to me. "If I just cut and paste I can't do the analysis to understand."

"Waste of your time," she responds with a shrug I can't miss.

"What do you know about this anyway?"

"I fix code from time-to-time," her non-chalant answer catches me by surprise. "For the company. My family's company."

"You? You're still in high school."

"So was Bill Gates when he learned how to code, back in the days when there weren't coding academies like today. I mean I've been coding since I was in elementary school. Debugging took longer because I had to learn logic. Six-year-olds seldom understand logic. When we do, we never tell an adult."

"Hey. I got to admit you seem to understand a whole lot of shit I never would have expected you to. But coding? Debugging? Fixing logic errors in code? That just seems a stretch to me."

"Only because it took you a long time to learn it. It took you a long time because you're not a natural. You're a writer who's been shoehorned into a coder's body. It's not you. You've had to remake yourself to be good at what you do. I have no doubt you're good. But think about it. Did you do every math problem the teacher gave you just to see if you could, or did you only do the required ones?"

"I did what was expected," I admit, afraid I know where she's going.

"But you didn't love it. Do math problems in your dreams. Spend hours trying to solve the hardest problems just because they were a challenge in and of themselves."

"Nobody does that," I respond remembering my high school math classes.

"I do," she responds very quietly.

"You dream math problems," I'm not believing her.

"Sometimes it takes all night. When I wake up in the morning I have the answer. I leap out of bed and write it down in a notebook I keep next to my bed. This isn't a one-time thing for me. Happens several times a week. You should see my notebook. It's what got me a full ride at MIT. I showed it to the math department chairman. That was all I needed to do."

"I showed the math department chairman at Cal Pomona Poly my notebook. He recommended remedial calculus two." I admit not even thinking about what it says about me. "Okay. So you're some kind of math whiz. I can live with that. But what does it have to do with copying and pasting code fragments rather than trying to determine the cause? Would seem I'm the one who's trying to be more rigorous about this whole thing."

"Tell you what," She glances over at Aces who is doing his best to seem like he's not listening, but I know he's tuned into every word. "I'm really bored. Do you have another machine here? I could do these simple fixes letting you work on the hard things requiring your advanced degree and years of experience."

"Who said I have an advanced degree?" Where did she come up with that?

"You do, don't you?"

"Well… yeah, but I never told you I did."

"Didn't have to. You said you were a systems engineer. Just like you want to understand the larger world out there by reading War and Peace? You want to understand how the whole system works. Make sure the code supports the mission of the system, not just individual tasks it has to perform along the way."

"Damn. You don't sound like any sixteen-year-old I've ever met."

"I take it the last time you met a sixteen-year-old you were sixteen yourself."

"Maybe eighteen," I admit again without thinking. How does she do that? Get me to admit to shit before I've had a chance to engage my brain to filter it? I need to be more careful.

"When you were eighteen, there were people like me walking around. You just never met any of them. Today they're running labs and inventing shit you'd have never thought possible. How many new devices have you incorporated into your systems in the last year?"

I have to think for a moment, "I don't know. Couple dozen at least, maybe more."

"My point. Someone designed those devices. They were probably mostly the math geniuses you never met because they went to private schools or enrolled in college when they were fourteen or fifteen. Do you know what I'm saying? Do you think Rocketman will ever design a new network device you have to learn how to control and integrate?"

"Rocketman?" I laugh, which is probably not a good thing because Aces will tell him making it even harder to get along with

Rocketman. "What are you saying?"

"Let me fix your nits. I can you know. Not a big deal for me. Then you and Aces and Rocketman can tell what's her name…"

"Modor," I confirm and instantly regret.

"…that you're being more productive than usual. Getting more problems fixed, which means your customer satisfaction should go up, she'll be able to sign up more cocooned families because of her customer satisfaction scores. Then maybe she'll give you and Aces and Rocketman a bonus for all the new business you brought on."

"Not gonna happen…" I counter her enthusiasm. "But I see where you're going. Let me see if I can find a machine… only it won't have any communications programs. Can't have you telling anyone where we are."

"Okay with me. Just want to do something other than math problems in my head."

I know there's no extra hardware here, so not sure where I'm going to find a machine she can use, but I need to humor her for the moment. "I'm gonna have to search around…"

"Let me use your machine for now…"

"No can do. I let you on my machine you'll tell the world where to come look for us. You already said you're a programming genius or some such shit. So no. Anything we find for you won't have any communications programs. I need my machine to find one. So just sit back and relax. This is gonna take a while."

She steps back realizing her ploy isn't working out the way she hoped. I glance over and see Aces staring at me as if to say, 'what the fuck are you doing?'

I pull up the inventory list and scan down for a barebones internet machine. I find one, but it's in San Leandro. Will take a day or more to get here if I request it now, but I'm not sure if I should or not. Do I really want to put her on line? Could be a major mistake. I hover my cursor over the requisition button. Do I or don't I?

I push the button for the requisition. Once it arrives I can always just lock it up somewhere if I decide it's better not to let her have it.

Rocketman comes in talking on his cellphone. "Yeah. Got it. Now?"

He listens to whoever he's talking to, nods and disconnects. "Okay ladies. The auton is going to be here in ten minutes so pick up everything, erase any indications we were here. Most particularly any indication she was here, including fingerprints. Got that?"

Oh, shit. Forgot we are leaving so soon. The machine will show up here and we'll be long gone.

Chapter Nineteen: Jazmin Braveheart

Aces stands up and looks at me. I realize instantly he would be just as happy to break my neck.

"Where to this time?" Stash asks Rocketman casually.

"Wherever the auton delivers us. How the fuck do I know?" Rocketman seems really annoyed with Stash.

"Just thought she might have told you since she keeps calling you."

"You want her to call you next time? Be my guest," Rocketman holds out his phone to Stash as if suggesting he should call Grendele's Modor and suggest she should call him next time. But Stash shakes his head and begins to pick up his computer.

Rocketman clearly doesn't like Stash's response, "You gonna wipe the place down?"

Stash looks at Rocketman, "Why me? I thought we all needed to."

Aces picks up a cloth. He begins to wipe down the area where he'd been working.

"Get the bedroom, since she was in there most of the time," Rocketman instructs the still unhappy Stash. "Make sure you look for anything she might have left as an indication she was here."

"Like what?" Stash responds, annoyed by the specificity of the instructions. "She doesn't have anything to leave behind."

"Fingerprints, saliva, maybe she blew her nose and wiped it on something. How do I know? You seem to think you should be in charge, act like you are. Figure out what needs to be wiped away. You

104

got seven minutes to do it.

Stash disappears into the bedroom. I see him wiping down nearly everything I could have touched. But since there isn't any furniture in there, it's mostly the walls, window and the area on the floor where I'd been sitting when he came in. It doesn't take him long. I see Rocketman wiping down the kitchen countertop where he'd been working before nodding to the door. I put my hands behind my back and lean against the wall to leave a set of prints from my right hand and then push away to follow after Aces who is nearly to the door by now. Stash comes out of the bedroom, must have seen what I did, because he wipes across the wall where I'd been, then the floor below it where I'd been sitting when we first got here. Guess he figured out he needed to make sure Grendele's Modor doesn't come back after him if anyone finds this place and finds my prints here.

A moment later Rocketman is out the door ahead of me. Stash is right behind as I put on my facemask. As soon as he steps out, Stash wipes down the door handle and locks the door. The auton is waiting at the curb with Aces and Rocketman already inside, watching us approach. I glance around the underground parking garage. No one else around. As I take my seat I begin to think about autons. They have cameras inside to monitor the passengers. Thermal cameras to identify anyone with a fever. Something required by law because of the constant pandemics. Anyone with a fever is restricted from travel and public places. The autons are programmed not to move if a fevered passenger is detected. But who is monitoring the images those thermal cameras are sending back? At least I have to believe the images are going somewhere. If a crime occurs in an auton, the police are going to want a record of who was in the vehicle. Someone could identify me, if my image had been sent out. I have to think it was. Jason would first thing, given some of the systems our company builds. I make sure I look right where the camera would be, to make sure the algorithms can match my image with the file photo of me.

The auton begins to move, which tells me two things. No one in here has a fever, so I shouldn't have to worry about catching something from one of these guys. I remove the face mask. The second is there hasn't been a match where the police would disable the auton and lock the doors so we can't get out. I remember a video lesson on how the system works. How is it possible no one has discovered where I am?

Rocketman shows me a crooked grin, "Disappointed?"

"About what?"

"This is a private auton. Not on the grid. Nobody's gonna know you're here, who you're with or where you end up. So just forget about the cavalry coming to your rescue."

I wonder how he knew what I was thinking. I should have figured it all out when we came to this place. But I guess I just wasn't focused yet on what was really happening. *I'm focusing now. This is becoming all too real because Stash and Rocketman at least are becoming more than just shadows who are watching me. The only thing I know about Aces is he doesn't say much and is brutal in his response. I would rather stay as far away from him as possible, but right now it's simply not possible.*

As the auton comes out of the garage, I get to see the neighborhood where I've been the past few hours. It was barely more than a day, I think, although I've lost track of time completely. Having no social media systems feeding me is causing me to go into withdrawals I think. I'm disoriented because I don't have a constant feed of information coming at me. I don't have instant answers to my many questions. This is causing me to have to spend more time figuring things out. But so far the one thing I want to figure out more than anything else is how do I get away from these guys and back home. I have little or no insight as to how at the moment. Since this is a private auton, there is little chance anyone is going to see me, recognize me or have any idea where I am. Including me. Rocketman was careful not to answer Stash's question about where we're going. I think he knows, but doesn't want me to know. Not that I could do anything with the information at the moment, but you never know. Things could change. Something might happen. I could communicate with someone. But even Stash is very concerned I not have the opportunity.

HAPPINESS

As the auton turns onto a busy street, I see people walking. They all wear the same hospital masks as us. Aces has a ski mask covering even more of his face. About the only thing of him I see is his eyes, dark brown, almost black, or so they seem to me. But I'd rather not look at his eyes because they seem cruel. I wonder how he got that way. *How do people become cruel? Is it because someone was cruel to them? Or did they just wake up one day and think they ought to be cruel because it's more fun than being nice? Some of the girls in my school are cruel to other girls, but because they want to isolate someone. Make sure they don't have friends because maybe they could be a threat if people liked them. I could be wrong. Probably am since I'm not someone who tries to be part of any given crowd. Don't think I need anyone to validate I'm popular, or one of the people others should hang with. I don't have time to worry about it. Been too focused on getting into MIT since it's the only school I wanted to go to. It's where Jason went and Gramps went. Didn't want to end the family tradition.*

No one seems to be paying any attention to the auton I'm in. Is it because they are such a common sight there's no reason to look? Does a private auton look any different than the public ones you can summons to go nearly anywhere? I guess I've never thought about it. But then I'm never out in the world making everything I see new. Maybe that's why I tend to look at everything. Nothing is common place for me. Does my incessant study of everything make me different? Certainly not different from the other kids at my school. We're all cocooned. All live apart from the rest of humanity. Is that why I'm struggling trying to figure out how to deal with these three guys? The fact I never spend time with others face-to-face without a monitor between us?

The auton leaves the populated area and enters the highway. Now I see the city skyline, but it's not a city I've seen before. *Densely populated, but not a major city where certain buildings are recognizable. This could be anywhere. Could be California. I just don't know.* The auton moves to the left and we enter the high-speed lane. *Means we're not headed anywhere close. Why are we moving so often? Does it mean someone has figured out who has taken me? Are they closing in? It might explain why we have to move. Or is this all out of extra caution? Keep moving so no one becomes curious about us. Not stay long enough for anyone to come by more than once. Not even the pizza delivery guy. But then Rocketman made sure I was no where near the door where the pizza delivery guy could have seen me.*

Aces finally stops staring at me, closes his eyes and is apparently going to take a nap. Must mean he thinks this is going to be a longer move than the last one, which wasn't far. But I'm surprised Modor would be willing to send us a long way from where the issues are they're trying to resolve. *Why would she? I wouldn't. I'd want to keep them in the area so Rocketman could go out and fix things without having to drive an hour or more just to fix something. Inefficient if you ask me. It would absolutely kill the response time. I know Jason's not happy if something goes out and isn't back up almost immediately. I've got to think he's not unique.*

Looking out the window the question I have is how far from my home were we to begin with? *It doesn't look like the bay area to me, but I've not travelled very far north or south. Could be only a few miles away and I'd not recognize it at all.*

It's afternoon and the sun is to my left, so I think we're driving north. As I finally start to get a little orientation the auton moves right and follows a ramp to another highway now taking us what I infer to be east. I don't see the distinctive California mountains, so I come to realize I know less about my whereabouts than I thought.

Rocketman is deep into his phone screen, flipping through what is likely social media sites. He isn't stopping to read anything, just taking in what I assume to be one photo after another. I'm not seeing any reaction to the images, nor does he slow down and look at any one for very long. Tells me he's not really interested in anything, but killing time until we arrive at our next safehouse.

Stash, on the other hand is reading something on his phone.

"War and Peace?" I ask quietly although I know the others can hear because the auton is just too small for a private conversation.

"Just re-reading a couple chapters," Stash admits, although tentatively as he looks at Rocketman to see if he looks up. Rocketman doesn't. "It's been a while but I wanted to refresh my memory on a couple things."

"Like how such a difficult writing style could deliver a classic?" I wonder aloud.

"If you or I were to write this today, no one would read it," Stash acknowledges.

"Then why are you?" Rocketman interjects still scrolling and not looking up.

Stash doesn't respond to Rocketman, but shakes his head as he looks back down at his phone. I touch his arm to let him know it's okay to read War and Peace even though Rocketman has a different opinion.

Chapter Twenty: Stash

The auton climbs a steep driveway to a one-story ranch-house sitting up on a bluff. It is nestled in a deep grove of Eucalyptus trees. We're up a ways, but the trees effectively block the views of the valley and high plain we just crossed to get here. The house may be all of two thousand square feet. Clapboard siding and a red tile roof in the Spanish style. No garage or out buildings here. No other vehicles so we are apparently the only guests. We're a ways from the town we went through on the way here, so getting food will require a special trip by a delivery vehicle. Everything is delivered or made on site these days so just have to take into account the delivery time when we get hungry. Speaking of which…

I'm the first one out as the auton comes to a stop. Rocketman follows and then the girl. Aces appears to still be asleep so I call him, "We're here." It takes a moment for him to look around, apparently sense the auton has come to a stop and then he follows us to the door as the auton leaves us. *I used to get uncomfortable about being in a remote place like this with no transportation on site. Not anymore. The autons have become dependable and ubiquitous. Modor will send a private auton out for us if she wants us to move on or go someplace as she did for Rocketman when he went out to Wilshire to service the control string.*

I hear the lock click open, apparently there's a facial recognition camera somewhere. We must be registered with the control system to let us in. *Nice of Modor to look out for us. Wouldn't want to be here if we couldn't get in.*

Entering the house I find it fully furnished in a western motif. Looks to me like someone lives here as there are personal effects, photos in frames, art work on the walls. I go to the kitchen and open the refrigerator to find it fully stocked. Even a small wine rack on the countertop which has a half dozen bottles of California cabernets.

Guess I won't have to worry about pizza delivery here. The girl should be happy as there's boxes of grains in the cupboard and fresh vegetables in the refrigerator. She follows me into the kitchen, "Can you cook?" I ask.

"I've never tried..." she responds tentatively.

"Can you follow directions... the ones on the label?"

I hand her a box of couscous and point to the directions on the back. She quickly reads them with a puzzled expression.

"Do we have something to measure these amounts?" she points to the label.

I open other drawers and cupboard doors until I find measuring cups and spoons. "Yup," I point them out to her.

She nods, "Between us I think we can figure it out," she responds as she looks in the refrigerator, opens a bag of full-sized carrots and takes one out, which she instantly begins to eat. I imagine she must be starved as I don't think she's had much, insisting she has to stay on her prescribed diet. I never thought she'd make it this long. I don't know if Modor decided she needs to keep her healthy or what. But in any event the kid should be able to find something to eat.

The kid moves away from the refrigerator. I poke my head back inside, discovering hamburger patties. They appear to be fresh. I also find mustard, and pickles in the door. I pick up the patties and look for a skillet to cook one.

Rocketman comes in and inspects the patties, "You making enough for all of us?"

"I can," I respond deciding not to call attention to the fact the kid won't eat one. But that's okay. Don't need to call attention to knowing more about her than he does.

I find the skillet and put three patties in to let them cook while I look for rolls and ketchup. I find both and note the rolls appear to be fresh. Must have been delivered in the last day or so.

The kid finds a pot and is looking at the directions to make up the couscous. "Make enough for all of us. If there's more than we want to eat today we can have the leftovers tomorrow or the next day."

She looks puzzled, "You eat food that's not fresh?"

The kid really is a cocoon baby. "Yes. All the time. Some leftovers are actually better than when they are fresh."

She wrinkles up her nose to tell me she can't imagine, but I just laugh and flip the 'burgers so the other side will begin to cook. I notice her looking at the burgers. "You want to try a bite?"

The emphatic shake of her head communicates just how strongly her meatless diet is ingrained. "How can you eat an animal? I mean they don't eat us… anymore."

"Certain animals would if we gave them the chance…" I suggest.

"Like who?"

"Lions and tigers and maybe even bears, oh my!" I say to see if she knows the reference.

"My name's not Dorothy." *she tells me without looking, probably not wanting to call attention to her real question which is where are we.*

"Surprised you would know that reference," I respond to see how she takes it.

"Ophelia made sure I watched what she called the classic movies when I was younger. It was a mother-daughter thing. Do you know what I'm saying? Something we could share. Whenever we got into a difficult spot she could always remind me of a character in one of those movies and how she handled a situation. She would dare me to be as creative or courageous or whatever it was the heroine did to get to a happy ending."

"So she used it to inspire you," I reflect how Gran did the same with me. *Only she made me read the book rather than watch the movie. On more than one occasion I would watch the movie in hopes I could answer her questions without having to invest so much time reading the story. But she would always catch me and make me read it. I can still hear her saying, 'it's not the same. Some director's vision is always different than the author's intent. Has to be because the director is showing you and the writer is telling you and has a lot more to tell...'*

"What inspires you?" she responds to my question. *I should have expected her to do so, but didn't.*

"It's hard to get inspired when you're an IT fixer," I respond without thinking, but recognizing the feeling behind the comment. "Life is more about endurance than inspiration," I offer to hopefully send her off in a different direction.

"I once heard someone say, 'Life's a bitch and then you die.' Is that what you're talking about?"

"How would you know?" I instantly respond to her comment. "You're a cocoon baby. Been one your whole life. For you, life is one rose blossom after another. Eternal spring. There's no downside for anything you look at because you're gonna be fine no matter what happens in the world. Money does that. Power does that. You've got it all and the rest of us... not so much."

The hamburgers are ready. I scoop them out of the skillet into a roll and put one each on plates next to the condiments. "Rocketman, Aces. The burgers are ready," I call.

In a moment they both come into the kitchen, take a plate, add their condiments of choice, grab a beer from the refrigerator and disappear back into whatever room they had set up to resume work. The girl and I are alone again. I see she wants to finish the discussion we were having.

"How many people are there in the world?" she asks.

"Approaching ten billion," I respond giving her the last data point

I remember seeing a while ago, but is probably still valid.

"How many of us are cocooned?"

Stash backs away from the cooktop, scratches his ear with a grimace and shrugs, "Best guess is… we talking U.S. or world-wide?"

"U.S."

"Fifty or seventy-five thousand at most."

"Out of over four hundred million people," she notes.

"Probably half of a percent if my math is correct," I offer. "Does that tell you how privileged you are? The politicians used to rail on and on about the one percent of Americans who controlled everything. You're from a tiny part of the people who live a parallel life to the rest of humanity."

"Tell me about the ninety-nine-point five percent," she asks earnestly.

"You don't have time," I respond reflexively.

"I want to know," she looks at me with those big green eyes and a completely deadpan expression. She wants me to think she's wanting to know something no one has shared with her. She wants to know if she's not like the rest of us, why not?

"What makes you happy?" I decide may illustrate the difference.

"A good day for me is learning something about this world I live in," she responds without thinking. Tells me she really feels that way.

"Would you like to learn about all the homeless people who are starving to death, becoming infected with viruses, and have no privacy in their lives because they live on the street where anyone can see what they are experiencing at any given moment?" I start to rant, but pull myself back.

"I would…" she responds to my surprise.

"You don't give a shit about the rest of us, so don't humor me..."
I respond bitterly.

"How many?" she asks next.

"Homeless?" I respond. "What city are we talking about?"

"In total. If there are half of a percent of us who live in cocoons,
how may have no place to live?"

"Why do you want to know?" *I can't continue this charade. She
doesn't care.*

"If a million of four hundred million are homeless something can
be done by the private sector... my family company and all the others.
If it's forty million, it will take the government to spread the costs
across all of us," she is making this assumption I'm not sure is valid,
but makes me stop and think.

"It's somewhere between, but I can't tell you an exact number," I
try to sidestep her.

"Then the private sector can't do it alone," is all she will offer.
"But we can help if given a chance."

Chapter Twenty-One: Detective Stebbins

How can a sixteen-year-old girl disappear? There is always a trail. Something linking the girl to the person who has taken her from her home. But in this case I'm not seeing the link. Not seeing why someone would want to take Jazmin Braveheart from her home early one morning. The events were well planned out. Someone knew exactly what they were doing. Knew exactly what it was going to take to remove her from the cocoon residence without being detected. Someone knew too much to be a casual observer. But who? No one has stepped forward to say they've seen the girl, even though her profile is out there everywhere for law enforcement to react to a sighting. But there has been no sighting. As I said, someone knew exactly what it was going to take to remove her from her cocoon. Yet we haven't seen the person. At least not yet.

Jason Braveheart appears on my wall monitor. "Yes Jason."

"I don't want to ruin your weekend, but I've had a thought."

"You're not ruining my weekend," I assure him. Any clues are always welcome, whenever they may come forward.

"It occurred to me Jazmin was profiled in an article in the community magazine about two years ago. I didn't give it any thought because it was a local publication. I didn't think many people other than neighbors would see it."

"What do you mean by community magazine?"

"You know… those local publications where they're trying to get you to buy ads if they say something nice about you. They profiled Jaz for her work in algorithm development for my company."

"I don't understand," I respond. "What are you saying?"

"Let me send you the article. You can judge for yourself if it may have identified her to a potential abductor."

"Please," I respond, still not sure what I'm about to receive from Jason Braveheart.

The article arrives with the headline: 'Teen prodigy has bright future'. I quickly scroll through the article and now understand Jazmin was identified as having intrinsic value. She was not just a target of opportunity to get money from her rich father. She had value in her own right. Maybe someone's understanding of her value explains why we've not heard from the kidnappers as yet.

"How wide is the circulation of this article?" I pursue now having more appreciation for it.

"No idea, but it's local so maybe twenty-five thousand or so," Jason responds.

I've not seen this particular publication so I'll need to do some homework. "If this was the source, it would most likely mean the suspect is also local," I point out.

Jason nods, "But I still have no idea who might have seen the article and been in a position to remove her from our home."

"Maybe the individual involved is not the one who saw the article," I suggest.

"What are you suggesting?" Jason responds immediately.

"Maybe someone saw the article locally, knew someone who might be interested and forwarded it," I suggest. "Maybe there is a local collaborator, while the people we are looking for may not be local."

Jason considers my observation. "You know… you're all over the map. Do you really have any idea who's responsible?"

"If you were listening, you'd know we aren't foreclosing

anything," I shoot back. "You were the one who raised the article as a possibility. All I did was acknowledge and try to determine how what you were suggesting might have played out. By no means have I tried to indicate we have no idea how this went down or who is responsible. We have narrowed down the field of possible suspects. The proof is not sufficient to eliminate the most likely suspects. So we are trying to continue to gather whatever information would solidify the case or clearly excuse someone, including your business partner. I'm not convinced we're focused on the right people. Seems to me each case is weak or unclear why the suspect would risk so much to remove your daughter from her home. Someone took a huge gamble they would not be detected. There was some objective, overpowering to the point they took the gamble. Not knowing the objective keeps me awake at night. Trying to understand what could possibly have made the gamble worth it."

"You come back to the fundamental question of motivation," Jason points out.

"You haven't given me enough insight to really understand why someone would risk so much. Have you given insight to Peter Tate?"

I see Jason Braveheart wince. Obviously not a question he wanted me to ask. "I've shared anything relevant."

"Depends on your definition of relevant. You may not think to share something the kidnapper either discovered or already knew."

Jason shakes his head, "There are so many reasons someone would want to take a piece of my business. The technologies I invent and build are in great demand. Someone who had one of a dozen technologies I created could become wealthy from just one business opportunity. But the hardest thing for most people is understanding how to make my creations. It takes a company like I have to produce these game changers. Having the intellectual property is only worth so much. It all comes down to being able to produce it in sufficient quantities and with sufficient quality the market will move to you from me. What's so troubling to me is I don't know anyone able to take my intellectual property and reproduce it at a cost point advantageous over what I currently have in the market. So why would someone go to this extent to get something likely to have little actual value?"

"If your company isn't the target what is?" I have to ask.

Before he can respond, Ophelia Braveheart enters the picture, comes up behind Jason and puts her arms on his shoulders. Reflexively he puts his right hand on her left as it rests there. "Detective," she acknowledges me and then continues, "Would you excuse us for only a moment? I need to ask my husband a question. It has nothing to do with the investigation so we'll be right back."

Jason rises and they leave the room rather than cut off the call. I use this time to look around the room where Jason has been sitting. Small at home office. Antique wooden desk and comfortable ergonomic chair. He has a tablet input device apparently for making engineering drawings. You just don't see them very often now. Everything is voice activated. Intelligent systems back them up with a depth of global databases feeding any conversation or answering most any question. But Jason builds things. So apparently he needs different tools to develop precise products. For whatever reason he apparently doesn't think whoever has his daughter is after what his company makes. Up until now it had been my assumption as nothing else really makes sense.

Ophelia returns without Jason and sits in his chair. "Detective, while my husband attends to an errand I gave him I wanted to speak frankly with you."

"Please do," is all I can think of to say, but I'm now hopeful I may get the perspective I've not been getting from Jason.

"Peter tells me you seem to be very early in this investigation. Says you really don't have a prime suspect."

I was afraid this would happen. Should have known Tate was going to make me look as bad as possible so they will give him a free hand to do his thing. "If anything we have too many suspects. All have plausible reasons to want something from you and just as plausible alibies the night she disappeared."

"Have you eliminated all those possibilities?" Ophelia responds still cautiously.

"Not entirely. Detectives see a lot of not so pretty things. After a while we get a gut feeling about a case because they either fit a pattern we've seen before or they don't. This is a new one for me. That's why I've spent more time than usual discussing the case with colleagues who have worked different types of crimes than I have. I've been drawing on their experience, their pattern recognition skills if you will."

"What are they telling you?" Ophelia still sounds like she's skeptical I'm really trying to find her daughter. I'm sure Peter Tate has been feeding her skepticism.

"First of all they are telling me to be cautious of experts whose experience is global and not local. This is a local crime. This is not Uganda, or Uzbekistan, or Uruguay. There are a lot of cultural differences between what happens here and what happens here."

"You're cautioning me not to put all my eggs in Peter Tate's basket." Ophelia has been listening.

"The experts who have solved similar crimes locally are telling me people who cut a wide swath with media trailing sometimes attract the wrong attention and the result could be tragic. I would ask you caution Mr. Tate not to turn this investigation into a media circus."

"I understand how Peter can be threatening to someone like you. While I generally don't trust him, in this instance I do. Media circus and all. Peter will bring Jaz home, while I don't think you can."

Chapter Twenty-Two:
Jazmin Braveheart

Stash has me wondering things I've not before. Homeless people? I've seen pictures. Never met one. But probably only because I just don't go where they are. Spend time out in the air? Nobody I know does because it's too risky. All kinds of invisible things in the air you can't see but make you sick or may kill you. Jason once explained the air filtration system we have at home. Said the air is sterilized so many ways no airborne virus could survive to infect us. Even the packages delivered to our cocoon are quarantined until they are appropriately sterilized. But I can't talk about any of this with Stash. He will dismiss me even more than he already does as just being a rich bitch. Someone who could never understand what life on the streets is like. In all reality I think I need to know. Ophelia is the one who always tells me it's important to know enough about many things. Great to be the absolute best at something, but I also will need to be flexible if I'm going to succeed in life. Too many things are outside my control. If I can't adequately prepare to respond to those things I won't succeed.

The couscous is finally ready. I take it off the heat and run the serving spoon through it to make sure all the liquid has been absorbed, but also make sure it's not sticking to the bottom of the pan. "Ready to try this?" I ask Stash.

"Did you put any butter on it?" he asks looking at it and smelling it.

"No, I don't eat butter because it comes from animals."

"What do you use instead of butter? I seem to find it in almost everything." Stash seems truly confused at how I'm going to answer this question.

"How about olive oil? Lots better for you than butter," I point out.

"Doesn't have the same aroma or taste," Stash concludes, "But hey, you're the cook, so make it the way you like it. The rest of us will deal with it."

I look around the kitchen for olive oil. Finally find it in the cupboard, next to the ketchup. I put a little in the pan and stir it in, add a little more so the couscous looks shiny. I scoop a small amount of the couscous onto a plate. A fork full goes into my mouth. I move the pearls around, tasting them. The texture is about right, the oil gives it a smoky flavor but probably adds a whole bunch of calories I don't need. Just means a smaller portion.

Stash puts a scoop on his plate and also tastes it. "Not bad. Would be better with butter. If I had to limit my diet to only two things it would be butter and bacon."

"Really?" *I can't understand those choices.* "Why?"

"Fat. Your body craves fat. Don't you know that? And the taste, although I'll admit it might be acquired. Not sure many people would eat plain butter. It's better in something or on something like bread."

"Do homeless people like fat? Don't think I've ever seen a skinny one in pictures." I ask expecting this will take us in a whole different direction.

"You're saying poor people only eat fat because they can't afford anything else?"

"Do you know any homeless people? Personally? Like you've had conversations with them and know them well enough to speak for them generally?"

Stash frowns. "I've talked with a few when I've been giving them loose change."

"So the answer is no, you don't know them well enough to speak for them."

Stash half nods although reluctantly. "So what's your point?"

"Everyone would probably eat healthy if they understood what they are putting into their mouths, and could afford to buy healthy foods. But healthy foods cost more. Fat is fast and cheap because rich people don't buy much of it."

"Why wouldn't I eat bacon if I knew what was in it?" Stash decides to challenge my logic.

"Look it up. I think you'll be surprised."

Stash pulls out his phone and looks it up on Wikipedia, scrolls down, asks, "You're wanting me to look at the health concerns section," he keeps scrolling and then stops to read, finally reading the last section aloud, "According to the World Health Organization regular consumption of processed meats such as bacon increases the likelihood of developing colorectal cancers by 18%."

"What else does it say about health risks?" I push sure there's more to it. I got this lecture once, a long time ago when I asked why my diet was so blah tasting.

Stash reluctantly reads more, "Studies have consistently found the consumption of processed meat to be linked to increased mortality, and to an increased risk of developing a number of serious health conditions including cancer, cardiovascular disease and type 2 diabetes." Stash grimaces as he looks up at me.

"Ready for some bacon and eggs?" I inquire trying not to sound too triumphant.

"Think I'll stick to just the eggs," Stash starts to put his phone away.

"Cholesterol."

"What?" Stash isn't sure he wants to know anything more.

"Eggs are high in cholesterol."

"I thought someone decided eggs are not all bad. Just when you eat too many eggs or something. But the same is true about most things, I think. You eat a pound of sugar… not so good for you. An ounce, on the other hand…"

"Refined sugar's not good for you either. An ounce or a pound. Your body gets all the sugar you need from fruit and other natural foods," I inform him seeing he's not liking this conversation one bit.

Stash is getting frustrated, "The next thing you're gonna tell me is I shouldn't drink milk."

"Look it up," I suggest.

Reluctantly Stash pulls out his phone again, looks it up and grimaces, "Milk and other dairy products are the top source of saturated fat in the American diet, contributing to heart disease, type 2 diabetes and Alzheimer's disease. Studies have also linked dairy to an increased risk of breast, ovarian and prostate cancers."

Stash shakes his head as he puts his phone away and looks toward the door rather than at me as if to say he is done discussing this particular subject.

"Saturated fat is the reason I don't eat anything from animals including dairy products."

"So you don't eat cheese?" Stash asks without looking at me.

I shake my head so he will have to turn and look at me to get the answer to his question.

He finally does so I shake my head again. "Explains why you wouldn't eat the pizza. Cheese."

"Does my diet make more sense to you now?"

Stash looks at the couscous, takes another bite and I watch him really taste it rather than just swallow. "You know, for no butter, this isn't half bad."

"You want some more?" I decide to test his new found enthusiasm.

He holds up his hand and shakes his head. "Let's not get too excited just yet. But you've made your point."

Rocketman and Aces finally arrive. Rocketman looks at the pan and then at Stash, "What's this shit?"

"Couscous," I respond.

"You made this?" Rocketman begins to scoop out a bowl. "Never would have guessed you could cook."

Aces scoops out the remaining couscous, samples it and shrugs. They both disappear again, ladling the grain into their mouths without comment.

Stash slowly eats more of the couscous, "Guess they didn't even notice the olive oil." Then Stash seems to mull something. A moment later he looks at me with his thought, "You eat this stuff because you want to live longer. For the rest of us there's not much incentive to want to live longer. So maybe we eat what we do as a form of gradual suicide."

Now I'm the one who is confused, "Why wouldn't you want to live as long as possible?"

Stash takes another bite, mulling my question. "Think about it. What do we have to look forward to? I mean every day is pretty much the same. Go fix something. Troll social media. Collect a paycheck and pay your bills. That's life for almost everyone I know."

"What do you do for fun?" I ask reacting to his dire description.

"Fun? Everyone's different. Rocketman goes to bars and hangs out with his friends. I have no idea what Aces does. He probably doesn't do anything. Some people go to professional sports or concerts or movies, or hike in the woods, or play organized games like baseball, or shoot hoops, or go boating."

"Even with all the virus and pollution concerns?" I'm surprised.

"Everyone takes precautions, you know? It's just part of what you've got to do to be safe and all. Go to a bar and most everyone has a hospital mask on. Anyone coughs or sneezes and it clears the bar and they wipe the place down. They have cameras scanning people as they come into stadiums and ball parks. Anyone with a temperature gets turned away. Some people travel, but it's the same thing. They can't get on the plane if they have a temperature, are coughing or display any other symptoms. We figure it out."

"What do you like to do?" I wonder aloud again since he hasn't offered this yet.

"I do crazy shit." He says this in such a way he's discouraging me from asking.

"Like what?"

"Bungee jumping off bridges, went skydiving once, but parachuting was expensive so won't do it again, dirt biking on trails, even tried surfing – wet suit and all with all the ocean pollution. Like I said, crazy shit."

Chapter Twenty-three:
Jazmin Braveheart

Bright light on my face pulls me out of a deep sleep. Probably the deepest since… well, since I woke up on the other side of the looking glass. Or the other side of the cocooned world I've inhabited my whole life. A world I'm finding is challenging my notions in an unexpected way. Guess I never really thought about who was keeping the cocoons up. Always thought it was the systems. Jason builds systems so of course they always work. At least I've never been made aware of the systems failing. Maybe Jason knows all about the support required to keep things working. He must. He has to support everything he sells. But we never talk about it. The boring part of the business. I wonder if Stash could work in Jason's support business. He seems capable although uninspired, at least until I got him talking about what he does for fun. His enthusiasm showed me a whole different side of him. A side I never would have imagined from everything I'd seen until then. Made me stop and wonder about what I'm missing out on living in my cocoon. No fear of anything because everything is so controlled all the way down to the very air we breathe.

Rocketman sees my eyes are open and calls to me, "You think you could make us some breakfast?"

"You might be taking your life in your hands," I suggest to see if he's serious.

"You seemed to do alright with whatever it was you made last night. It was edible."

Must be his way of offering encouragement, although I'm not quite sure. "What do you normally eat for breakfast?" I ask expecting another discussion about healthy eating.

"I'm not a big breakfast guy. Usually just a bagel or roll of some kind."

"With butter and jelly?" I wonder where his diet goes off the rails.

"Just plain. The other guys want to eat heavy stuff. If Aces doesn't get his bacon and eggs... well, let's just say it's not a good day for anyone."

"He hasn't had it in the last few days," I muse aloud.

"Believe me, it will be a much better day for all of us if you give the guy what he wants."

I react to his comment thinking I'm not at all sure what it is Aces wants. I still have trouble swallowing from the way he held me up in the air by my throat. Every once in a while I catch him looking at me in a way I don't think is necessarily friendly.

"I've never cooked breakfast either, but I'll give it a try."

"Cook the bacon first," Rocketman advises. "When you get the bacon grease melted in the fry pan then you cook the eggs in the bacon grease. He'll love it."

"Do I cook the eggs in with the bacon or take the bacon out then?" I'm confused by his instructions thinking bacon is supposed to be crispy from the pictures I've seen of it. Never had it so not entirely sure.

"Cook them together until a lot of the fat has melted off the bacon. Then set the bacon strips aside so it will crisp up."

I'm not entirely sure what he's suggesting, but decide if I can make Aces less hostile it will probably be a good thing.

I ache everywhere as I get up. Stretching helps a little, but not enough. I'm still rolling my head and listening to the bones cracking as I enter the kitchen. I'm realizing I've been in these same clothes, I've lost count how many days. All I want is a shower and clean clothes.

But I don't see a shower in my near future. As I open the refrigerator, I find the eggs in a container up on the top shelf right hand side. "How many eggs?" I call to Rocketman.

"Try four," comes the response, "Two each ought to be enough. Eight to ten pieces of bacon should do it. We don't want them going into a food coma."

Why is Rocketman treating me like a person? He wasn't in the other place? Was it because I cooked the couscous and he decided maybe I can do something of value for them? Don't know, but there certainly has been a change in the tone of his voice when he's talking to me. I find the bacon in a refrigerator drawer, open the package and strip out ten slices, laying them in the skillet I found under the cooktop the night before.

I turn on the heat to six, thinking the Goldilocks range of not too hot, and not too cold. But hot enough to cook the bacon relatively quickly. As I hear it begin to sizzle, I can smell it cooking. I can't guess how many nano seconds pass before Stash is looking over my shoulder. I hear Aces approaching the kitchen as well.

Stash checks out what I'm doing. "Heat at six?" he nods to himself. "Ten slices? Who all's eating this?"

"Just you and Aces," I respond. "Rocketman said he's not a bacon and eggs guy."

Stash looks over to where Rocketman is working on his laptop. Shrugs, "Fine by me."

"Even after our discussion about the health effects?" I push him to see if it made any difference.

Stash looks at me like he's trying to remember the conversation, "You're the one who's cooking it. What should I be thinking?"

"This could all be for Aces," I suggest. "Maybe I don't care what he eats."

"Are you saying you care about me?" Stash reacts to the implication of my comment.

"Do you care about me?" I push back knowing this is going to be hard for him to respond to.

Stash shrugs, clearly not wanting Rocketman to hear his response, although I note Rocketman is watching this whole interchange.

"You should have a bagel with Rocketman," I suggest and remove one from the bag on the counter next to the refrigerator. I put it on a plate and hand it to him.

"I'm having bacon and eggs," he informs me. I set the bagel plate down next to the cooktop, tear a piece off and eat it myself to demonstrate I'm walking the talk.

Stash glances at Rocketman, then whispers to me, "One egg, two pieces of bacon and half a bagel. Enough of a compromise?"

I smile at him because it's a step in the right direction. At least half the fat and cholesterol he was expecting. Even though he is clearly wanting more.

I break the eggs, and add them to the skillet after pushing the bacon to the edge of the pan. "How do I cook the eggs?" I ask hoping someone will give me directions.

Stash looks at Aces who is watching this whole process but not giving any direction. "I think he likes his eggs sunny side up, which is just like you have them. For my one egg… well, normally I'd ask you to flip it and cook it more, but don't bother. I can handle it the way it is."

"I remove the bacon from the pan and set it on a dish to crisp up. Eight slices for Aces and two for Stash. The eggs start looking crispy around the edges so I remove them one at a time. Three for Aces and one for Stash just as he asked. I add the other half of my bagel to Stash's plate and hand them to them.

Aces nods once and heads back into the other room. Stash goes over to the kitchen table and sits down with his diminished breakfast. I bring him a glass of orange juice to go with his plate and sit down across from him. "What do you think?"

"I wish we'd never talked about food last night," he admits. "I'd have a lot more of the good stuff on my plate."

"Good stuff…" I respond to him.

"Good tasting stuff, even if it's not good for you," he admits.

"You know there's hope for you yet," I suggest. "You'll most certainly live longer than Aces, but I think Rocketman has a head start on you with his morning bagel."

"Why is a bagel better than this?" Stash asks as he takes a bite of the bacon.

"Made entirely from grains. No sugar, no fat, entirely healthy," I respond.

I pick up my half of the bagel and take a bite. I chew slowly and savor the flavor although I'm thinking Stash would prefer butter and jelly. He takes a bite as well and kind of shrugs at me as if to say, okay, I know what you're saying, but this just isn't what I'm used to eating.

Aces is back with an empty plate which he drops in the sink. He seems to be expecting me to wash his dishes too? Ophelia's rule is if you eat something you clean up your dishes. But the cocoon cooks everything, we just need to put our utensils and plates into the washer. I look around and find the dishwasher next to the sink. Okay, I'll clean-up for him even though Ophelia would make him do it.

After Aces disappears back into the house, I rise, carry my bagel with me and rinse off his dishes and place them into the washer. I take the last bite of bagel, chew it for probably longer than necessary, but then finally swallow. In the few minutes I've been at the sink, I note Stash has inhaled the egg and bacon, but is just starting on his bagel. The orange juice helps him get it down with multiple sips as he chews.

Rocketman finishes his orange juice, places the glass on the plate and pushes it away from him. I get the message and retrieve it, bringing them over to the sink, rinsing off and placing into the dish washer. Stash evidently sees what's going on. He brings his plate and utensils over, rinses them himself and places them into the washer. Stash glances up at Rocketman who is ignoring him, but I get the sense he knows exactly what Stash is doing and doesn't approve.

Stash leaves the kitchen as I put my plate into the washer and begin to follow him out, but Rocketman stops me with a question, "What are you going to make for dinner?"

"So I'm the cook now?" I let him know I hadn't volunteered.

"It's either you or take out. I think I've had about all the fast food I can handle for a while."

"What do you normally eat?" I expect it to be totally unhealthy since fast food generally is.

"I only eat fresh vegetables and grains. Pasta and vegetables is kind of the holy grail for me, just with an olive oil sauce."

"You vegan?" I'm surprised at his answer.

"I eat what I have to," Rocketman responds wearily. "We all do. If I have a choice I never eat fast food."

"Why don't you generally have a choice? I don't understand."

Chapter Twenty-Four:
Jazmin Braveheart

Stash seems distracted. He walks up to me as I sit on the couch on the back porch overlooking the many Eucalyptus trees. "We need to have a chat. In the bedroom," he nods in the appropriate direction.

"What's the problem? You want lunch too?" I ask, not understanding what he wants to talk about.

"Now!" he practically yells at me, conveying a sense of urgency seemingly out of the blue.

I know I must frown in response to his order, but I'm trying to understand why he's in such a hurry. I finally get up and follow him, although he keeps looking over his shoulder at me. I don't know if it's to make sure I'm coming or whether he's preoccupied with something else. This isn't like Stash. The only thing I can think of is Aces has said something he wants to tell me about so I can be prepared if Aces does something.

Once we are in the room and the door closes, I immediately ask, "What's the problem?"

Stash holds up his hand as if he wants to hear something, but what? So I listen too. I hear voices from the other room. *Does this mean Aces is talking with Rocketman? Complaining about me, maybe? Is Stash hoping to keep me from hearing the complaint? But I haven't done anything to elicit a response from Aces. I've just ignored him like I have right along.*

But then for no apparently reason Stash steps forward, puts his hand over my mouth and pushes me down on the bed, coming down next to me. *What the fuck is he doing?* With his hand over my mouth,

133

I'm having trouble breathing. I try to inhale through my nose, but he's partially blocked it. I try to tell him, but it comes out muffled. Even I don't know what I'm trying to say. I try to pull his hand away, but he pins my arms down with his other arm. I bite at his fingers as I squirm and try to break free, but the lack of oxygen is already starting to have an effect on me. I'm doing everything I can to bring in more air, but I'm getting light headed. I rock side-to-side, kick and try to break my arms free to pull his hand away from my face.

But Stash gets up on top of me. *Holy shit! Stash? He's the one who was going to help me get away, at least in my best-case scenario. Now he's going to rape me!?? Why is he doing this to me?* But all he does is adjust his hand over my mouth so I can't call out. He's not trying to get into my pants. At least not yet. *What's he doing? I hear the voices again. Unfamiliar voices. Is somebody here? Someone who could tell the police I'm here? Help me escape these lunatics? I try to listen. See if I can hear what they're saying. If someone has come to this house why are they here? Is it neighbors welcoming us to the neighborhood, or have the police come to arrest them and send me home? Doesn't matter. I've got to figure out a way to get free, to let them know I'm here. Make them understand I'm not here because I want to be, but because they took me from my home.*

I notice Stash has relaxed the pressure on my mouth, but keeps his hand there so I can't call out. I try to tell him he needs to let me go, needs to let me breathe because his hand is making it difficult. But he continues to sit astride of me, keeps the hand over my mouth so I can't be heard.

My heart is beating furiously and with his slight relaxation I'm getting more air, which helps me think more clearly. Small consolation. But he still has my arms pinned to my sides, has me so I can't move, or get away or even scream for help.

I'm listening again, trying to hear anything being said. Stash has relaxed the pressure on my mouth just a bit. I bite his fingers. His instant reaction is to pull his hand away. But he realizes what's happened before I can make a sound. He has his left hand pressing hard against my mouth again, reducing my air and the light headedness returns. I see Stash looking at his right hand. I apparently broke the skin. He's bleeding, but can't do anything about it at the moment. He deliberately lets the blood drip on my forehead. He watches me looking at it. Watches me feeling the impact of each and every drop of blood hitting me. The blood runs down my face. Alongside my nose. It then follows his hand along my cheek. What else can I do to let them know I'm here? Can I bite this hand too? What would he do if I did? Probably put a pillow over my head. Would that suffocate me? What else can I do? I've got to let them know I'm here, but how?

While Stash keeps the pressure on my mouth, and reduces my air, I try to listen. Someone other than Rocketman and Aces is here. I can clearly hear voices, but have no idea what they're saying. I recognize Rocketman's voice. Sounds like a conversation and not him protesting being taken away.

I hear the door close. No voices. My chance at escape is gone. I feel my hope vanish. Stash takes his hand off my mouth. I take a deep breath and exhale before I can do anything else.

But then I have to try, "Help me? In here! The bedroom. Help me!"

"You're wasting your breath," Stash looks at me and then back at his bleeding finger.

"Why am I wasting my breath?" I demand, feeling angry, scared and unsure and still pinned down by him. "How about getting off me."

"In a minute," Stash responds.

"Who was here?"

He doesn't answer, but continues listening to see if they come back he can ensure I'm not heard. A few more minutes pass. "All clear," Rocketman finally calls out.

As Stash gets off me, I punch him in the balls as hard as I can. He doubles over in unexpected pain. I push him off the bed and scramble away from him towards the door. As I rip it open, Rocketman is standing in front of the door apparently wanting to see how Stash kept me quiet. He looks at the blood on my face and then past me. He sees Stash on the floor, doubled over with a bloody hand.

"Looks like it got a bit rough," he remarks.

I demand, "Who was here?"

Rocketman shakes his head, "You gonna live?" he asks Stash.

"Give me a minute," Stash responds as he slowly tries to get to his feet. Once up Stash takes a deep breath and moves towards the door.

I glance over my shoulder at Stash, and sidestep Rocketman to get away from both of them.

Chapter Twenty-Five:
Ophelia Braveheart

"Where?" I ask Peter Tate as I look at his image. Apparently he is riding in an auton somewhere. I see him on the wall display of our wood paneled study. This is the room I always go to when I want to be alone. Jason never comes in here since he has his office and I never go there.

"Near Stockton," he responds trying to lower my expectations, but raise my hopes. I know what he's doing. "It was only a fleeting glace, girl riding in an auton with several other people. The woman who saw the girl had just seen the bulletin and admits she had it on her mind."

"Meaning you don't think it was her," *I know him too well. He did this to me how many times when we were together? He's always trying to manipulate the situation. Make sure I think he's doing all he can when in reality he's not put much into it at all. Peter rides events, he doesn't cause them. But despite his many shortcomings he seems to be a lightning rod. People who otherwise wouldn't pay attention do. Maybe Peter just takes advantage of his fame. Whatever it is, he's more likely to bring Jaz home than detective something who just doesn't seem to have any energy when I talk with him. Seems to be there, going through the motions. I just don't see what he's doing to bring her home.*

"The sheriff went house-to-house afterwards. Apparently didn't come up with anyone matching her description. Makes me think whoever the woman spotted probably doesn't live in Stockton. May have been just passing through. Most likely wasn't her, but we're not assuming anything."

I recognize his pattern. Says he's not assuming anything, which just means he hasn't taken the next step to do anything other than ask the Sheriff to check around. I'll bet the Sheriff didn't do much. House to house? Probably left a voice message asking if they'd seen anyone who looks like Jaz. "The Sheriff's not doing enough, Peter. She's my daughter. You need to treat this like she's yours."

"Is she?" he puts right back at me.

I don't answer him.

"Always trying to renegotiate the terms of our relationship," Peter responds. "Some things never change."

"No, some people never change. I understand Barbara filed for divorce too. Who were you cheating with this time? The sixteen-year-old baby sitter?"

"Word does get around," he notes mockingly. "What, is there a Peter Tate former wives club or something? You all get together over a glass of expensive wine I'm paying for through my alimony and compare notes on how the relationship fell apart?"

"I've been off your payroll a long time, Peter so I buy my own wine."

"I was fortunate with you. I still have three payments a month going out…"

"And will soon have a fourth…" I throw at him to let him know I'm enjoying the digs.

"Ah yes, another one bites the dust. Barbara lasted longer than anyone. Don't know if she was more tolerant of my failures or enthralled of my cocksmanship."

"I have to admit it's been a while. Maybe my memory isn't perfect, but I don't remember being enthralled, Peter. At best you're only average."

"I do bring out the worst of your memories, don't I?"

Peter seems to want to move past this discussion. Since he seems to be getting the worst end of it I don't blame him. "My worst memory was waking up to find Jaz gone. I'm counting on you to help me create my best memory, which is Jaz coming home safe and unscarred by this whole event."

"I hear you babe."

Peter almost sounds like he means it. Somewhere along the way could he have grown a conscious? In all the years since I left him I never thought it possible for him to do so. He's just so narcissistic. There's no one else in the world as far as he is concerned. He has the ex-wives to prove it. Tells me he could never close the deal with someone unless he married them, or for whatever vainglorious reason he only wanted women who were unattainable any other way. Marriage was certainly the only way he was getting into bed with me.

I hear Peter's phone ring, he looks down and notes, "Your Detective Stebbins calling. You want me to patch him in?"

"Please," I respond only because I want to hear what Peter is hearing, when he hears it so he can't filter it later.

"Mr. Tate?" I hear as his image comes up in a window on the display.

"Mrs. Braveheart is also on the call, Detective."

"Mrs. Braveheart, this will save me the next call I was going to make. Mr. Tate, I understand you are on your way to Stockton, correct?"

"How did you know?" Peter asks surprised.

Detective Stebbins' tone changes to more challenging than inquiring, "Am I correct?"

"Yes," Peter finally acknowledges apparently answering his own question.

"Good. Your going will save me a trip," the detective's tone changes back to more informing than challenging. "I spoke to the Sheriff just now. He was following up on the status of his search triggered by the call he got from Mrs. Wilson." The detective apparently moves his eyes to look at my image on his screen. "Did Mr. Tate inform you of...?"

"Yes. He told me someone reported possibly seeing her."

"I don't want to get your hopes up as it was only one person who reported it. If it had been more than one I'd give it more likelihood of being her. But I asked the Sheriff if he would check out the listed bed and breakfasts in the area. I was thinking if someone brought her there, they wouldn't take her to a hotel as too many people might see her. More likely they would take her to a private residence someone was letting out on short term rentals."

"Makes sense," I agree. "And what did they learn?"

"Sheriff just called me back to say they visited sixty-two properties. Of course no one acknowledged having seen Jazmin. But of the sixty-two he is keeping an eye on five as something the residents said or their behavior raised questions as to whether they were telling the truth."

"Did the Sheriff say whether he just visited the B&Bs where people moved in on the day Mrs. Wilson thought she may have seen Jazmin?" Peter asks. I didn't think to ask this, but it's a good question.

"Actually he visited all the listed B&Bs regardless of when people arrived. Just to be sure he didn't overlook someone. Hard to establish if she has been there a day or several days. She's been missing what? About a week now?"

"Six days," I confirm. "Seven hours and twelve minutes since we discovered she was gone."

"Since the girl who looked similar to Jazmin was seen yesterday, if this was her, she's been someplace else for five days. It may mean they're moving her around. They may not have known exactly when they were going to move her here."

I see Peter nod, considers the logic for a moment before asking, "What did the Sheriff tell you about the five places he's watching?"

"Not much," the detective responds as if he's wondering if he should have asked for more information. *I could be wrong.* "In each case the deputy who made the visit didn't see all of the people who they were told were there. In each case the reason for their stay in the Stockton area was vague and the purpose of their visit didn't seem to match with something they said or did while the deputies visited."

"No specifics?" Peter pursues apparently hoping to better understand why the deputies picked those five.

"As I said the Sheriff didn't say much about them at all," the detective responds matter-of-factly. "I suspect he's trying to respect privacy rights as much as possible. Doesn't want anyone outside his office harassing people who aren't involved in the disappearance."

"But it makes it harder for us to decide if any are," Peter pushes right back.

"The Sheriff has access to the same databases we do, so I'm sure he's already checked backgrounds to see if there's anyone of the five and possibly more who have priors. If they do they may warrant further investigation."

"You seem satisfied the Sheriff is doing everything he can," Peter begins. "So what are you wanting me to do while I'm up here?"

"If she's there, I'm sure they'll keep her out of sight. Particularly if the Sheriff paid a visit," the detective states the obvious. "But if I were going up I'd talk with the deputies who went out, I'd talk with Mrs. Wilson and better understand how sure she was the girl she saw was Jazmin. I'd try to see if anyone could track down the auton company of the vehicle the girl was in…"

"Mrs. Wilson didn't think to check for a car number or anything?"

"Sheriff said she looked but didn't see anything."

141

"Probably a private vehicle then," Peter responds but clearly still deep in thought.

"The Sheriff's assumption, but still worth checking out. Then I'd drive around the community and talk to people in shops and parks and restaurants. Try to understand why Stockton? Why did they possibly bring her there?"

"It's a Goldilocks town," Peter responds. "Not too big where lots of people will see you, but not so small people know everyone else's business."

"So you think it's the kind of place someone may have taken her?" I ask Peter.

"Fits the criteria I would have if it were me," he responds although I can tell he's already thinking about something else.

The detective nods, "Mrs. Braveheart, I take it there has been no contact with you as yet from the kidnappers?"

This time I shake my head as I can't respond at the moment, brimming with hope someone has given us the first real clue as to where Jaz may be, but having as many fears this may not be her.

"Call me after you've had a chance to talk to people there," and the detective is gone from the screen.

"What do you want me to do if I find her?" Peter asks.

"Kill them. Kill them all and bring her home to me," I respond in a voice even I don't recognize as I feel a desire for vengeance new to me.

Chapter Twenty-Six: Jazmin Braveheart

If anyone was going to rape me, I thought it would be Aces. Stash was supposed to protect me. Now I don't know if I can assume he will. I couldn't move with Stash on top of me. I've never felt so helpless. Never been restrained where I couldn't even move. Biting him didn't do anything other than make it worse. And nothing I did would have stopped him.

I notice I'm still shaking from the experience. I pull inward, have my feet up on the couch in front of me and wrap my arms around my knees, leaning into them to make me as small as I can be. When I get stressed out I tend to think about someone far away who I've talked with but never met. I can have a conversation with them in my mind because it's not so different from talking with someone on a wall display at the cocoon. I see them, we have a conversation but it doesn't have to be a real conversation. I never touch them. Never notice the smallest details about their mannerisms only evident when you are with someone. Phoebe was the last person I talked with. Even she was acting like she was concerned about her own safety when we talked. She heard sounds. There could have been someone in her house. Her family was away. What would she have done if there was someone there? What did she do? All of a sudden I realize she was in the middle of dealing with something in her house when the lights went out in mine and I lost the signal. What happened to Phoebe? I don't know.

Did someone rape Phoebe while her parents and brother were away? Did someone even try? Was someone in her house? She's my best friend of the moment and I have no idea what happened to her in what may have been her hour of need. And she has no idea what happened to me, either. Does she care? We're not really close for best friends of the moment.

Stash comes by again. I wouldn't talk to him when he came over the first time. Must be hours ago by now. Still not going to talk to him.

He completely shattered my expectations of him. Thought I could trust the kind of person he is, but it's clear I can't. I'm here on my own. If I'm to ever get home, it's going to be because of what I do, not because any of these assholes takes pity on me. Fuck it.

"You ready to talk about it?" Stash asks looking down at me. He's apparently not willing to sit down. Probably concerned I'll bite him again. I see he has a bandage over his finger now. At least it stopped bleeding.

Then I realize I still have his blood all over me. Yuck. I need to go wash up. Put this behind me.

I shake my head and get up to go to the bathroom. I want his blood off me now. Then I notice it's on my top. Shit. I could take it off and wash it. But since I don't have any other clothes I'd have to wear my wet top. Not going there. No wet t-shirt competition for these bozos.

With the door closed behind me I look into the mirror. The blood ran both ways. Into my hair and down beside my nose and then along my cheek. Somehow it dripped down onto my top. It looks like fingers of blood have drained across my chest. I so want a shower, but am not going to give anyone an excuse to take advantage of me naked even for a moment.

I scrub the blood off my face. Try to wash it out of my hair, even though doing so makes me look like a wild woman. I use the bar of soap on the counter to try to wash my hair as much as I can, rinse it out and towel it as dry as possible. No comb or brush in here so I use my fingers to run through my hair, pushing it back and hoping it will dry. At least my hair is now cleaner than the rest of me. Sort of. I suppose I should be happy about small gains in the quest for hygiene.

My top is the next issue. I look at it and am disgusted. I'm not going to continue wearing this with the blood stains. What is it about blood? Something about it brings the worst out in people. I've got to rinse it out and wear it. I'm just not about to go around looking like this. The hair should scare the shit out of them if nothing else does.

HAPPINESS

The top comes off. I'm reminded of the morphing Phoebe did of me just before… morphed me into having normal sized, or slightly larger than normal sized breasts. And how different I looked. I probably should be glad I'm a little underwhelming in my development at the moment. Note to self: being sexy isn't always a good thing.

As I rinse the blood out of my top I look up in the mirror. A pasty-white, anorexic girl looks back at me from the mirror. And now with wild long brown hair. No wonder I've not been raped already. I probably wouldn't be turned on by me if I was a guy. Probably also a good thing at the moment, but do I really want to look like I do now for the rest of my life? I already know the answer is no. But why? I want to be attractive. Do guys think they want to be attractive as well? I don't know. I have to think they want to be attractive, but what turns a woman on is different than what turns a guy on. Guys want big boobs and an attractive face. They can deal with the rest if it's not perfect. Women want a strong, rugged attractive face, reasonably in shape and can deal with the rest if they make a lot of money. Smart is a bonus, but highly prized. No one wants to be married to a dumb guy. Clearly wasn't what Ophelia went for in Jason. Smart and rich. She was lucky to have gotten a shot at him.

I wring out my top as much as I can. Want it as dry as possible so it won't cling to me. I have no idea if even my meager chest will have the wrong effect on Stash, or Aces or Rocketman. I really trust him the least of all of them. I don't know why. The fact he's a vegan should be a good sign. But there's something in the way he looks at me. As if he knows this whole kidnapping isn't going to end up well. Seems he doesn't want to know me at all. Impressions are dangerous when they are merely impressions.

I try wringing my top one more time, but I'm simply not strong enough to get any more moisture out of it. So I pull it over my head and pull it away from my body so it won't cling, but of course it does. It's wet. I can't expect it not to cling. I look at myself in the mirror. No more blood. Well, if nothing else I've accomplished my primary objective. Wish I could take a shower and change my clothes. Not going to happen any time soon from what I can tell. Guess I need to be thankful for progress.

I return to the couch on the patio and resume the same position I was in before Stash came by. Back into the same smallest space I can inhabit. Knees up, arms around the knees and my head down. My mind won't shut down and I find myself looking out over my knees. I wonder who came here when Stash seemed in such a panic. Someone was here. I heard the voices. Was it someone looking for me? Must have been or they wouldn't have reacted as they did. Was Stash just doing what he thought he needed to do to keep me quiet? Quiet so whoever came to the door wouldn't find me here with them? Makes more sense than anything else I can come up with. And even if it were someone selling Girl Scout cookies, they wouldn't want her to know I'm here. Keep me out of sight. Make sure I don't make any sounds, thus the hand over my mouth. Not even Stash wants anyone who might come by to know I'm here.

I look out through the trees surrounding this house. Eucalyptus. I've heard about them. The problem seems to be Eucalyptus trees secrete an oil. But it takes a long time before they start the secretion process. So the trees are mature before anyone knows you have a fire bomb in your back yard. A lot of the California wildfires are a result of the prevalence of the very trees I'm looking at. The documentary on wildfires I watched made it clear any wildfire coming through this way would have taken these trees out a while ago.

Off in the distance I see something moving. What could it be? A bear? No. Couldn't be a bear up here, and then it comes closer. Five deer, one with antlers and four does approach the house. I've never seen deer, actual live deer before. Always a picture on a monitor in the cocoon. But there they are. Live deer. They seem very alert. Looking in all directions, grazing on the grasses covering the fields just beyond the trees surrounding the house. Low grasses. Probably the perfect kind for deer to feed on. Just a guess since I don't know anything about deer. For a long time all I knew was reindeer pulled Santa's sleigh. But something made me look them up. Probably a question from someone in one of my classes. I learned all about Bambi and movies about deer and how tragic it is when hunters kill the mothers of baby deer. From then until recently when someone asked Jason if he wanted to go on a deer hunt I'd not thought about deer. He mentioned the trip to Ophelia, who was all against him going. Out in the wild. Rampant diseases. He could die. If anything happened to Jason, what would happen to the business? It supplies the money we need to keep living in the cocoon.

If Ophelia were the one who had been kidnapped, she'd be totally freaking out. No doubt. She simply couldn't handle this since she'd be breathing unpurified air. Having to be around men, who knows where they've been? Have they become infected with one virus or another? After all these years of purified air would any virus or bacteria simply overwhelm her body? I'm sure she would be lying here prostrate, sure she was about to die. So if Ophelia would handle all this so poorly why am I not doing the same? I am my mother's daughter. But I'm not. Why?

Maybe because she has her view of the world already worked out. I'm still trying to decide what it is I think about the world I live in. I'm not convinced all the precautions we go to are necessary. Especially now. There are a lot more people who live out here than in cocoons. They seem to be doing just fine, although money for them seems to be in short supply. But money can't be the sole arbiter of the value of a life. Can it? Is my life more important than anyone else who is out here? I don't know the answer to the question having only a sample of three to compare. But I have to believe there are many worthy people out here.

Stash comes by again. Notes I've cleaned up from what I was sure was going to be a rape, but now I've come to the conclusion he had other intentions.

"You look better."

I still don't look at him, continuing to watch the deer feed, and surveil the area for anyone who would do them harm and maybe set me free. Am I like the deer?

"Look, I'm sorry I treated you so roughly, but I didn't know what else to do."

147

I glance up at him, but only for a moment, then reengage with my deer friends, who are keeping their distance from us at the moment. Their behavior suggests I need to do the same with Stash and the others.

"Are you going to accept my apology?"

I don't respond. I can't give him any indication treating me the way he did is okay in any way.

Stash glances over to Rocketman who sits just inside the front door, as if he is guarding it in case someone comes to visit. His behavior confirms someone did. Whoever came was not a welcome visitor. But then maybe he's expecting someone to show up like Grendele's Modor, whoever she is.

Stash returns to me. "Hey. If you're willing to cook something for dinner I'll help you. Better than take out or another pizza delivery, which I know you won't eat and I shouldn't."

I keep my gaze on the deer. He killed any enthusiasm I had for cooking or helping my captors in any way. At this point I'm a prisoner. I have to think if someone unexpected found them they will decide to do something about me sooner rather than later.

"If I cook a vegan meal, will you eat something?"

I'm now a hostile prisoner. How can I make this as unpleasant for them as it is for me?

Chapter Twenty-Seven: Rocketman

Modor hasn't called me back. I'm not sure what I should do. The deputies were clearly not convinced by my story. The fact I had to call her to vouch for us was not good news. What caused them not to take my word for why we are here? I even showed them my work badge needed to get me into infrastructure control boxes. The badge should have been enough, but they didn't buy it. I'm sure she's going to say we have to move her again, but for some reason she's hesitating. Maybe she's changing where she wants us to take her. Some place where we're less likely to be seen. I still can't figure out who saw us. We never left the auton. Kept a low profile everywhere we went. The kid didn't do anything to call attention to us. I kept an eye on her and I'm sure she didn't.

At this point I'm not even sure if Modor's called the girl's parents. She's got to know the police have their place wired to trace any contact. Probably why she's waiting. Hoping to figure out a way to make the contact in such a manner it can't be traced. But contacting the parents is not my problem. All I got to deal with is getting the girl to wherever Modor tells me and handing her off when the deal is done. Then I get my payday and disappear to an island where nobody knows my name or gives a shit.

Stash approaches me, "She's not coming around."

"Need to turn up the charm…" is all I can offer him. Keeping the girl from going off the rails is his problem. I'm not going to get involved. Modor's paying him to keep her quiet, "So fucking do it."

"I'm going to cook something to eat…"

"She's not helping I take it. After you did such a good job with breakfast…"

"The cops coming gave her hope."

"No, you were too rough. You spooked her," I push back on his simple but inaccurate explanation. "She won't get over it any time soon. So as long as she just sits there quietly I'm okay with life."

Stash looks at the girl. Still in the same position on the porch couch, looking out into the distance. If Stash hadn't been rough she might have screamed and alerted the cops. Stash stood up and did what he had to do. Glad he did it. I'm feeling new respect for him since I wondered if he would. Thought he'd never do it. If he hadn't we'd all be sitting in some jail cell right now. So okay. Cut him some slack. He did what he had to. Now let's just get on with it.

Stash shakes his head and heads off to the kitchen. "How about a risotto?" I call after him.

"What's risotto?" he responds.

"If you don't know, don't bother trying to make it." I respond. "Whatever you decide will work for me. I'm sure Aces could give a shit as long as it's edible."

I see Aces look at me with a puzzled look, but it only last a few seconds and he's back into whatever it is he's working on.

The girl continues to sit in the same position, looking out into the distance. Stash isn't going to get through to her after restraining her. Probably should have had Aces do it and kept Stash the good guy. Lesson learned. Too late to make any difference now. I look down the driveway to make sure the cops aren't coming back. I have a bad feeling and expect a return visit at some point. Hopefully we'll be long gone by then.

I walk over to the couch where the girl's sitting. "You shouldn't be pissed off at Stash. He only did what he had to."

The girl doesn't look at me. In fact, there's no reaction from her.

I put my hand on her knee. She instantly puts her legs down and turns away from me. Clear message.

"Someone came by. We couldn't let them find you. Stash had to make sure they didn't know anyone else was in the house. Since Stash has never done this before, he didn't know what it was going to take to keep you quiet. Take pity on the guy. He's doing the best he can."

She still doesn't respond, so I put my hand on her shoulder, expecting the reaction I get, which is she pulls away from me, gets up and walks to the window.

"Look," I begin. "You're just a payday to us. Nothing more. We agreed to keep you out of sight until we're told to hand you over. You cooperate and you'll be home as soon as daddy does what he's asked."

She continues looking out the window at something in the backyard. I look out and see a group of deer probably three hundred yards from the house. Apparently what she's been looking at all this time. "Have you ever had venison?" I ask expecting her to freak out since she's already said she's vegetarian.

She looks at me with pure and unadulterated hatred. There's no question what she's thinking. But she's also not answering my question.

"I only ask because a lot of rich people think it's a delicacy. A lot of not so rich people view it as game. They like to go out in the woods and bring a deer home in season so they can feed their family. For some of those families, they need to kill a deer because they make so little money. Including people who work for your father's company. Have you ever looked at the salaries he pays people?"

She finally stops looking at the deer and engages my eyes. Still not going to say anything, but at least I have her attention.

"Not everyone who works for your father's company can afford to live in a cocoon. It's not a matter of the value of the work they perform. All work is important. People establish their identity by the work they do. They establish their self-worth by their work. But you father makes a lot more than anyone else who works for him. All the other people have their livelihoods at stake. For them if they lose their job, their family starves. Did you ever think about what happens if someone loses their job? If the company goes out of business you lose your cocoon, maybe. But they lose their identity. Who they are as people. They aren't the ones who caused the company to fail. Your father did by decisions he made, not them."

The girl looks at me with a strange expression. Not sure I've ever seen one like it before. Still she says nothing, but the stare goes right through me.

"Don't give me a look," I shake my head and step closer. "You know what I'm saying is true. You know because now you've left your cocoon, you see what the real world is like. You see not everyone goes to MIT and becomes a clone of her parents. Not everyone eats a vegan diet and maintains a precise weight."

She turns away from me, seems to be looking for the deer again. Apparently has decided what I have to say is of no significance. I'm just saying things to get her upset, hurt her, question what she believes. But she has seen enough. She has seen how we live, what we eat, how we work. She knows there's more to the world than she has seen. She should question even more as she thinks about it the world as it is.

I walk over and stand between her and the deer in the field beyond. She continues staring even though I know she can't see them. I squat down so I am looking directly into her eyes. I knew it would only be a matter of time before she looks at me. She does so quicker than even I expect. "I know you want to go home. Hell if we were in the opposite places here, I'd probably want to go home even more than you, because I know what it's like out here. I know what it takes to survive in this world. But you don't have to worry about surviving. And all those movies we've both seen? What's the moral of every story? You can go home where you'll be safe, secure and happy in the loving arms of your family. The story mankind would have you believe. The story Hollywood always tells. But do you believe it? You've seen there isn't necessarily a happy ending for everyone. People die out here. From the virus we can't see, from the pollution in the water we drink and bathe in. From the violence arising from those who don't have enough, and those who have too much. There's no means of balancing out the needs of everyone. This isn't your world, or at least you're thinking it isn't. But I've got news for you. It is."

Her gaze is steady. I can't tell if she's thinking about what I'm saying or she's just totally cut off listening. Letting me go on and on, but not hearing a word I've said. I decide to see if what she would have me believe is true. I stand up and look down at her. "I'm sending you on to the next place."

She looks up at me. I see a concern in her eyes I didn't see a moment ago.

"You're wondering why, aren't you?" No reaction from the girl. I reach out and grab her thin wrists. She begins to struggle but in only a moment Aces is next to her, holding her still from behind. I tape the wrists together with electrical tape, reach down and tape her ankles together as well. "Too bad you didn't want to talk with me, because now I have to make sure you can't talk with anyone. I put the tape across her mouth, but make sure it doesn't block her nose so she can breathe.

Aces grabs her under her arms and lifts her up. I take her legs. She struggles, but we hold on tight. Between us we carry her to the front door. Stash comes out of the kitchen, "What are you doing?"

"She's going for a ride," is all I'll say trying to hold onto the bucking bronco.

He comes closer and looks at her as if not sure what we're doing. "Is this Modor's idea?"

"Open the door," I nod. He does and we carry her out. Aces opens the trunk and we put her in. I hear her trying to protest, trying to roll out of the trunk, but I push her back and slam it shut.

When Aces gets in the car, Stash gets right in my face, "Not a good idea. Sending her with just him."

"I can't trust you alone with her, even after you kept her quiet."

"And you trust Aces?" Stash is really asking whether Aces raping the kid is better than him letting her go. Since the latter will ensure I end up in jail and what Aces does doesn't. I'm making the better decision for me, but I'm not about to tell him why I decided to send her with Aces. So I adopt the girl's tactic and say nothing, returning to the house. Stash gives up on me and watches the auton move slowly down the long drive towards town.

Chapter Twenty-Eight:
Jazmin Braveheart

The road is rough. The auton bounces me around in this dark trunk. *I'll be lucky if I don't have bruises everywhere by the time we get wherever we're going this time.*

I try to clear my mind, listen to the world outside, and try to imagine where we might be going. *Rocketman deciding it necessary to bind me and tape my mouth is not a good thing. Means this is getting serious. People must be looking for me. Someone came to the house asking questions.* I have a moment of hope. Then I realize it's only good for me if they find me before one of them decides to dispose of me.

Dispose. Not a term I would have thought of before this happened. I had an unlimited future. Everything just pointed to things getting better. Forever. Never thought of the future as having any constraints. No bounds. No end. The future is the future isn't it? I mean it just goes on and on. And now, all because of something I don't even begin to understand my future has a possible near-term end. Like days or weeks. Hours maybe. And then what? The worst thing is I have no idea how to answer the question.

The auton comes to a halt. *Must be in the city near the house where we were staying.* I listen hoping to hear voices. People nearby. *Someone who might hear me if I make noise even with my mouth taped shut. I could kick on the back of the trunk. Knock on it with my bound hands. Something to draw attention. But if I don't hear voices, then it's not likely anyone would hear. And since someone is in the auton, if I make noise and no one hears it's likely whoever is in the car will make sure I can't make noise at the next stop where someone might hear me and ask questions.*

The auton starts up. No voices. *No one I can count on to help me. I'm back right where this whole thing started. Unable to change anything. Totally at their mercy.* I try to see what else is in the auton trunk with me. Spare tire and a whole bunch of lining. Not so much to make this space comfortable, as it clearly isn't. *But to cover up all the wiring and electronics. Even though I can barely see, I decide it's time to see if I can do anything to affect my future. But how with the tape on my wrists and ankles, to say nothing of my mouth? If he hadn't taped my mouth I could have pulled on the tape on my wrists and maybe gotten it off. But my fingers are free so I should be able to pull it off my mouth, let's see.*

I pull at the corner of the tape. *Owwwwwww. God-damn. Electrical tape across the mouth. But it came off.* Now I try to see if I can unwind the tape on my ankles. I feel along until I find the seam, find the corner and give it a pull. In only a moment I have enough up to start unwinding it. Doesn't take long. Now I can yell or kick if I hear someone. But the real test is to see if I can catch a corner of the tape around my wrists with my mouth and get my hands free. I run my teeth along the top but don't catch anything. I turn my wrists and find the underside. I do the same. And in a moment I have a tiny corner and pull the tape away from my wrists. I have to pull it across the top and then down around to the bottom again. I come around and catch the loose tape with my mouth. I have to try a couple times before I have it firm enough to pull up and across again. *Three turns around and I'm free!*

Oh shit. What do I do now?

I seem to remember something about a trunk release in most cars, in case someone gets trapped inside. I start feeling around hoping to find my ticket to freedom. Still too dark to see something but I finally feel a handle. No good to pull it when we're motoring along. Need to wait until the next stop. But I have no idea how long until then. *Nothing I can do. Just wait.*

I hold onto the handle. Close my eyes and try to relax while I wait. *I feel the road. Still rough. Tells me we are still likely on local roads. Interstates are going to be a lot smoother. They're designed for higher speeds and every bump is magnified at speed. So we're still somewhere near the house. Somewhere near where someone was looking for me. Be patient. Your chance will come.*

We ride along at a low speed. Don't know how slow, but most cities are thirty miles per hour. Likely what we're driving. We're likely still in the populated areas of whatever town we were close to. I need to be ready to pull this handle if we stop. *But as I think back, I don't remember stopping many times when we came in. But I wasn't really focused on how many times we stopped. I could be wrong. Wish I knew.*

As I'm waiting, my mind wanders. *Who is the good guy here? I thought Stash was until we went into the bedroom. Now I don't know anymore. Thought Rocketman was the least sympathetic, but now I don't know. He seemed to be sharing his vulnerabilities with me when we were talking food, but what does his conversation mean? The fact he thinks about nutrition the same way I do? We have one common bond and it's kind of impersonal. And his whole condemnation of Jason and the family business? Did he realize he was condemning me too? Aces? He seems to view this whole kidnapping thing as a Royal pain in the ass. From what I can tell he'd be just as happy if the whole thing was over. I would too, but not in the same way he views it.*

The auton seems to speed up. *Have we passed out of the downtown area? Out on the open highway? If so then I'm not likely to get a chance to get away until we arrive wherever it is we are going. I have absolutely no idea where we will end up since I have no idea where I've been. Am I a mile from the cocoon? A hundred miles? A thousand? No idea, and it's all because they put me out when they took me from the cocoon. Don't have any idea how long I was out. Could have been an hour or a day or a week.*

Now we're apparently out on the highway, I listen carefully. *I'm hoping I'll hear whoever's in the auton talking to someone about where we're going. But nothing. No radio, no phone, nothing.*

The road gets smoother and the auton seems to have accelerated. *No doubt, I'm back on the highway again. The car rocks. Not sure if the rocking is from the uneven highway or wind or could be uneven tire pressure. Never gave tire pressure much thought, but now I have nothing else to think about. I guess my mind will be looking for ways to entertain me until we slow down enough and I can try to get away. Only I'll have no idea where I am, if I'm successful. What if they don't speak English? What if I can't tell people who I am? Tell them I need help? A very real possibility.*

If I had something to write on and with I could write my name on a piece of paper. I could give it to whoever finds me. My name on a piece of paper would solve the language problem if there is one.

What was Rocketman trying to do by telling me he's a vegan? He had nothing to gain. No reason other than to make me feel some affinity to him. But if I'm either going home soon or they're going to kill me... I stop for a moment. This is the first time I've really admitted the possibility to myself even though it's been in the background the whole time. In the background until Stash showed how easy it would be for him or any of them to rape me. Until Rocketman taped me up like he did, it never occurred to me I might not go home. But now I wonder. Did something change? Something I'm not aware of? Did what's her name call Rocketman or Stash? Did she make a call? Would explain why I'm tied up in the trunk of an auton. Something definitely changed.

The auton seems to react to traffic by moving to the left suddenly. It seems to be slowing down, like there is some issue on the road ahead and it adjusted in some way. *Is this my chance? Will we slow enough I can pop the trunk and run away? If I do, will whoever is in the auton with me follow? Will he bring me back? Since I got out of the tape it's not likely he would tape me up again. What would he do?*

The auton doesn't come to a stop. It seems to be travelling slower. *Is it slow enough I can get out without hurting myself? Could I get away without someone coming along behind us running over me? A distinct possibility I can't dismiss. Autons are reliable in a lot of ways, but something totally unexpected like me getting out of the trunk? Would the car's radars even see me at close range? I don't know. With only one chance to get away I can't pull the handle until I'm sure. Not being able to see anything I have to trust to my hearing alone. Not a desirable situation to be in, but it's where I am. Now what?*

158

HAPPINESS

I wait for the auton to come to a stop, but it doesn't. I wonder if I pull the handle could I sit here, looking out the back until we come to a stop or would whoever is up there know the trunk is open? Have to believe there is some sensor here and an indicator in the cabin to notify whoever is in there. *Can't afford for Aces or whoever to see the indicator, find me untied and do whatever he might to restrain me. Whatever it might be won't be pleasant.*

The auton apparently picks up speed. *I feel the difference. My chance has passed. Now I just have to wait until the next opportunity.* I close my eyes again, even though there is little difference with them open or closed since it's dark in here. But there's a serenity with them closed. I've chosen the blackness engulfing me rather than having to endure one imposed on me by nature or someone else.

The road smooths out as the auton picks up speed. Whatever was slowing us down has cleared. Now we are on our way somewhere totally else from where we were. *What's her name... Modor, I think, isn't taking any chances in my being discovered. But what does she want? I have no idea? I've never met her. Never did anything I can think of to bring me to her attention. How does she even know I exist, other than her team keeps our cocoon up? Did one of them tell her about me? And if they did, what do they know about me? What made me of interest to someone who maintains systems? None of this makes any sense to me.*

I try to shut down my mind. I want to stop thinking. Relax so I'm ready when we get wherever we're going. Rather than thinking about all the things I don't understand, I just recite to myself, '*OMMMMMM*'.

This lasts about ten seconds. Then my mind seems to reengage me whether I want it to or not. I reconsider what do I do if I escape? *Where do I go? What do I say? Would anyone listen, or care or do anything to help me? The worst thing I can think of is escaping and being recaptured. Given how brutal all of them have been to me at one time or another it's not likely things would be any better.*

I feel the handle in my hand. *This is my ticket out of here. My ticket home, maybe. But there's no assurances. And even if I go home, can I feel safe having been taken from there once? What has Jason done to make sure it can't happen again? Did he figure out the vulnerability? Plug whatever let them come in and just take me away? And why me? Why not Ophelia? What made me the preferable target?*

I'm assuming Jason wasn't the target because whatever it is they want, he's the one who will have to give it to them. To her. Modor. If she's even the one behind this. I suddenly realize she may not be the one who is. And if she's not, then the motivation becomes even murkier. But it actually makes more sense to me. *I haven't been able to figure out why someone who maintains cocoons would risk her business to kidnap someone from one of them. She has to know someone will eventually figure out her role. But someone else doesn't have what she has at stake. For someone else this may have only upside. For her, it's only downside because it's likely when this is all over she won't be able to continue supporting cocoons. Did Rocketman, Aces and Stash sign on because they knew there was no going back to the way things had been? They know their current gig is going to end soon, so cash out and fly far, far away? Makes sense to me, but what's really going on? I have no idea. On the other hand it would explain why Stash seemed to change in an instant.*

I try to wash all of this realization out of my mind so I can relax and be ready when the opportunity presents itself. The opportunity to test the reality of my situation. See if I can get away or whether I'm on a short list to oblivion and the end of my existence.

The auton seems to slow to a crawl. I don't hear voices, but I pull the handle anyway and....

Chapter Twenty-Nine: Stash

I can't help thinking none of this will work out in the end. I never thought Modor had a foolproof plan. But she seemed to think there were enough safeguards worked in we would come out all right. *She was going to protect us. Make sure only Rocketman would still be here when the handover occurred. He wouldn't actually be here. He would tie her up and leave her where she could be found. Me and Aces would be long gone. Only Rocketman had to worry about being caught. We'd have our money. We'd have our freedom. We'd never have to worry about keeping anyone's cocoon up ever again. Unless we were stupid and ran through our money too fast. Lamborghini? We want a Lamborghini lifestyle, we clearly chose the wrong parents. No way would the meager payout cover a Lamborghini kind of lifestyle. But we signed up to a payday. A payday we're gonna get if we don't screw it up. If Rocketman delivers the goods when instructed to. But I don't have anything to do with the handover. Rocketman has all the risk. I have to assume he's gonna get a bigger payday than I am, even though Modor said no. But at least I'm pretty sure I'm gonna get mine.*

Rocketman sits down across from me. We're still in the Stockton house, waiting for the sheriff to come back with a search warrant. *Looking for her. We know it's coming, so why are we still here? Letting the Sheriff take pictures of us. Run us through his database. He's not gonna find anything since I have no prior convictions. Rocketman's were all juvenile and those records are sealed. So we're virgins.* Modor said no records is the only reason we have a chance at this opportunity. *Opportunity is the word she used.* This 'opportunity' to make a lot more money than we'd ever make fixing code and cocoon hardware.

"What the fuck were you thinking?" Rocketman hits me hard. "Did you think she was gonna say it's all right we took her from her home? Everything's all right now? You can just go on back to your office? I'm having a good time with my friends here? I'll be happy to come home when Daddy gives Modor what she wants? I'm okay even though I have no earthy idea what this is all about?"

I shake my head because I wasn't thinking about what he's just described. "Chill," I suggest even though I want it to sound a whole lot more forceful and know it's not coming across the way I want.

"Great," Rocketman turns away like he's talking to an imaginary audience. "You're living in a fantasy land if you think anything other than she's the enemy. She's gonna do everything she can to make sure we get locked up. We fucking kidnapped her. Do you realize it would be a federal offense if we took her out of state? She doesn't know where she's been or where she is. Some prosecutor asks, she won't know. She won't say, 'no I never left the state'. By then we're all in Federal court. You, me and Aces."

"And Modor," I remind him.

"And whoever she's working with… maybe. But don't count on it. She's got this thing wired more ways than we can see. She's not going anywhere."

"They'll figure out who we work for."

"Nine to five. But how do we link her to the after-hours? The safe houses? She gives them the time sheets, they show we worked projects the whole time. She paid us for those projects. What's our tie to her beyond 9 to 5? I don't see it. She was very careful. Everything's been verbal. Yeah there are calls from us to her, but she can easily explain them given our time sheets showing we were working projects for her having nothing at all to do with the girl."

Shit. Rocketman has a point. I'm really getting depressed. Why did I ever sign up for this?

"So when the Sheriff shows up?" Rocketman asks tentatively. "We invite him in and suggest he check us out, which we know he's already done. He comes through. Looks everywhere. Is there any indication anyone other than us has been here? No. I tell him we're nearly complete on the on-site work we needed to do here so we're

162

likely to head on to our offices to finish the project design. May be back to confirm things to suggest why we have the place for a week. Just so they know we're leaving. Nothing to do with their investigation. We're just slave to the project and the work we need to do is back in SFO. We finish it up there, maybe come back to check something and then on to the next project."

"Why are you so sure they're coming back?" I push him having not been out here with him to see how it went.

"Just a feeling," Rocketman responds. "How they looked at each other. Like they were making notes of all the holes in my story. I don't know. I've not spent one minute with cops in a very long time, so I don't know how they think. But it just seemed to me they weren't buying what I had to say. I've been there before, with my old lady. Same shit. She never believed me even when I told her the truth."

"What was the deal?" I ask him, surprised he would tell me about his mother.

"Deal? With my old lady?" Rocketman turns away like this is not a topic he wants to explore. But for some reason he continues. *Maybe only to kill time until the cops arrive.* "I was the youngest. Three boys. So by the time she got to me, she'd seen it all and told me over and over and over."

"Seen it all?" *I'm not following coming from a family of three girls and only one boy, me.* "My brothers weren't exactly angels. They got into a whole lot more shit than I ever did. My old lady... she had her own waiting bench down at the jail. All the cops knew her. Mostly because of my oldest brother. He was probably fathered by the mailman or something because he never fit in. Couldn't be more different than my old man. And they hardly ever spoke, probably because my old man knew my brother wasn't his. But it was my old man's fault for marrying my old lady without checking into who she'd been sleeping with."

"So your old lady got around." I offer to try to understand what he's telling me.

"My old man too. He was no saint. Seemed to know most of the women in town by their first names. He kept slipping up with my old lady. She'd say Mrs. Brown and in response he'd say something about Vivien or Sheila or Keisha. When he did she'd just shake her head and turn on her heel. She knew he'd slept with the person they were talking about. Saw it I can't tell you how many times. And every time my old man would follow her into the bedroom and an hour later they would come out all lovey dovey. His arm around her. She making jokes about one thing or another. It was like foreplay for them. He'd get her all riled up about who he'd slept with and then she'd want to know if she was better in bed than the other woman. Of course he'd tell her she was. And then she'd be all smiles. Sick if you ask me. But the way it was."

"How did you get out of there?" I ask, not sure he'll tell me. *But since he's waiting for the cops, maybe he will just to pass the time.*

"You think I'm out of it?" Rocketman shakes his head. "I mean I get the calls now. Not there to watch it, but my old lady still calls me to complain about my old man. I think she uses me as a whip. Keep hitting him with his infidelity so he'll get a hard on and come satisfy her, because if she doesn't whip him he can't get it up."

Apparently he's right. I hear a car approaching. Slowly progressing up the drive. I stand up and see the same auton they came in the day before. Before she left with Aces. I go sit in the back porch and pick up a magazine. *What the fuck is this? Southern Living? Not something I'd ever read.* I put the magazine down not wanting it to be so obvious I'm reading something I have no interest in. I pull out my cell and begin to scroll through social media sites. This would be more believable.

Rocketman goes to the door. A third person is with them. I wonder who they got to join them? *Why would they bring this person out?* Means to me they spotted something and this guy is here to confirm we're the ones holding her. I dive into the social media sites and just look at pictures because nothing I would read now would have any meaning for me anyway.

"Afternoon Deputies," Rocketman greets them at the door. "Sorry, I forgot your names."

"We wear name tags," the older male responds. He was in the car the first time, I remember seeing him as the auton approached the house. "This is Mr. Tate." Apparently there is a head nod greeting before they continue. "He works for the family of the missing girl. So we're cooperating with him as much as possible. We said we were coming out to ask a few more questions. He asked if he could come along. In the spirit of cooperation we absolutely want to take advantage of any help we can get."

"I understand. So what would you like to ask?" Rocketman responds.

"First, we'd like to search the premise," apparently a search warrant is handed to Rocketman, who I guess doesn't even bother to look at it.

He immediately responds, "Sure. Don't need a warrant. Do you want a tour or do you prefer to do this alone?"

"Deputy Reynolds and Mr. Tate will look around," the male deputy responds.

They both come out on the porch, she asks, "Who are you?"

I look up from my cell, "I work for Systems Maintenance, Inc. too. We're scoping the new infrastructure project as part of an RFI." I know this is what he told them earlier as we rehearsed it. The guy comes around behind her, glances at me for only an instant, checking out the room and the area behind the house in a fast sweep of his eyes. *I've seen him somewhere before.* I don't have a warm comfortable feeling seeing him. *He's famous or something.* "Anything I can tell you?"

Deputy Reynolds and Mister Tate shake their heads and disappear into the rest of the house. I go back to my phone, suspecting it's absolutely the best thing I can do at this point.

"Have you left the premises since we were here earlier?" the other deputy asks Rocketman.

"No. Why?"

"Have a report an auton came up this way."

"Meal delivery," Rocketman responds without having to think about it. "They brought up lunch about one or so. We were working on pulling data together to send back to the proposal team and worked through lunch. You know it's better to eat a bigger lunch and lighter dinner? You gain less weight if you do. Also cheaper for the company as lunch is always cheaper than dinner."

The house isn't very big, so Deputy Reynolds and Mister Tate come back to the doorway after a brief tour. I look around to see what's going on. Not going to join them as don't want any questions directed my way. Deputy Reynolds shakes her head, but Mr. Tate keeps looking around as if he's burning every square inch into a memory.

The deputy asks, "The report said it looked like there was someone in the auton when it left."

"Did you have a report of whether anyone was in it when it came up here?" Rocketman thinks to ask. *I never would have been as quick. Probably why he's the one to hand her off.*

The deputy shakes his head with obvious regret his ploy didn't work.

Tate speaks up, "You're not who you say you are. There's no proposal for Stockton infrastructure. I asked. So why are you really here?"

Chapter Thirty:
Detective Amare Stebbins

The voicemail from Peter Tate was most curious. Just the one word: Maybe. And of course he was unavailable when I called him back.

Even more curious, Jason Braveheart wants to talk. *Right about now*. And sure enough Jason appears on my live wall. "Detective. We were contacted about an hour ago."

"Why did you wait to call me?"

"In a moment. No disrespect, but they gave me a deadline on a response. I had to find out if what they were asking for was even possible."

"Do you know who you're dealing with? Whether your daughter is safe?" I have to ask since he omitted those details.

"They say Jaz is in a safe place, wouldn't tell me about her. For now I'll have to take their word for it."

"No proof of life," I seek to confirm.

"Only a picture they apparently took when they removed her from the house. She appeared to be asleep. But she could have been drugged. I really don't know."

"The picture was to prove they took her. And they ask you accept she's still fine, even though…"

"They said if they put her on she might say something to compromise their ability to safeguard her until they have what they want."

"Sound like your daughter?" I ask as from the little I know it seems like a plausible reason, but I need Jason to confirm it.

"Yeah. Sounds like Jaz. She would figure out some code to tell us something. A clue to lead us to them eventually. It wouldn't be obvious, but apparently she's said or done enough she's spooked them."

"So this would be the contact we've been waiting for. And if so, who are they?"

"Nobody," slips out of Jason's mouth in such a way he apparently expects me to just accept it.

"I have to admit I've never had a victim or a victim's relative say nobody before."

"They're nobody. No big corporate body trying to achieve global domination of their markets. No ideological group who wants to defeat communism. No hegemon, who wants to conquer Canada. They're nobody in particular."

"I don't get it. They must have an agenda or they never would have gone to such lengths," I protest. *I'm starting to get pissed off at Jason because he's jerking me around and I don't like it one bit.*

"They're clever. And they've done their homework. They knew exactly what to ask for in such a way most people wouldn't have any idea why they want it."

"But you do?" *Why is he beating around the bush? He's not going to tell me.* "And if you do, what does all this mean about releasing your daughter?"

"I don't know why I never thought of…" but Jason doesn't finish the thought.

"Jason, if you want me to help you bring your daughter home, you'll need to tell me who we're looking for and what they want. Without those two key pieces of information, you're just delaying bringing her home," *he's not listening to me.* "I'm sure your wife would be very unhappy to learn what you're doing."

"My wife?" Jason looks up at my image on his screen.

"Ophelia Braveheart. The mother of your daughter."

Jason looks over his shoulder as if he's heard someone or something. *But I suspect he's just been reminded his wife is waiting for him to do something to bring their daughter home. If she were to find out he delayed it for even a nanosecond, I'll bet she would not be kind to him.* "They said there would be an exchange. They will let us see her when I deliver the package. Then they will tell us where we can pick her up."

"Are you going to negotiate or just take what they've offered?" *Why do I think there's so much more to this story than he's telling me? Does Peter Tate know more than I do? If asked to wager I know where I'd have to place my bet.*

"Well, I had to determine whether what they want is even feasible first…"

"Now you've determined it is, what are you doing about giving them what they want?"

"Is keeping them from harming my daughter worth a few lines of code? You've got to be kidding. Of course I agreed, once I was sure. Now negotiating… once I have the code, then is the time. Once they know what they want is a mouse click away? In this instance I'll be able to get them to deliver her to the house in a Lamborghini auton if I want. And leave the keys to the auton. Once they know what they want is real, it exists and they're about to have it…" *Jason smiles this funny little crooked smile I've never seen before.*

"Of course you'll have it too. Whatever it is they want."

"My having it won't be a problem for them. There's nothing I can do with it to keep them from getting what they want. Although they may be underestimating me. Underestimating what I might be able to do with it." *The same crooked little smile.*

"Jason!" I try to get his attention.

Jason continues considering something he won't share. Same look. Same total absorption with a concept I am apparently unworthy of being given.

"Ophelia, Ophelia, Ophelia!" I repeat in an effort to get his attention.

Jason again looks at my image on his monitor. "What?"

"Your wife. Your daughter. We're trying to get them back together again. Remember?"

"They will only release her if I deliver what they want," Jason responds as if confused why I keep dragging him back into this conversation.

"When you've told me what you're not telling me, and I go out, find your daughter, and bring her home, then maybe you can make this super whatever-it-is just for yourself. You wouldn't even have to share it with them. Sound like an appealing opportunity for Jason Braveheart businessman?"

Jason looks at me, but then I see the light go out in his eyes. "You haven't been able to figure out where she is so far, why should I think you could do it now?"

"I haven't done it so far because you've made sure I'm totally in the dark about the nature of the transaction they want," I push back as hard as I can. "I can't do much until we establish a motive. You know the motive. You're still you're sitting on it and not sharing. You know something about who has your daughter and all you'll tell me is they're nobody. I can't do my job when you don't share what you know. You obviously aren't as eager to bring her home as your wife. Do I call her and tell her? So she will stop calling me and telling me I'm not doing my job? Up to this point I've not pointed the finger at you. I've tried to be respectful of your relationship. But I can't keep doing this. Not when you have information crucial to solving the kidnapping you won't share."

Jason apparently thinks through what I'm saying for the first time. Apparently thinks through how his wife is going to take it if I tell her he's keeping their daughter from coming home. A small shake of his head. The funny little crooked smile is gone. "Who are they?"

"If you know you need to tell me. If you even have a guess as to who they might be, you need to tell me. If you don't have any insight, but based on what they want you could infer who might be involved, you need to tell me."

Jason again looks over his shoulder. Suddenly I see Ophelia Braveheart standing behind him, she leans forward and puts her arm across his chest, kisses him on the top of his head.

"Mrs. Braveheart," I acknowledge her. Then see the change in her expression.

Her voice is strained, "What news, detective?"

"Your husband hasn't told you they contacted him?" I inquire, surprised by her question.

Ophelia Braveheart, stands away from her husband, "What's he talking about, Jason?"

Jason's expression tells me all I need to know. I can either drop off the call at this point and let them work through the issues they have as a couple or stay on and see if Jason will tell her in front of me what's really going on. I decide the latter strategy will probably get me where I need to be much quicker. So I just wait to see if Jason cuts me off.

After about ten seconds he hasn't. *Maybe he'll forget I'm on. Let's see.*

Jason reaches around. Ophelia comes with him to sit on his lap. "I got a call…"

"And you didn't tell me? What the fuck is going on Jason. This is our daughter... Jazmin. The one person who can take all the compromises we've made... and create a better world. She's the most important person in our lives. What are you doing to bring her home... to us... to me?" Ophelia is crying as she takes his head in her hands.

"Jaz is okay," Jason begins again. "They want an algorithm. Nothing more."

"Why haven't you given it to them?" Ophelia Braveheart asks as if she can't understand why this whole nightmare is continuing.

"Because it doesn't exist. No one has written one to do what they want. Explains why they went to such extreme measures."

"Kidnapping... to get you to create something you probably wouldn't have otherwise."

"I don't know... I might have created what they want if I'd thought of it. Just wasn't something I'd ever considered."

"The team is writing the code?" Ophelia looks him steady in the eye. The camera gives me a bird's eye view of her on his lap, but unfortunately I can't see his face.

"They started about an hour ago."

"When will they have it?" Ophelia asks clearly letting him know sooner is better than later.

Chapter Thirty-One: Jazmin Braveheart

The trunk rises slowly. I see autons queued up behind me in the rain, which is steady, but not a downpour. All the autons are moving very slowly. The people in the one behind us haven't recognized the trunk is open. Haven't recognized I may be stepping out in front of them even though we are moving along at a slow rate of speed. I can get out, but will the car behind hit me before I get off the road? *I have to hope the radar will tell it to stop.*

I swing my legs out and step away from the auton into the rain. Right into the path of the one following. I see the people in the auton deeply engrossed in their handhelds. They're not paying any attention. The auton doesn't stop and hits me between fifteen and probably twenty miles an hour. Before it can knock me down, I put my hands on its wet windshield and jump up and onto its short hood to keep it from breaking my legs. I spin from my left so I'm now facing the auton I've just escaped. Continuing to roll, I push off of the trailing auton, jump down and to my left as fast as I can to keep from being hit again. The auton hits my trailing foot. The impact spins me around. I fall backwards deliberately to roll away from the moving cars. Lying on my back by the side of the road I look up into the falling rain. Through the drops I watch the autons progress along. Apparently whichever of the three musketeers is in the auton didn't notice my escape. At least I'm hoping he hasn't. The fact the auton hasn't pulled over makes me think I'm right.

A big sigh of relief. I relax for only a moment before regaining my feet. A quick glance around and I run away from the highway in the covering rain as fast as I can move. I suddenly realize I'm out here without a mask. *I'm breathing who knows what in the air. I could catch a virus and die like tomorrow. Holy shit. What have I done?*

Too late, just keep moving. Got to put as much distance between me and whoever's in the auton as possible. I soon come to a road. Not much traffic, but which way do I go? If I had any idea where I am it wouldn't be such an existential question. If I go in the wrong direction it will take me a long time to find help. At least I guess it may take a long time. No tall buildings I can see from here. Looks like houses down to the right, but I've never thought the first appearances to be the best long term. Better to go to a commercial place than a home. People are much more likely to help me. I start walking as fast as I can to my left. Even though I don't see anything close. *No traffic coming this way either. Should I try to hitchhike? Get in the car of someone I don't know? Someone who might be infected with who knows what? Someone, who would transfer a virus or disease my sheltered body simply can't cope with.*

I walk along now, drenched, but I don't care. I'm free. I look over my shoulder periodically for a trolling auton looking for me. *Can't let them pick me up again.*

What do autons do when someone's hitchhiking? My guess is it wouldn't know what to do and would simply keep on going. So I guess I shouldn't be expecting anyone to give me a ride to the next town. Unfortunately, I don't have a biometric credit account since I use Jason's or Ophelia's when I need something. So how do I get home?

I break off the road and cut through a field towards a small town I see in the distance. What am I walking through? Seems to be wild grasses, sparse and tall. Blowing in the wind and rain. But doesn't seem to be a crop of any kind. Nothing here to harvest and eat. Must be fallow land. Letting it go wild for a few years. Plow under all the grasses and repopulate the soils with the nutrients it needs to support the next crops coming along. If not this year, maybe next. What have they grown here? Last year or the year before? No indication. Makes me think maybe strawberries. Nothing needing nurturing over many years like grape vines. Nothing with trees like the citrus grown here for decades and has now almost disappeared. Strawberries can be planted each year without a problem of needing last year's plants to grow successfully this year.

HAPPINESS

Ophelia again. Learn about everything, even if it's not what you're interested in at the moment. You'll discover things you can use. Deeper and wider understandings all at the same time. Jason never advised me to think about crops grown in California. He didn't care about it. Thought it was a waste of time to even consider it. But here I am. Ophelia's daughter, understanding the situation I'm in better because I took the time to explore broadly. Took the time to learn about curious things, but not necessarily related to whatever it was I happened to be researching at the moment. Took the time to consider the wider world I inhabit, she inhabits, Jason inhabits... and now I'm finding it's a much different world than I thought with a whole lot of others whose plight I'd never considered.

I continue to trudge through the soaking fallow field. Towards the small town not so far away. The rain obscures my vision as my wet hair has fallen into my face. No one seems to be objecting to my crossing their property. *Would Jason ignore people crossing his? Not likely. He'd prosecute them to the full extent of the law. Make sure they never thought of taking a shortcut through his property. We don't have much. A few acres. Not nearly as much land as I'm crossing at the moment.* I hear a buzz. *Drone??* I don't know, so I try to see if there's something following me through this field. If there is, I have no idea if it's the landowner upset I'm crossing his or her lands, whether it's the local law enforcement following up on a description sent out on my disappearance, or it's Modor trying to locate me after I escaped her auton. Could be any of the three. I can't be sure how to respond to it. But from what Jason has said in the past, probably the best thing I can do is keep from looking at it. *Try to prevent it from getting a picture clearly identifying me.*

The buzz is coming from behind. *So I don't look back. Don't look up. Keep my head down but all the time looking out the corners of my eyes to make sure it doesn't come down low to get a better look at my face. As long as I keep my head down, it shouldn't be able to recognize me. As much as I want Jason and Ophelia to find me, I don't want Stash, and Rocketman and Aces to find me. Don't want Modor to find me, even though I have no idea who she really is. There's too many people who want to find me I don't even know. So got to stay off the communications grids as long as possible. Hopefully I can find a safe way home.*

I'm trucking through the field when I trip and fall forward. What the f…?"

"I'm sorry," a small man, probably not taller than five feet is curled up in the field. I've tripped over him. He has a rather large head and much smaller body. Not a dwarf, but a person of small stature. His clothes are soaked and shabby. Hiking boots I notice. He looks around. "How did you ever find me? I thought this was the perfect place to disappear forever."

"Why would you want to?" I have to ask, even though I am more interested in who he is and why he's here.

"Disappear?" he looks at me. "When you're beautiful, you want to be noticed. When you're not… well better to disappear on your terms than to be noticed and forgotten or dismissed instantly."

"Who is dismissing you?" I have to ask now he's raised the issue.

"Everyone…"

"I'm not," I point out hurriedly to make him understand he's making assumptions.

The short and plain looking man rises and looks at me with his wet and stringy long brown hair hanging in his face. I notice he wears his hair in a pony tail. "Why are you walking through my field? I didn't give you permission."

"This is your field?" I have to admit I'm surprised. I also rise to stand looking down at him, since I'm taller.

"I own everything as far as you can see," he gestures as he informs me but with a pride missing I would expect.

"I would love to own this much land. But you don't seem to be proud of it. Why?" I press the short plain man.

"When you're attractive like you, everyone pays attention. When you're not…"

"Not what I've seen. Some of the most unattractive people who are rich get a lot more attention than those who are pretty but poor," I respond to his comment, not even thinking about it.

"Pretty but poor can marry unattractive but rich and change the whole dynamic," my mysterious field fellow comments, although I have no idea what he's talking about.

"So marry someone attractive but poor," I suggest since it seems to be his perception.

"No one really attractive would have me. Believe me, I've tried and tried and tried. I'm like the frog who was once a prince. Only no one wants to look back at what I might have been, once… Look beyond what I am today."

I'm feeling sorry for him, but then one thing leaps to my mind, "Why are you out here? In the middle of an empty field?"

"Everyone seems to have the same problem. You look at what it is today and say… empty field. I can cut through here because I'm not disturbing anyone's crops. But you don't look at what it may be next year. This year it doesn't deliver any revenue so it's useless. Next year I plant strawberries and I make millions from one crop. No one looks at potential. They only look at what it is today. No one looks at the millions I'll make next year. No one looks at my potential. They only look at what I am today."

"What are you today?" I ask to see where he thinks this conversation is going.

"I'm an unattractive guy who has a lot of land, but not a lot of cash. I don't go around flashing wealth like so many do. But if you want to look at balance sheets? I blow away most of those flash-in-the-paners."

"Why are you telling me this? I'm just passing through."

"The fact you're just passing through is why I'm telling you. Just passing through. You're one of all those people who just ignore me. Think I'm no one of consequence, but I am. Someone of consequence. Not a lot happens in this valley without someone from one of my companies involved. Not a lot gets decided unless one of my people agrees. My people. Maybe the problem is I've let my people take over. Now I'm just the person who counts the money when all is said and done."

"What's wrong with counting the money?" I ask, still not understanding his angst.

"There's nothing wrong with it..." he acknowledges. "But for me... it's just not fulfilling. People have to deal with my people, but they never deal with me. Do you know what I'm saying? I'm here but everything gets decided by others. People I pay to take care of things for me. Do you know why?"

"What? Put other people in charge?" I ask. "I would assume it's because you couldn't do it all yourself."

He shakes his head, "I could have. But everyone in my social circle said to me, 'Why would you? Other people are quite capable. Use them.'"

I look at the town, not so far away now. "Do you live there?"

Chapter Thirty-Two: Rocketman

"She's gone?" I can't believe what Aces is telling me as we talk on my cell. There's no way she'd be able to get out of a trunk when she was tied up. I tied her up myself. Oh shit. What is Modor going to say? She's fucking gonna say no payday. "Well Fucking find her. And I mean now."

"Gone?" Stash has been listening. He has turned pale. Apparently he's thinking the same I am. No payday, no job and the whole world looking for us if she tells her story. "Where? How?"

"When he got to the new safehouse he found the trunk open and no girl," I shake my head still not believing Aces let her get away when I was afraid Stash would. *Called it wrong.*

"I told you sending her on with just Aces was a bad idea," *Stash just has to remind me.*

"Not helping find her," and then I have to push back on him. "I suppose this wouldn't have happened if I'd sent her with just you."

"No, it wouldn't," he looks me straight in the eye. "I never would have put her in the trunk. Which was your idea. So don't blame Aces. This is all you."

"Fuck you," is all I can think to say. "Doesn't matter anyway. We signed up together and we go down together if we don't find her now."

"How?" *Stash is eliminating possibilities as we talk. I see it in the way he keeps shaking his head like a half shake or something. Not an overt action. Probably doesn't even know he's doing it. Only does it when he's trying to work through a solution to a system problem.*

"You got a license?" suddenly occurs to me.

"For what?" *Stash isn't following my logic yet.*

"Drive a car. We could rent one, follow the roads to the new safehouse. Look for her along the way. Aces comes the other way. Maybe we'll see something leading us to her."

"Like what? Camera crews from the evening news?"

Stash doesn't think my idea will work, but at the moment I'm not quite sure what else to do.

"Do you have a license or not?" I push.

"I take it you don't?" *Stash realizes the predicament I have.* I make an assumption as I dial Aces, wait a moment, "Rent a car and back track. We'll meet up half-way." Next I order a car to be delivered to the house. "Twenty-minutes," I tell Stash, "Since you're the bigshot engineer, reverse engineer where you think she might have gotten free."

"What are you gonna do?" Stash always has to see the whole picture.

"I'm gonna try to figure it out too. Maybe between us we'll zero in on a place where she was likely to have made her escape. Go there and start looking around."

Stash goes over to the table where I'd left the electrical tape. He comes to me and, "Hold out your hands."

"What are you doing?"

"Reverse engineering. I'm gonna tape you the same way you taped her, sit you down on the floor of the bathroom and time how long it takes for you to get the tape off. As close an approximation as we can make. Anything else would be a guess with an infinite margin of error."

"You are a fucking engineer," I tell him holding my wrists out. I'm surprised he apparently was watching what I was doing. He turns the tape around my wrists the same number of times. Then walks with me to the bathroom. I sit down on the toilet as Stash tapes my ankles. Then I see the smile in his eyes as he pulls down my hospital mask taping my mouth shut.

Stash steps back, sets the timer on his phone, "Okay, see what you can do."

I look at the tape on my wrists. The first thing I can think of is I would use my mouth to pull the tape off my wrists, but then realize my hands are free and I can pull it off my mouth. I start to peel it off, but it pulls on my beard. Then I realize the girl doesn't have facial hair so I give it a yank, which is what she probably would have done. "Owwwww."

Stash grins at my pain, clearly enjoying this whole thing. "Payback's a bitch," I caution him. Next I use my mouth to grab a corner of the tape on my wrists. Takes me a moment to work up enough of it so I can tug on it. Finally get it and pull as far as I can. I let go and bring my arms up trying to grab the dangling tape from the other side. It's awkward. I have to keep working on it to finally grab it with my teeth. I pull around and all the way to the other side. I let go of the tape, try to pull my arms apart, but still too tight. I repeat the attempt to grab the tape from the other side. It's hanging longer down so I try to catch it in the middle. Catching it is harder than I expect since it's all the way around the other side. I have to grab it right next to my arm. I nibble at it and finally grab it, pull, but it's tighter here, probably because I pulled on it. The tape slips out of my mouth. I have to try again. This is taking much longer than I thought. I wonder if the girl had this much trouble? *Doesn't matter because this is all just an attempt to get an estimate. A minute or two isn't going to put her in a different county or anything.*

One more try. I get a firmer grip on the tape with my teeth. This time I bring it all the way around and the tape falls away. Now I reach down and easily unwind the tape around my legs. I look up with a satisfied look to see Stash stop the timer. "How long?"

"Three minutes and twenty-six seconds."

"Really? Holy shit she could be somewhere between here and Stockton," I realize.

Stash shakes his head and looks away. "She would have waited for the auton to slow down or come to a stop. More likely a stop. So likely first place she might have tried to get out would be Stockton. Can we get a read out from the auton about where it stopped and where it was travelling really slow?"

"Probably not," I respond. "The only one with the information you want is Modor. Enough said?"

Stash puzzles. "No, we don't want her help at this point."

"I'm surprised you would describe it as help. More like a nuclear explosion taking us both out."

The dual use auton arrives. It drove out in autonomous mode, but we can override it and drive wherever we want. *At least Stash can with his license.* As we walk out to the auton Stash turns to me, "Autons drive according to conditions including the route they select. We don't know what route it took to the safehouse. Modor input the destination and the auton did the rest."

"What are you saying?" I'm not sure where he's going with this.

"We don't know what route it took. Doubt Aces was paying any attention. Maybe we should ask Modor to send the auton back here so we can…"

"Can what?" Stash is working the problem and has forgotten Modor isn't going to help us.

"Hold on, I'm still working my way through this. We need a reason to access the vehicle she sent. Once we have it we can set the destination and it should follow a route nearly the same. Probably the closest we will get."

"You're saying you driving isn't a great idea."

"Different autons have different route planning software. They don't optimize on the same parameters. They don't select the same route. I'm not even trying to optimize as a driver, so I'm likely to go with a different route than the auton did. May not even go through the area where she got away."

We stop at the vehicle before getting in. "We don't have time to make this perfect. We got to find her so I vote we turn on the auton's self-drive mode. Follow it as far as it goes before stopping or slowing. There you take over and we explore the area. See if we find any trace of her."

I hear Stash give a sigh, he apparently has come to the conclusion I'm right. But then he looks down the drive. "What do we do if deputy dog is waiting for us down there?" he nods to the driveway.

"I don't know why you think he didn't accept my explanation this time," I toss back as I get in the back.

"Because the other guy clearly didn't," Stash responds. "I watched his eyes as you explained we serve private homes and not cities. Told them our proposal is for a group of individual homeowners and not the city. A possible development of cocoons outside the city. It hasn't needed to file for building permits as yet."

"Hey. I thought it was brilliant because they can't go look at public filings since I said it hasn't been filed yet."

"Generally when someone is spending money on a development, they go have informal conversations with the city staff. I'll bet he went back to them and discovered there hasn't been any conversations about a cocoon colony."

"Look. I got it covered. Put in the address of the safehouse so we can get started looking for her."

He looks at me blankly, "You never told me where we were going. Do you even know? Usually Modor just sends an auton and it takes us there."

Damn. I don't. I can't call Aces because the police will be able to monitor the call. Same with a text. How do I find out where they were going when she got away? Fuck, I can't play this game. I dial Aces, "Where is the halfway point?"

"He says try Roseville. Northeast of Sacramento." I repeat for Stash.

"Why there? Roseville's a long way from here."

"He didn't say, but he has a better idea about this than we do because he was at least in the auton when she got away."

Stash sits in the driver seat, enters an address in Roseville. The auton closes the doors and begins to take us there.

"Roseville," Stash repeats as if he's trying to remember. "Something happened there."

"The Roseville fire? Bombs or something blew up in the rail yard when a rail car caught fire. Happened a long time ago."

Stash looks at the map on the dashboard. He's following the route we're taking, hopefully looking for places the girl might have escaped from the auton.

"There's something else about Roseville. Wish I could remember what it is," Stash continues to mull.

Chapter Thirty-Three: Peter Tate

I know bullshit. These guys were bullshitting me. The only question is why? Do they have anything to do with Ophelia's daughter? I can't tell. But they were clearly making up the conversation as they were going rather than telling me the straight scoop. Been around way too many bullshitters in my time.

We've now visited five different suspects. Only the one still remains on my list, although I think the Deputies haven't eliminated some I have. Not because they have any more information to work with, but simply because they're a little more indecisive than I am. Probably because they haven't seen as many extreme situations like I have.

"Why do you keep going back to those two infrastructure guys?" Deputy Reynolds asks me as I sit in the back row of the police auton. She and her boss are in the front seats with their back to the windshield, looking at me.

"You get to the point where you just don't believe people anymore," I respond.

"You apparently believe the others we interviewed." She responds. "What's different?"

"The others didn't have to clarify things multiple times. Explain why their first answer doesn't work," I note for them. Looking to see if they heard the same thing.

Deputy Reynolds, responds. "Seemed to me they were legitimate, just you made the wrong assumption about the proposal they were making."

"You know I've noticed something. When police are confronted with a set of facts they tend to doubt their understanding. For private detectives, we tend to doubt everyone but ourselves. Why? Something about someone who expects to get paid for the results versus someone who collects a salary and it doesn't matter?"

Detective Reynolds bristles at my analysis. "I don't agree," she engages my eyes. I'm noticing for the first time she's not unattractive. In fact, under her uniform she might be more than attractive. "As public servants we're obligated to give the public the doubt. Afterall no one is guilty until a jury of peers judge you so."

"If I used your approach I'd never find the bad guys. Have to assume they are likely involved until they can prove beyond a shadow of a doubt they aren't. Those two guys? There's more than a shadow of a doubt in my mind."

"But there was no sign of her," Deputy Reynolds continues. "Nothing would indicate she was ever there. How do you continue to assume probable guilt when you have nothing other than a certain evasiveness to hang your theory on?"

"A friend of mine is a banker. Lends money to people for their businesses. He once tried to explain to me there are three C's in credit. When he first tried to tell me about this I had no idea what he was talking about. Credit only has one c, anyone who can spell would know he's wrong. But then he explained it's not the spelling, it's how you make a decision about whether to lend or not. The first C is cash flow, do they have enough money coming in to pay their monthly payments. The second is collateral, do they have assets you as a banker can seize and sell to recover the balance of what you're owed if the cash flow disappears? The third c is character. Is the person you're going to lend the money to going to step up when things go bad to make sure you get your money back?"

"Your story is a way of telling me it's all about character?" Deputy Reynolds asks.

"It is," I affirm for her. "You get a sense for people. Who is trustworthy and who is going to screw you if the economy tanks. I hate to say it, but our society has made it so hard for most people to make a living it seems to me there are a lot more people willing to screw you than there used to be. Also seems there are fewer honorable people who will look out for your interests because they owe it to you."

Deputy Reynolds isn't buying my conception of what we've become. "I'm a Catholic. I believe things I know you probably don't…"

"How do you know what I believe? I could be Catholic too."

"You're not," She responds firmly.

"My point exactly. You don't know me at all. But you've made certain judgments about me based on a few things I've said. All I'm saying is I've done the same thing, not about someone's religious affiliations, but about how they respond to people. There's no ambiguity about who you are. You come at people straight. You're Catholic. You believe in forgiveness and redemption and heaven, even though there is no proof for any of what you believe. You're able to suspend your disbelief because you were raised to believe. Your family and friends said it's okay to believe in fairy tales. You don't need proof. You just need to believe."

"And your point?" Deputy Reynolds isn't buying what I'm saying.

"Members of the church have been abused by priests, children have been abused by priests, nuns have been abused by priests, and yet priests are still God's representatives on earth to point the way to heaven," I point out to her although I doubt she's listening anymore.

"All you have done is point out man is fallible, whether a butcher, a banker, or a priest," she shows she is indeed listening. "Man has free will. It imposes a bigger burden on all of us to make the right decisions. To do not only what is morally right, but what is in the interests of mankind writ large."

"Our two friends aren't concerned about either," I point out.

"How do you know?" she responds instantly, clearly not accepting anything I'm saying at this point. "They could be more

187

devout than either of us. They may give ambiguous answers to questions they've not had to answer previously. We should have asked if anyone else questioned their reasons for being in Stockton."

"They haven't been in town long enough to have anyone question them. Got here yesterday. Planned to stay a week, but they're already finished and ready to leave. Smells to me like panic. Someone has come ask them about why they're here and already they want to leave. I would have been fine if they said they were just getting started on their assignment. But they've already gathered all the info they needed after a single day? Doesn't pass the smell test."

"I understand what you're saying," Deputy Reynolds continues. "But not everything works out the way you expect. I can see they may have gotten all they needed in a full day of research. California is legendary as being a bureaucratic nightmare for most people. But the reality is California isn't nearly as bad as some people paint us. We react when we absolutely need to. But when it's not important… well then things take the time they will take."

Deputy Reynolds is defending her state and her government of which she is a part. They pay her salary. They indoctrinate people about what to say and what not to say. Been there at the national level, so I recognize it here. "Tell me, are you ready to take them off the list of suspects?"

"No, but I'm also not ready to remove any of the others you apparently have."

I engage her eyes. Pretty blue eyes. Lighter than the sky, but full of color and good humor from what I can see. "Everyone's a suspect until you catch the person who is going on trial. They're still a suspect since no one is guilty until judged so by a court of your peers. In your world, no one ever becomes more than a suspect until the jury acts and no one is every taken off your suspect list until then either."

She exhibits a soft and gentle smile. I could get to like Deputy Reynolds. "The jury decides. Not you. Not me. At the end of the day it all comes down to the jury."

HAPPINESS

Her supervisor looks up at me from his cell phone. "You finished?"

"Depends… what do you have?" I respond.

"I don't know. A traffic management report of an anomaly."

"You have my attention," I offer. "What kind of anomaly?"

The detective hands me his phone. I see the image of someone getting out of a trunk, gets slammed up against the windshield of the auton following in the rain, spins around and falls away. It all happens so fast the images are blurred and even more so in the rain. But the person could have easily been a young woman. Could easily have fit the general parameters of Jazmin Braveheart's profile. I play the sequence again. Still not enough image clarity to see what I need to see. But just someone emerging from a trunk raises all kinds of questions. The most important for me is could it have been her?

I hand the phone back to the deputy. "We have a location on the image?"

"Near Roseville, on highway 80," the deputy responds.

"Any idea how fast they were going when this happened?" I have to ask. *If it was at high speed, which the interstate would indicate, there is little likelihood the person in the image would have survived. But if for some reason the traffic had slowed, she might have walked away. And the key question is, if the traffic was moving along, why would the person have chosen there to bail from the trunk?*

"No," the deputy responds. "Just one of many problems with these clips. They don't give you anything other than an impression of what may have happened. I have to say someone getting out of a trunk is kind of unusual in and of itself. At this location? I'm not sure there is anything we can read into it. No indications your girl is in this area. Particularly if you think these two guys here are trying to hide her. But like I always say, you can't ignore evidence. The one thing you ignore is the one most likely to explains things."

189

"You going to reach out to your brothers…"

"And sisters…" Deputy Reynolds inserts.

"…and sisters, to see what they can tell us about the clip? I know it came from traffic management rather than the police department. But the cops should have some idea if a body was picked up along the highway last night."

"No body last night or this morning," the deputy responds.

"So the person in the clip survived," I note more to myself than to them. "Where did the person go?"

"Jazmin Braveheart did not check in with the local police, which if she had just escaped from her captors one would think would be the first thing she would do," Deputy Reynolds reads from her cell phone screen.

"Think I'll be heading up. Right after dinner," I say hoping Deputy Reynolds will join me at least for dinner…

Chapter Thirty-Four:
Ophelia Braveheart

I look at the clip from the auton. The problem is the angle. Whoever came out of the trunk ahead never looked up, only down. So all I am able to see is the top of the head. The cameras also had difficulty focusing because the vehicle is so close. The image is blurred as much from the rain as the speed of the event and the proximity. When the person stepped out, he or she was right up against the windshield in an instant. Made contact above the camera used to judge distance between vehicles. The person spun around and was gone before the camera could focus. I want to think it is Jaz, but when I look at the image, I can't be sure.

"What do you think?" Peter asks, staring at me from the active wall in my library. I look up at him and all the rage I used to feel about him passes through. But I try not to slow it down. I want it gone before I have to answer him. After all, he's doing this because I asked him. There's no other reason he would have taken this case.

"Too fast," I give him a shrug.

"Yeah, what I thought too, but I was still hopeful you would spot something tying the image to her. A distinguishing mark, an article of clothing, her shoes maybe."

"Are you even sure it's a woman?" I have to ask, because I couldn't be sure from the blur I watched.

"No," Peter finally admits. "Most likely not her. But I wanted to check with you and be sure before we widen the search again."

"Widen it?"

"If she was in Stockton, likely we've put enough pressure on to cause whoever has her to move her from there. They would want to get away from the attention we are bringing. Afraid someone would remember something if enough questions are asked."

"Should we pull back and wait, now they've contacted us? Now Jason is working on getting them what they want?"

"No. We need to continue the full court press. Keep them on the run, if they are. Make sure they don't have a restful minute between now and the time they release your daughter."

"Advice from someone who only gets paid by obtaining her release earlier than would have otherwise been the case."

"I'm not doing this one for the money, O."

"You say you're doing it because I asked you."

"This will be one I never talk about. Never acknowledge I was a part of. I'll never talk about this one because you and your daughter don't need the publicity. Don't need the public to know it ever happened."

"If I thought this would just be another credential for you, I'd never have called in the first place."

"You called because I get results. All I'm saying is you need to let me get your results. The ones you asked me to get for you when you called."

I don't know what to do, so I ask another question, "Have there been any reports of sightings of her anywhere else?"

"Lots of calls. Everything from her robbing banks with a tall dark stranger to her performing miracles in Assisi. Every call is looking for the reward. Every call is most upset when I ask them to tell me where she is now so I can verify it is in fact her."

"Are you sharing all the calls with the detective?" I wonder aloud.

"Stebbins? Yeah, I pass him a summary. There's nothing he needs to follow up on."

"What about the video?" I ask suspicious now he is telling me not all evidence is treated alike.

"I've not shared it yet. I will. But I wanted you to see it before he did. See what you think before he sends a thousand people off to Roseville if there likely isn't anything there."

"Are you going to Roseville?" I ask curious with his description.

"If you had given me any indication the video could have been her, I would. But since you can't, it's probably not worth my time. Still nothing tying her to there. I'm really more concerned the people Jason talked with are just playing you."

"What do you mean, playing us?" He's raised a whole different possibility than up to now.

"The photo they showed Jason."

"What about it?" He's lost me completely now. I saw the photo. It was most certainly Jaz.

"Taken when she was asleep or drugged. Not a photo of her doing whatever it is they have her doing now. I would have expected a short video clip of her doing something. A video clip establishing she's alright. A clip would show she's not been mistreated. The photo doesn't tell me anything."

"You think she's... dead?" I can barely ask the question.

"I don't know. I hope not. But my experience tells me the photo is not a good indication."

Oh God, what do I do now? If Jason gives them what they want but Jaz is gone... all this would have been for nothing. I sit back in my chair and just feel overwhelmed. Peter gives me a moment.

"I'm watching a couple guys who are potential suspects. We came across them in Stockton, but we searched their premise and there was no sign of her. Doesn't mean she was never there. But if they had her at one point she was gone when we got there."

"I don't care about your suspects. I care about Jaz coming home. So far you haven't been able to find her. You said you would. Said you've worked cases much harder than this. So why isn't she home Peter?"

"I'm just trying to prepare you for whatever we find…"

"Whatever we find?" I practically go into orbit. "What kind of bullshit is this Peter? You stop preparing me, stop making excuses. Find my daughter and bring her home."

Peter nods contrite. His image fades from my wall screen. I understand he's doing what he can. They're all doing what they can, but none of them are bringing her home.

Jason is in his office working on the algorithms the kidnappers asked for. He said not to disturb him until he comes out of there. *Couldn't tell me how long it would take, but this is like the early days when he'd show up with a gang carrying cases of Red Bull and they'd get on their machines and code until they delivered something. It usually had to be reworked, but they had the first version. They had the working prototype. They could see if it did what they wanted. See if it would change anything. And the more they did this, the more new ideas they would generate. The more new prototypes they would drop. It was an exciting time. It seems Jason is reaching for the same result. The ability to drop a prototype before he goes to sleep. But there's a major problem.*

I get up and walk to Jaz's bedroom. I haven't been here since the day after they took her. Haven't been able to face the reality she's not here. *I keep telling myself she's just sleeping late. She does frequently. Tell myself she's fine, just doing her studies, getting ready for her first semester of university lessons. Getting ready to follow in the footsteps of her father and one day run his company. We all know it's her fate. Follow in the footsteps of her father and grandfather.*

HAPPINESS

I see her bed, where she slept the last night. *She never makes her bed. Expects me to make it for her. I usually do when I come through and see it like this. But I didn't then. Didn't touch a thing. Didn't have the heart to make the room look like she wasn't here. I just couldn't. I touch the screen to see what she had been studying last. Advanced algorithm development. The heart of Jason's company. Creating tools to marry data in such ways they provide insights, ideas, and suggestions on how to do something differently. Jason and Jaz have both been doing this as long as they or I can remember. I page through the lesson. I've seen all this before because Jason and I met when I was studying these same lessons. I was writing algorithms for a university professor. Working towards my doctorate in advanced mathematical concepts. Algorithms are just one expression of those concepts. Jason came to me and said I didn't need to worry about finishing the degree. Unless I wanted to teach, nobody cared. Of course my dissertation advisor strongly disagreed with Jason. Said having the degree would ensure I never had to worry about going up against someone who did have it. Jason told my professor he only had a bachelor's degree and was making in a year probably nearly what the professor would make in his lifetime. It wasn't what you knew, it was what you could do with what you knew.*

I go back to the menu and look to see what else she had been looking at. I come across the whole conversation with Phoebe. *I've already watched it from start to finish several times. Nothing there other than she was worried I'd not approve of her changing her hair color and certainly wouldn't approve of body sculpting. She was right of course. I would never have signed off for her to do either. But now... I certainly won't stand in her way. I won't do anything to make her unhappy. Make her think we don't want her here with us.*

I see when she comes home our relationship is going to be different. I'd not thought about it until just now. I can't be as hard on her as I have been. Can't be the task master making her do what she needs to do to be successful. She's got to figure it out. I can't make her do anything. She has to make herself do things. Does this mean I've finally figured out she's nearly an adult. If I want her to be successful I need to start treating her like one.

195

What do I do with Jason when it's just the two of us? This time has not gone well. We've not pulled together as I would have expected. He seems even more into himself. I don't know what his behavior means. I can only guess he's blaming himself for what happened. Trying to figure out what he did wrong. How he fixes it. I know he loves Jaz as much as I do. She's almost a clone of him in so many ways. When they get into one of their discussions it's like there's no one else who can contribute to the solutions they are creating together. I've never tried to compete with Jason, even though I have things to contribute. I wanted her to have a bond with him since he can be very remote. I wanted them to have something just theirs. Something drawing them together. Something they shared, loved to do together and would cause the other to reach out and engage. I've seen the strategy succeed. But now, I'm wondering if I created a monster in the process? Jaz is almost as proficient as Jason, maybe more so since he's turned a lot of the development over to his team. And that's part of the reason it's taking so long for him to develop the solution. Deliver what they want. Jaz isn't here to help him.

Chapter Thirty-Five: Jazmin Braveheart

Sanders Rose takes me to his Roseville home. Not large or elaborate. Not a cocoon. It is spotless. "How do you keep it so clean?" I have to ask as he hands me a towel and gives me a tour while drying off himself.

"Housekeeper comes in every day. I don't like messes. Don't like things dirty. So her job is to just make sure everything is put away and everything is clean. She carries disinfectant wipes everywhere she goes. Just to make sure no virus can take hold."

"We have air filters making sure nothing gets in the cocoon," I offer.

"Waste of money. If you don't have many visitors and you keep everything sanitized you'll never have a problem," Sanders informs me. From the tone of his voice it would appear he's spent a good amount of time researching the issue.

"Then why do so many wear the hospital masks?"

"It's a concession so people won't be afraid of you. Afraid you have something."

"What is?" I'm curious about his alternative view of the dangers in the world. This is different than Stash and different from Jason. I wonder who is right.

"You only have to be afraid of people who think you have something they want."

"Like money?" I suggest looking around.

"Some people think you know the truth about something and everyone wants the truth, even those who spend their lives making sure no one else knows the truth."

"Everyone wants truth," I reply surprised at his answer and having to think about it for a moment.

"Or they think you have an insight, able to help them be more successful," Sanders Rose notes and studies my reaction.

"Everyone wants to be successful," I continue to test what he's saying.

"Absolutely. The people who want my money? They don't want me to give it to them, although if I did they would certainly take it. What the money represents is success. The ability to fit in with a social circle of people who are also successful in their own right. No, the people who come to me would rather have me give them a job where they can succeed than a one-time check, even for a lot of money."

"How did you get your money?" I'm trying to understand his viewpoint.

"I earned every penny. On my twenty-first birthday my trust fund was turned over to me and I was made Chairman of Rose Industries, a company in the family for six generations."

"Your parents must have been extremely trusting of you to make you Chairman at such a young age." I note and watch his reaction.

"My parents died in a fire when I was eleven. I was the only child so..."

"I'm sorry. It's got to be tough losing your parents..."

"You adjust," is all he'll say about what happened to him. *I see him dealing with a lot of feelings and emotion wrapped up in it. I catch him glancing at a picture on a table across the room. My impression is it's a picture of his parents, but I don't want to seem nosy.*

"I take it you live here alone?" There doesn't seem to be anything of another person about.

"I do. I've become used to it."

"This is where you grew up?" I guess to see what kind of reaction I get.

Sanders Rose smiles for the first time since I met him in the field. "Would you like something to eat? I have to admit I have terrible manners since no one visits me here."

"I'm vegan, I have to warn you."

"No problem, Mrs. Watters will make whatever you like."

"Are you not going to eat too?"

"Mrs. Watters!" he calls. In only a moment a short dark-haired woman enters the other end of the room.

She waits for instructions.

"Our guest will be staying for dinner and the night. She's vegan. Could you make something appropriate and arrange for her to clean up?"

"Vegan," she repeats, "Let me see, no animal products, so how about a vegetable salad with grain, beans and olive oil?"

"Fantastic," I can't believe a normal meal and shower are close. "I've been waiting for a good salad and shower for too many days now. Oh, no more than eighteen hundred calories."

"Thank you, Mrs. Watters," Sanders dismisses her to prepare the meal and arrange a room for me. He then motions to chairs next to a fireplace. He picks up a remote device and the fire starts. The chair looks large when he sits because he is barely five feet tall. "You still haven't answered my question about why you were wandering through my field or where you were going."

"I'm on my way home," I respond, trying to be cautious about what I tell him. He seems like a nice person, but I'm just not confident he's not connected to Modor in some way. I'm not sure how to determine whether he is without revealing too much.

"Home is San Francisco?"

I nod.

"So what are you doing in Roseville? We're not exactly on the beaten path. We were a very long time ago when the transcontinental railroad first came out of Sacramento. This was an early stop and why the railroad is still a major employer here. But you don't look like you have anything to do with the railroad."

"I don't. My family is into tech."

"Oh, you're one of those," Sanders Rose intones as if I were a leper or something. "Coming from San Francisco I can't imagine you'd not have something to do with tech. What's your role?"

"I help my father with whatever he needs help with. He owns the company."

"So you understand about families and money, then."

"I don't really get into the business side much. I'm more fascinated with the technology solutions we develop."

"You really should consider your family obligations," Sanders responds knowingly. "There will come a time where the business side will be all you care about. From my experience it will come much sooner than you wish or expect."

I hear the voice of experience calling me to consider things I would have never even thought about. But from what he's said, it sounds like life took a very different turn for him very early. *Earlier than this whole kidnapping event has changed things for me. I'll never feel safe again. Never. So I need to listen to Sanders. I need to consider his experience, knowing it's been different than mine and will be.* "I want to thank you for making me think about things I wouldn't otherwise."

"Your parents haven't raised these issues to you?" Sanders seems curious about my comment.

"No. Guess they wanted me to have a normal childhood."

"Normal," Sanders reflects. "What does normal mean to you?'

I'm not sure how to answer his question. "Normal is just what is from day-to-day, I guess."

"What is normal day-to-day for you?"

I don't know any other way to explain, so I just start, "I live in a cocoon. Life is pretty much structured from the time I wake up until I go to sleep. I have a prescribed breakfast, a daily exercise routine, studies all morning, a light lunch, more studies, dinner and then I work with my father on company projects most evenings."

"Studies? You've not completed your degree?" Sanders seems surprised. Not sure why because everyone tells me I don't look much older than twelve.

"Guilty as charged," I smile at him.

"Child prodigy?"

"Hardly. I'm just real focused on some things," I respond trying to make it seem not worth discussing further.

"Like technology," Sanders puts two and two together. "What you do with your father most evenings. Am I correct?"

I nod, "Lot's more interesting to me than the other things he tends to talk about."

"The business matters?" Sanders guesses.

"Not so much. He has a very strong CFO who advises him how to make a profit and keep the bills paid," I almost quote Jason.

"What else does he like to talk about then?" Sanders isn't going to let this go. I regret bringing it up.

I decide I need to steer this off in a different direction. "Family history mostly. Who was who, who married who, which kids went on to be doctors, dentists and lawyers, and which ones started their own businesses."

"All traditional indicators of success," Sanders notes. "So he's trying to instill in you to value success?"

"Could be," I respond cautiously, like I'm agreeing but not confirming.

"Mrs. Watters will have our dinner ready shortly. But what I'd like to talk about over dinner is what fun things have you always wanted to do but you've never been able to locked away in your cocoon."

"Fun things?" I instantly reflect on the discussion with Stash. He's probably on his way to Mexico by now. Afraid I'm going to identify him to the police. But then I remember the conversation more completely and one of the things Stash mentioned I thought about later. "You know I've never gone for a hike in the woods."

"Really?" Sanders Rose seems amazed. "Connecting's like a primordial right. Everyone needs a connection with her or his environment. You know this is a railroad town. The California Zephyr Amtrak goes through Truckee. From there we can hike in the Tahoe National Forest or even go down to the lake."

"Lake Tahoe?" I ask surprised.

Chapter Thirty-Six: Stash

The auton slows down as we round Sacramento. Would she have tried to get out when the traffic was still moving? I close my eyes and try to feel what she probably felt. The vehicle is moving. I look at the dashboard to see we are still moving about forty-five miles per hour, even though it seems slow in comparison to the eighty plus we have been traveling at to get here. Too fast. No way could she get out without falling and someone following running over her. If she tried then there's no way she would have survived. "We need to check hospitals to see if anyone died in a road accident."

"What are you talking about?" Rocketman looks up from his phone.

"We're assuming she's still alive. But what if…"

"What if?"

"She's not. What if someone struck her after she got out? What if she rolled out and hit her head on the pavement at eighty miles an hour or even forty-five. We just need to realize there are alternatives we should check out before just walking away."

"She doesn't have any identification," Rocketman informs me. *First I've thought about it.*

"So if she did die as a result of injuries, whether a following car or just the impact, no one would be able to identify her."

"DNA."

He's right. "If it's a DNA identification her parents will know almost immediately. Modor will too."

"Is she still tapping their communications?"

I didn't know he knew. I put the tap in, what was it? Six months ago? Somewhere around then. As far as I know she's still recording and getting daily summaries. I nod but don't vocalize an answer.

"Then the point where she calls in we're screwed," Rocketman reflects.

"If the girl's dead then Modor probably already knows. I haven't heard from her. Have you?"

Rocketman looks at his phone, "No."

"Then we assume there's been no call and the girl is still out here somewhere," I suggest. I wonder if I really believe it for I see my hand is shaking. Clearly I'm not as confident as I'm trying to sound. Rocketman is looking at me. I think he knows it too.

"Since the auton slowed here, do you want to take over and go investigate? Take the access roads, drive into the towns, and cruise around hoping to see her or something telling us she was here?"

I shake my head, "Roseville is half way. I think we go there, see if there are any congestion points between here and there. See if there is any sign of her."

Rocketman doesn't respond, but goes back to his phone, reading something.

"What are you reading?"

"Just an article about Costa Rica."

"Vacation?" I'm confused.

"Where are you going to go if this all goes to shit?"

"I have a friend in Buenos Aires," I inform him even though I hadn't intended to. It was just a backup plan I never seriously thought I might have to execute. "He has a place and invited me to come visit.

Should give me enough time to work out a job and find a place there."

"Habla Española?"

I shake my head, "Yeah, I know. Gonna be a problem until I can figure something out."

"So not a realistic plan," Rocketman dismisses it.

"Is yours really any better?"

"At least I studied Spanish in high school. Been a while, but I think it will come back. The real question is what do we do about Aces?"

"What about him?" I'm completely lost given the tone of his voice.

"Aces knows everything. We can't let him go to the police."

"We talking about the same guy?"

"What do you mean? Aces… the one who lost her. I can see him plea bargaining if he's caught."

"Aces doesn't talk to anyone," I point out. "Do you really think he would talk to the cops?"

Rocketman seems puzzled by my response. "Why do you think he keeps to himself?"

"Do you know something I don't?"

"He was in. Folsom. He beat a store owner he was robbing when he was still in high school. The story I got he was coked out and running with a gang. They all got away, but left him behind when he twisted his ankle. He never identified any of the others."

"How'd he get a job with Modor?"

"He got his two-year degree while inside. He's no dummy. But he learned a major lesson. You don't rely on anyone but yourself. You don't talk to others and you don't do anything anyone would remember. Aces likes to blend into the background. You ask most people who spend a day with him who they were with, almost all will identify others but not him."

"Explains his short fuse." I'm surprised to learn all of this, but some things seem to be falling into place.

"Modor needed someone who could do what it takes if things really go bad."

"Wasn't he working for her before? I thought I was out with him a few times on site."

"Wasn't Aces," Rocketman sets me straight.

We ride in silence for a while. Thinking about the way this is likely to go down. We both know it's a long shot. She just has too long a head start. But the good news is haven't heard from Modor.

I see the first signs for Roseville. Aces is likely already here. I let the auton take us into town, watching carefully, hoping for any sign she may have been through here. I take control from the auton so we can cruise streets starting with the main street. I'm looking for the bus station to see if she's hanging around there. She has no money or identification. So how is she going to get home? Either she has to find someone to give her a ride or get a job somewhere to make enough money to buy a ticket. But then again she has to find a place to stay. The more I think about it, I don't know where she starts. Getting home may be a lot more difficult than I thought. "Maybe we have time."

"Reverse engineering. I drop you off here. No identification and no money. How do you get home?"

Rocketman keeps looking out the window while he thinks. "I go to a truck stop. See if I can hitch a ride."

"Would you if you were a young girl who's been locked up in a cocoon most of her life?"

Rocketman considers my question and ultimately shakes his head. "You're right. What would a girl do?" Rocketman thinks about the question for a long time. "She would walk into town and go to the Police Station. Turn herself in. Have them send her home."

"If you lived in a cocoon, would you? Go to the police?"

"If I thought we would be coming for me, I'd be looking for someone to keep us away."

"But if she had, we'd have heard from Modor by now."

"True. Maybe she'd go to a restaurant. See if they'll pay her to wash dishes or wait tables I guess."

"Got to have identification to get a job," I point out.

We drive past the bus station. I pull over and park the auton. Rocketman and I get out, slowly walk around where the buses load. Then we enter the waiting area from different ends. We walk through checking everyone. Rocketman goes to the rest rooms. He waits to see if she comes out. I go over to the ticket seller. I have the picture of the girl in my pocket. When it's my turn I push the picture to the woman and ask. "Have you seen her? She's my niece. Ran away and I'm trying to find her."

The woman picks up the picture, "She asleep or something?"

"It's an old picture."

"How old?" she looks at me as if she's trying to decide if I'm telling her the truth.

"Maybe a year."

The woman shakes her head and pushes the picture back.

"Thanks," I pick up the picture and go find Rocketman still

waiting across from the ladies room.

I sit down next to him. "She's not come through here. At least not yet."

"Where to next, Sherlock?"

"There's a mall not too far. Saw it on the map as we came in."

"Hook up with other kids?" Rocketman asks. "Maybe one of them will be able to help her get a ride?"

"You have a better idea?" I push since I'm coming up blank.

"Let's go for it." Rocketman rises and follows me out to the car. We drive on down the main street. As we turn on the street taking us out to the interstate I see the train station over a block. I think of all the stories of kids trying to get on boxcars and wonder if she might try. I turn down the street and drive slowly past the station. The Amtrak California Zephyr is just arriving.

"She doesn't have money for a ticket," Rocketman observes. "Besides, she wouldn't be getting on this train, it's going the wrong way."

"Let's check it out anyway," I suggest. "If she's not on a bus and hasn't gone to the police yet, this is one of the few other ways she can get home." I'm looking out the rearview mirror when I see an auton pull up. A short man and a taller woman get out and walk towards the station. I watch them all the way.

"But it's the wrong way," Rocketman repeats.

Chapter Thirty-Seven: Peter Tate

The auton is bringing me back to San Francisco from Stockton. I'm on Interstate 5 going south to catch the 205 which will eventually take me back into the east bay. *Not travelled this route much. Nothing brings me this way.* But I'm still feeling badly Ophelia is in such anguish over her daughter's kidnapping. *We may have had our differences, but I did and still do love her. Only I can never tell her. Wouldn't be right now she has a proper husband and nearly grown daughter. She sounded disappointed I decided not to go up to Roseville. The video just doesn't establish anything. I have to assume the kidnappers still have her. The video was just a faint hope Jazmin found a way to escape. But we've not heard anything leading us to believe she has. By now I would have thought she would have made contact with someone who would call her parents or the police or somebody.*

But still, in the absence of any other leads, I probably should go up. Do some inquiries. See if anyone has seen whoever was in the video, whether O's daughter or someone else. What was it all about anyway? I don't have anything else pressing today. I can afford to run up there and still be back in the office in the morning. Might be a late night, but at least I can tell O I went the extra mile. "Auton. Reroute. Roseville California police station. Off Interstate 80."

The auton continues on to the next off-ramp, exits and comes around to take me north. I sit back in my seat and glance out the windows, but I'm not really seeing the countryside. I'm still working the puzzle. Trying to understand why I'm so sure the two guys in Stockton have something to do with Jazmin Braveheart. *Maybe it was the obvious tension, particularly the guy who didn't say much who evidenced it more than the other. I expected him to come over and participate in the discussion, find out why we were there and what was going on. But he didn't. He let the other guy handle it all.* Seems he didn't want to say something possibly not tracking with what the other guy was saying. *Didn't want to give us a chance to trip them up. Seems most companies don't rent a house for employees who are only going to be somewhere for a couple days. Why a big remote house for two guys? Then they wanted us to know they finished early and wouldn't be staying much longer. Deputy Reynolds didn't say anything about either issue coming up in the first meeting. Then again she wasn't sure the other guy was the same guy who was there on their first visit. The second guy worked on something the whole time they were there the first time. On the second visit he wasn't working, just flipping through social media. Not a smoking gun of any kind, but it again indicates there could be more holes in their story.*

Time to call Stebbins, "Detective Amare Stebbins, Napa Valley Police Department," I request the auton to access the number in my phone so I can talk to him on the monitor in the auton. It is only a moment before I see the detective looking at the camera above his desk monitor.

"Mister Tate. What did you learn in Stockton?"

"Cops aren't willing to make decisions and move on," I toss at him to get him defensive so he won't push me too much.

"A broad generalization if I've ever heard one. What is your specific concern with the Stockton police department?" *Stebbins isn't going for the bait.*

"We interviewed five suspects they identified. They still think all of them may be our kidnappers, even though I'm finding no evidence linking them to Jazmin Braveheart."

"I take it you eliminated all of them?" Stebbins continues his guessing as to what I'm trying to tell him.

"One of their suspects has given me pause. Story doesn't seem to hang together even though plausible on the surface. Inconsistencies I noted the deputies apparently didn't see. Now for the others, their suspicions are based on circumstantial aspects of these individuals being in their community, like when they arrived, how long they were intending to stay, why they said they were there in the first place, rather than anything linking them back to the Braveheart's daughter."

"Tell me about the one you haven't dismissed," Stebbins is letting me lead him where I want him to go.

"Couple of infrastructure technicians. They support cocoon colonies like the one where the Bravehearts live."

"A possible first link," Stebbins seems to seize on the fact.

"Could be coincidental. They said they were in Stockton to do research for a proposed cocoon colony a developer wants to build. But I checked with the city. They've had no contact with any developers."

"How did your suspects respond to that news?"

"Said the project was still in the concept phase. Developer is doing some investigation on sites. Just overall project feasibility. They were supposed to give an estimate of how much to build out and maintain the supporting infrastructure."

"Why do you doubt their story?" Stebbins wants me to cut to the chase.

"Because I looked up the company they said they work for. The company doesn't do the construction of cocoon colonies. They maintain the systems, but don't build new."

"Does the company service the Braveheart's home?"

"I don't have the answer. Didn't think O, er... Mrs. Braveheart would know and I haven't spoken to Jason recently. He's supposedly working on what the kidnappers want."

"Yes, she told me," Stebbins considers my insight. "I'll run it down for you. Should be able to find out from the Community Manager. What's the name of the company?"

"Grendele's Support Systems, LLC." I read from the notes on my phone.

"They based on San Francisco?"

"Sunbury-on-Thames, UK." I read from my notes having asked the same question.

"Where?"

"I had to look it up. It's a suburb of London on the Waterloo line."

"Never been," Stebbins considers. "These techs are based here?"

"They work virtually, or so they said. No local office. If someone has an issue, the customer logs a request and a tech will respond as appropriate. At least it's the model they said they use."

"So the tech could be anywhere," Stebbins attempts to clarify what I've described.

"They said they have local people in the areas they serve. So if someone has to go out they aren't far. But the software guys could be anywhere."

"In the world?" Stebbins wonders aloud.

"Didn't say, but I would assume. Not sure it's relevant."

"But the fact they have local people could mean one of your suspects was the house painter who came and did the survey of the Braveheart house. I assume the Stockton deputies had their bodycams on?"

"I didn't ask. Refresh my memory of the housepainter."

"Came out about three weeks before the abduction. Walked around the house with Mr. Braveheart, but failed to submit a quote. Jason had forgotten about it until they discovered the kidnappers had cut the electricity to the home, which shut down all the sensors and communications."

"I remember now. I take it you're going to contact the Stockton department, get photos and share them with the Bravehearts?"

"If Jason will leave his lab long enough to take a look. He's the one who walked around with the painter. I'm not sure Mrs. Braveheart even saw him."

"Mrs. Braveheart can be very persuasive, as I remember," I respond. "There is one other thing I wanted to show you. I'm sending you a videoclip from an auton. Taken yesterday on Interstate 80 near Roseville, California."

I wait for him to receive the clip. He displays it for both of us to watch. The whole thing is less than fifteen seconds. Then he looks back into the camera. "What?"

"Would appear to be someone escaping from the trunk of a moving auton."

"Do you think…?"

"I showed it to Mrs. Braveheart. She couldn't identify anything in the clip she could positively tie back to her daughter."

"So you don't know if it's relevant or not?" Stebbins is wondering why I showed it to him.

"I don't think it is, but it is curious. Now Roseville? Why there? Why would someone take the chance of being run over by a moving auton? I can imagine a scenario where their daughter could go to an extreme in trying to get away from her captors. But by now I would have thought she would have made contact with someone who would have contacted her parents or the police."

"I can confirm there has been no police department contact on this case from Roseville."

"I appreciate you confirming. Tells me there isn't much I'm going to learn there. But I am going to stop by their department to see if they know anything about the clip. Did they find a body along the highway? Did someone show up in the emergency room with injuries possibly caused by what we see. I don't have an expectation of finding a link to Jazmin Braveheart, but I will inquire as to whether anyone might have reported seeing her."

"Understood," Stebbins responds apparently realizing we are almost done with this conversation. "I'll initiate a contact from here, advising them of your visit and the basic information on Jazmin. Hope you get full cooperation from them."

"I appreciate it."

I'm about to end the call when Stebbins turns his head as if trying to remember something, he turns back to look at me. "Roseville," he shakes his head. "I think I know their Chief. She was in the department with me in San Francisco before I moved out here. Loretta Sweeney was her name then. Seems she married so she'd have a different last name now. Very capable lady, although only a lady when she wants to be. She's what you'd call a tough cop. No nonsense. By the book. Follow the damn procedure or look for another job. Yes, I remember Loretta. If you get a chance to talk with her, she may have some insights about this case. Seems to me her sister was kidnapped when she was young. Similar circumstances as I remember. But something for you to consider: I think the sister never came home."

Chapter Thirty-Eight:
Jazmin Braveheart

I've never ridden on a train before. This is exciting. When we get there, I'll be able to hike in the woods. Maybe see animals, hear the birds for real, not some recording of them playing out on the walls of my room. And the lake. He said we could go see Lake Tahoe if we want. Not very far in an auton. I'd like to see a lake. To be there, not just looking at the image of a lake somewhere else. What is it about being someplace? Breathing the air and smelling the unique smells you only find in one particular place in the whole world? When you live in fear as we have, unwilling to go out of an air-filtered experience. Sealed away from the world at large, you never get to experience nuance about nature. You never get to feel the sun on your face, the wind blowing in your hair. This has started out as a nightmare... and yet there is the promise I'll get to be in nature. To feel what nearly every other person on earth feels every day when they wake up, but I don't.

As the train begins to leave the Roseville station, I look at the architecture of the tiny building. It looks like an old west movie set.

"Built in 1995 so it's nothing special," Sanders Rose apparently is wondering what I'm thinking.

"You said your family was one of the original investors in the railroad." I try to get him talking as we sit in our open car seats looking out on the slowly passing cityscape.

"We were. I was born in Roseville. My father was born in Roseville. And so it goes back to around the turn of the twentieth century. This rail yard we're leaving? It's the largest in California. We also have the largest refrigerated warehouse in California where local fruit and vegetables are stored until they move by rail to other parts of the country. So Roseville is actually very important in a lot of ways for

215

the entire nation and particularly California."

"You seem rightfully proud of where you live, your family and the railroad your family helped create. Do you take rides like this often?"

Sanders smiles again, "Amtrak isn't part of the Union Pacific. Just couldn't make money with passenger service after all the highways were built and airports went into service. Do you know what's the difference between roads, airports and railroads?"

"I don't," I respond earnestly.

"Railroads got land grants to go where no one lived yet. Was needed to build the transcontinental railroad. But the highways and airports... they've been built with federal money. You get to drive on the interstates for free in most places. You get to fly from most airports, where all you pay is a portion of a landing fee which is the operations but not the cost of building the airport. So the railroads have a long history of competing without all the subsidies the roads and airports get."

"You focus on the business side of the railroad and not the operations or technology or the real interesting parts of it."

Sanders shakes his head, "I get to learn about what we're doing. Things like the automated rail dispatch centers tracking the millions of boxcars, tankers and flatcars out there. Not only track them but are able to bill the party renting the use of the car to haul things from one point to another. There's a lot of computing horsepower at work."

"Clearly I don't know much about railroads," I respond and smile at him to let him know I'm agreeing with him and appreciating what he's saying although I've never thought of a railroad as particularly high tech. Then I decide to go back to the question I asked he didn't answer, "So when was the last time you rode on a train?"

"Sunday. I have a lifetime pass on Amtrak. I can go anywhere I want on their system. So I ride a train at least once a week unless I'm on a trip. I've gone across country and have been gone a couple months. Last year I went all the way to Boston and Washington D.C. Spent a week in each city, riding the local trains. The T in Boston. The Metro in Washington. I just love trains. Love to see where they take people. Love to watch passengers come aboard, huddle over their phones or a book or just look out the windows even when we're underground. There's nothing like a train ride to make me happy."

Happy. What makes Sanders happy? I guess what makes me happy is writing code, an algorithm pulling data from lots of sources and revealing insights our brain alone can't discern. But my happiness comes from a constrained environment. Would I be just as happy as a forest ranger looking for forest fires, or helping campers find a lost child, or keeping illegal loggers from cutting down majestic trees? I don't know, because I was never given an alternative. What's the value to society of a new insight versus a preserved forest trail people can hike as I am going to later today? I was surprised Sanders had hiking boots. Didn't know they existed. Special shoes to go walking in the woods. I never would have thought about special shoes to hike in. It was so nice of him to take me to a shop and buy me hiking boots. I didn't ask him to, but he said he wanted to. Said it was the least he could do for a cocoon baby. I don't know what he must think of me. Probably thinks I have so little appreciation for the things important to him. He would be right. I don't appreciate trains the way he does. I don't appreciate nature the way he does. But does my perspective mean I can't come to appreciate them from knowing him?

"Do you do this often?" I ask wondering why he is being so nice to me.

"Go up to Truckee?"

"I was thinking more about showing someone around like you are me."

"Just once. But then I've never had anyone literally trip over me like you did in my field when I was just trying to disappear."

"Why do you want to disappear?" This I still can't understand.

"Would you agree we live in an interconnected world, a world continuing to connect us more and more completely? How do you escape from it? You carry a phone connecting you to anyone or any media source or any information source you want. Anyone with your number can find you anywhere in the world, practically. I'll have to admit there are places out in the national parks and forests where there is no coverage. I think I've found most of them trying to get away from all the people who are constantly demanding I make a decision on something I could care less about, but it's like life or death to them," Sanders looks at me, shakes his head. "But you probably don't have to worry about people finding you, do you?"

Does he know about Rocketman and Stash and Aces? "People looking for me to make decisions? No, I don't. I have enough trouble making decisions just for me."

"I envy your innocence. Embrace this time because it won't last." I see a tear in the corner of his eye. I'm starting to see Sanders in a different light. He's not the titan of industry. He's a normal person carrying an extraordinary burden. He's doing the best he can, but finds he needs solitude to rebalance. I understand although I've never experienced it.

"So when was the last time you were in Truckee?"

"On Sunday," he says simply. "I was up here hiking one of my favorite trails. Just getting some exercise, fresh air and an opportunity to decompress."

"So why don't we go someplace you've not been recently or maybe not even at all? Let this be a new experience for both of us?" I suggest.

Sanders gives me the most curious look. "Why would you care whether it's new for me?"

"We could both notice things for the first time. You wouldn't feel the need to show me things since you've not seen them before either."

I watch Sanders consider my suggestion. He pulls his phone out

218

of his pocket. He looks up something. He muses for a long moment, then looks up at me. "You know there is this one trail. Never been on it. Keep saying I will someday. People tell me it can be spectacular, but mostly at sunset. I've never wanted to be out someplace late, or try to find my way back in the dark. You know what I'm saying? If you get off the trail in the dark, you pretty much need to stay put until morning. You'll never find the trail again with a flashlight. I'm all about a day trip, as you can see. I'm not even carrying extra water or a sleeping bag or any of the equipment I see the serious climbers carrying. I'm more of a hiking tourist than an actual heavy-duty nature freak. I love nature, but on my terms and not hers."

"How far would it be coming back in the dark?" I wonder aloud to hopefully help him frame his decision.

Sanders motions like he doesn't know, then looks at his phone again. I see him stretching the picture with his fingers and then using his finger to estimate the distance. He scrolls to another place on the map, repeats and then looks up. "My guess is to the best site, a high point looking down into a tree covered valley is like three miles. If we just go to this other point, it's a little more than a mile and a half."

"What are we talking about? In terms of time? I've never been hiking so I have no idea." I admit.

"For me, it's like a half hour to hike a mile. Other people go faster, but I'm never in much of a hurry. I want to see things. You know? Listen for animals, birds, wind in the trees. I want to inhale the clean air, not polluted by all the cars and trucks…"

I want to add trains and planes to his list, but don't think he would appreciate it.

"So from the place I'd want to take you, figure forty-five minutes to get back to the trail head. We'd still have another forty-five minutes or so to get back to the station to catch the train home. Doubt we'd get back to Roseville before midnight. Now for you midnight's probably not so late. But I'm usually in bed by ten."

"You're my guide. You're the experienced hiker. I'm all new to this, so I'll trust your judgment."

Again, Sanders gives me this very curious look, as if he's surprised I would be willing to trust him since I don't know him at all. *But here I am. Having an adventure I know I'll never have again. A first time for anything is never to be repeated because it won't be the first time the next time. I'll have a frame of reference. I'll know what to expect. Right now I only have a vague impression of what it will be like, but I know it will be very different from what I'm expecting. Every minute will be all new. I'm a virgin to this experience. And I wonder if Sanders can appreciate the fact he comes out here all the time has just made it all routine. Has it desensitized him to what others experience when they come out? But then again, he said he's only brought one other person out like this. So why me?*

Sanders shakes his head, "You want me to make a decision." I hear the distress in his voice as if this is not something he wants to do.

"Not if you don't want to. I'm happy going or not going to the spectacular point. Who knows when or if I'll ever get back here? Any trail will work for me. If you're good, I'm happy making the decision."

Sanders looks relieved. "You sure you want to be out so late?"

"I trust you wouldn't suggest something dangerous. If you thought there was a high probability we couldn't get back, I expect you to simply say so."

Sanders considers my comment, "You want to see the sunset, we'll see the sunset."

Chapter Thirty-Nine Stash

"What the fuck are you doing?" Rocketman asks as I turn around on the street just down from the Roseville train station. I pull up across the street and watch the man and woman get on the train. It only takes a few minutes and the train pulls away. I get out of the auton, go across the street and look for a sign showing the stops going in both directions. The next station east appears to be Truckee. *Given they weren't carrying baggage I assume they are planning to return today. Truckee's the last stop in California. Unless they're going on to Reno? Maybe.*

I trot back to the auton, where Rocketman looks up from his phone. "So end the big mystery."

"Truckee," I tell him.

"You got the address from Aces?"

"What are you talking about?" I'm completely lost now.

"Truckee's where the safehouse is."

"What? Didn't know that," I look around. "Is Aces here?" I can probably beat the train to Truckee, but I'm not sure how much time I really have to waste.

"I'll find him. Hold on." He apparently pushes a connection to Aces on his phone, "201 Pacific. Now." Rocketman looks up, "You gonna tell me what the fuck you're doing?"

"She may be on the train."

"What are you talking about? I didn't see her."

"Did you see the guy and the girl who got on here?" I ask,

expecting from his demeanor I know the answer.

"I wasn't paying attention, why?"

"Can't be sure, but it could have been her," I'm still wondering if I'm right. "It's the only thing we've come up with so far."

"You're reaching. I would have recognized her. The woman was too tall."

"You think so because of the guy she was with," suddenly comes to me. "What if he was short? Would she still be too tall?"

"How short?"

"Fuck it Rocketman. Work with me on this. You and I got nothing. We leave and go on hoping to find her wandering along the highway, or washing dishes in a restaurant. But we got nothing. I see this girl who could be her. We gotta go find out. If she gets off in Truckee… all the better. We nab her and take her to the safehouse and Modor doesn't know any different. She's where she's supposed to be and we're still in line for our payday."

"And if you're wrong?" *Rocketman is still skeptical. He's getting a bit paranoid as the reality of the situation is sinking in for him. He doesn't want to be wrong.*

"We got what we got at the moment, which is nothing. You want to stay here with Aces, I'll be happy to chase this one down by myself. Tell me what you want to do."

Aces pulls up in an auton. We get out and walk over to him.

Rocketman motions to him to get out as we stand just outside microphone distance from the auton. Aces doesn't look at me, only Rocketman. "Write down the address in Truckee and give it to me."

Aces feels around for a piece of paper and something to write with. None of us have anything and we each gesture. "Text it to Stash."

Aces looks at me, apparently unhappy about the request. I don't know if it's because he's sharing the information with me or he's sharing it period. He does as asked. I see it come up on my phone.

"So you staying with Aces?" I assume.

Rocketman looks around once with a grimace. Shakes his head, "This is worthless. We're not going to find her by just riding around. If this is where she got out, she's got to be long gone."

Aces looks around. By his body language it seems to me he probably agrees, although he isn't overly communicative in the best of circumstances so guessing what he's thinking is always dicey.

Rocketman turns to Aces, "Send your auton back to the barn and come with us. Worst can happen is we'll bunk down at the safehouse. Then we can figure out our next move in the morning."

"Sure you wouldn't rather go back to SFO and buy your ticket?" I push Rocketman to see what he's really thinking.

"Not yet," he responds as Aces walks over to the auton and gives it instructions. "Maybe after tomorrow. We got to see if we can make this right. I'm not walking away from my payday just yet."

I get in the driver seat and instruct the auton to take us to the Truckee Amtrak station. The screen shows it at 10065 Donner Pass Rd, Truckee, CA 96161. When Aces is in I instruct: "Auton: proceed."

The door slides shut. The vehicle moves out from the station parking lot.

"Why didn't you dismiss the girl like I did?" Rocketman asks once we're up on the Interstate and up to posted speed of 80 mph.

"I'm the first to admit she could have been the guy's wife or girlfriend. Actually more likely. From the distance I couldn't see her clearly. She never looked in my direction. It was all color, more than anything. She was wearing all black. I haven't seen anyone else here wearing all black."

"What was the guy wearing?"

"White shirt and khaki pants," I remember more than answer his question. "No luggage. Like they're taking a day trip, not overnight."

"I'll be ecstatic if you're right, but I'll bet you're wrong. Probably a girlfriend. Why would anyone go from Roseville to Truckee for a day trip? Doesn't make any sense. Sacramento's closer with a whole lot more to do."

"Could be going to North Lake Tahoe. I think the Truckee station serves both," I suggest. My mind has been working to answer the question. "Could be going to do dinner at a restaurant on the lake. There's shopping there too, but only the very expensive kind."

"Why would you take a train and spend so much time getting there if you have the money to go shopping in Tahoe? I would have expected a private auton or jet or something." Rocketman responds to my thoughts.

"Maybe they're making a day of it. Train in and flight back," I suggest, trying answer his question, although I have to admit he's probably right. *Not many people are going to spend hours on a train if they can afford to shop in Tahoe.* "What is there in Truckee?" I finally ask.

Rocketman googles it. "What I'm seeing is a whole bunch of nothing,"

"Not helpful," I respond without thinking. I instantly regret it because I know Rocketman won't take it well. "There's got to be something there."

"Donner Pass Bridge, a bunch of ski resorts, a small downtown and some trails. About it. Not where I'd take a hot date except in the winter to ski."

"White shirt and khaki pants," I remember.

"More likely dinner than hiking in all black. Never seen black hiking clothes." Rocketman responds to my question with a tone of authority I know he doesn't possess. "Too hot out on the trails for all black."

"But what if those were the only clothes she had?" I point out knowing Jazmin Braveheart only had the clothes she was wearing with her.

"Sure," Rocketman dismisses me. "Reach for whatever faint hope you can muster. Still don't think it's her. She wouldn't have had time to hook up with a guy in Roseville. Who the hell lives here anyway? I mean she's a cocoon baby. She doesn't have friends in places like this. Besides if she hooked up with someone, why didn't he take her to the police?"

The question of not checking with the cops has been bothering me. We're missing something. I can't imagine what it is. But I'm going to take full advantage of the fact she apparently hasn't gone to the police as yet. But I know it's likely only a matter of time. It's probably our last chance to salvage our payday. May be the only way to stay out of jail.

Rocketman scrolls through something on his phone, "Did you realize Truckee is almost in Nevada?"

I shake my head. I had no idea having never even heard of Truckee before now.

"You sure they're not going to Reno? Gamble all night, get a room at the casino and come back tomorrow? Makes more sense to me. If they screw all night they can have the hotel clean their clothes and deliver them to the room in the morning. If they're not married no one will be the wiser. They don't have to be rich to make it work."

I have to admit his scenario is a lot more probable than mine, although I still don't even know what my scenario is since going to Truckee makes no sense. Going to Tahoe makes no sense either if they're riding the train. All I come up with is the increasingly likely outcome it won't be her.

"Rather than going back to the fucking safehouse, we might

oughta should go on to Reno and gamble for the night," Rocketman suggests. "What do you think? What was it the gladiators were taught to say to the Emperor of Rome? Before they went out to fight knowing they likely wouldn't survive?"

"We who are about to die, salute you," I repeat from memory having seen more movies about ancient Rome than I can remember. I started reading a whole series of books on Rome when I was in high school, until my father told me I needed to stop wasting my time when I needed to learn about software development. Told me software was the future. I gave the books back to my grandmother. She couldn't understand why I wouldn't read them. She so enjoyed talking with me about the first volume, before my father came by and ended it. It was the beginning of the end of my literary thoughts. The one volume was the last resistance I put up in high school before capitulating to my father's vision for me. To be what he wanted me to be regardless of what I wanted. War and Peace was my rebellion when I got to college. But he told me if I read anything else he'd not pay my tuition any more. I'd forgotten all about this part of my life until the girl asked me why I knew about War and Peace. *She upended my whole life because all I keep doing is coming back to the fundamental question of whether engineering and not a writer is what I was really destined to be.*

Rocketman pushes against my shoulder from behind since I'm sitting in the driver's seat. "What do you think? Reno tonight and Costa Rica in the morning?"

Aces apparently looks at Rocketman who instantly responds to his look, "What are you looking at? I'm not going anywhere. Not with a payday still waiting for us as soon as we deliver the girl."

Chapter Forty: Peter Tate

Blonde Loretta Rose doesn't look like a police chief. Maybe ninety-five pounds soaking wet, barely over five foot. And yet there is something about her stance. Her balance maybe. Like a dancer who is ready to move in any direction she decides, gracefully, fluidly... with great strength.

"What is it I can do for you?" she asks in the tiny and well-worn police department offices. Maybe desks for five people. Latest technology though. Cameras on the major thoroughfares in town all on a display wall. She can see what any driver is doing, video tape their illegal maneuvers and levy a fine knowing none of the justices of the peace would ever not impose the appropriate fine with the evidence right here. Must mean most people aren't using the autons.

"Why Roseville?" I use as my opening gambit.

Loretta Rose cocks her head as if she's not heard my question in a while, "Why not is the better question."

I nod, "Amare Stebbins told me you might have some insights."

Loretta Rose steps back from the counter, "Amare? Been a while since I heard his name. Where is he now? Seems the last I knew he went out to the valley somewhere."

"Napa Valley department," I confirm. "Been there since he last saw you, he says."

"Seems about right. Always sucking up to the fat cats. He chief yet?"

"Apparently not sucking up enough. Still a detective," I confirm for her.

A wry smile and she looks away. "You know he could have had this job if he'd wanted it, but he said it was about time for a woman to lead a department. Said I'd do a better job than he would because it would be a struggle every day to get people here to take me seriously. You know he was absolutely right."

"But you succeeded," I point out to ensure she's going to help me.

"Some would say this is success," she responds with some irony. "So what did Amare tell you I could do for you?"

"Two days ago. Up on highway 80," I show her the clip from my phone.

She seems surprised, which tells me she's not seen the clip. I would have thought it mandatory for traffic management to turn over clips like this to the police.

"Someone took a hell of a chance," Loretta Rose responds.

"So two questions: Did anyone find a body along the highway? Would possibly have been a young woman." I slide the photo of Jazmin Braveheart Ophelia wanted me to use.

Loretta Rose takes a long look at the picture. "Saw her when it came through. No. No body and we've not seen her in town."

"So you may have answered my second question: has anyone shown up at the emergency ward with injuries fitting what we saw on the video clip?"

"Call doc Mukerjee," she speaks into the office communications system.

"Emergency Department," responds the voice across the office system. "What can I do for you Chief Rose?"

"Doc, you have anyone come through the ED in the last few days who might have fallen out of an auton up on 80?"

"What do you mean fall out of?" the doc responds warily.

"I just looked at a video. Shows someone climbing out the back of a vehicle ahead of them. Bounced off the windshield and rolled way."

"In the road or the shoulder?"

"Shoulder," Loretta Rose responds while still looking at me.

"Head trauma, maybe. Let me check: Dates last seventy-two hours, head trauma."

The doc apparently reads a report from his system. "Nothing here in the last seventy-two hours. One broken arm but the patient is the daughter of a local family, twelve years old who fell out of a tree in her yard."

"Anyone I know?" Chief Rose asks.

"All too well," the doc responds.

Loretta Rose nods to herself, "Thanks, doc," and hangs up.

She looks at the picture once more. "Pretty girl. I take it you're a private investigator working with Amare to find her?"

I slide my identification across the desk for her. She takes a quick look and slides it back.

"I'm not aware of her being here or having been here. Is the video why you think she may have come this way?"

"The video isn't conclusive. Even her mother couldn't identify the person as her daughter. So in reality I have no proof or even strong indication she is or ever was here. But I wanted to check it out personally just to make sure."

"I'm sorry I couldn't be more help."

Then I remember, "Detective Stebbins said you lost a sister under similar circumstances."

I see Loretta Rose's eyes pull back, as if she remembers

something painful. It takes her a moment to regain her presence, "I did."

"Would you be willing to share what happened? Detective Stebbins said it was a long time ago, but he thought it might have some similarities and be helpful in this case."

"Amare thought that? Must have been listening more than I thought." she responds with a weak smile.

I nod and wait.

"Why I looked at this one. Some similarities. No ostensible reason why my sister was chosen other than our father was prominent. People thought we had money, although my mother struggled every month to pay all the bills we had as a family."

"Is your sister's case why you became a cop?" I wonder aloud.

"One of many reasons," she responds looking at me and then away. "Lisa was fourteen. Smarter than me in every way. She was the popular one in school. All the boys flocked to her. She used to tease those who were too shy to talk to her. Athletic too. We both took ballet and dance since she we were six, but she took up running on the school track team. She was fast. I mean there was no way I could keep up to her. Don't know where she got her speed, but I certainly didn't have it. We had the same parents as far as I knew."

"Anyone ever suggest you had a different father from your sister?" I push the point since she raised it.

"You know how old people talk. They look for any explanation for something they don't understand and it usually comes back to someone screwing around. I never understood, were they making an admission they had when they were young, or simply wishing they had."

"What happened?"

"Our room was on the second floor."

"You shared a room with her?"

Loretta Rose nods misty-eyed, and then continues. "We slept with the window open because it was a warm summer. The house didn't have air conditioning. It was the only way we could sleep even without blankets or anything. Just sheets."

"You were in separate beds?"

"Yes. I remember talking with her as we always did before going to sleep. Mostly about what boy was trying to make a play for her and what were the other boys doing about it. She was always talking about them to me once the lights went out. Never with our parents around because they wouldn't have liked it."

"So you turned the lights out, the window was open and then what?" I'm making notes to myself.

"The next morning when I woke up she was gone. I didn't hear anything, didn't know someone had been in our room and taken her."

"Evidence of a struggle?"

"What the police suggested was someone brought a ladder to the window, climbed in with a hypodermic of something to put her out and then carried her down a ladder and drove away."

"Why didn't she make it?"

"Amare told you she didn't?" She looks sad.

I nod and wait for her to continue.

"My sister was strong willed. We don't know what happened, but she was found in a wooded area about fifty miles from my home. Severe trauma to the head. Whoever took her beat her to death. The police never found the person responsible. My family was never contacted about her with any kind of demand."

"What do you think I need to know about this case based on your sister's case?"

"When someone does something this desperate about the only thing you can count on is it won't go as anyone thinks it will. I'm sure whoever kidnapped Lisa thought he was going to get a bundle of money from my father and he would let her go. Would have been the end of it. I've thought of every possible reason he beat her, but the only thing makes sense is he probably had been wearing a mask or somehow keeping her from seeing his face. She must have done something where she could identify him. Probably threw him into an uncontrollable rage. Remember this guy is already desperate. He must have just started beating her and couldn't stop until it was too late. I'm probably wrong, but I have no evidence leading me to believe anything else."

"This has been incredibly helpful, thank you for sharing it. One final question. If Jazmin Braveheart had been in Roseville why would she not come here?"

"I can't put myself in her place. If she escaped, she may have been afraid her captors were watching for her to come here. I'm sure she would have a reason, but a young girl with no ID or money? If she was afraid to come here she probably tried to hook up with a guy."

Chapter Forty-One: Jazmin Braveheart

The three-hour journey from Roseville to Truckee goes quickly as Sanders and I are having a great conversation. I've not met anyone with as diverse interests. None of them have anything to do with tech or algorithms or MIT or anything I've focused on for as long as I can remember. It's like he has opened up the world to me, shown what I have missed in my narrow existence.

"Looks like we've begun to slow," I note for him as I look forward to see if I can see a station. Not yet, but I have the impression we are not far from it.

Sanders looks about through the windows, "Yes, we're very close. We probably ought to make our way to the doors."

"This really is a pleasant way to travel. Why don't many people do it?" I ask wondering why I never hear of people who have taken train trips in the US.

"They do. Just not enough," Sanders reflects.

"Are you making up for all the others who have decided air travel or driving is faster or more flexible?"

"I've never been on an airplane. Are you surprised?" Sanders seems to be testing me.

"Neither have I," I point out hoping he sees we actually have something in common.

Sanders follows me down the stairs. I note the Truckee station is actually larger than Roseville, which surprises me until I remember Sanders saying it also serves North Lake Tahoe. So there are a lot of people served by this station. I notice the deep forest seems to surround the town. I didn't really watch our approach. Didn't notice how the forest seemed to grow up around the tracks the further we went from Roseville. This community was carved out of the forest by the crews building the transcontinental railroad, Sanders told me on the way. Only a very long time ago. When Interstate 80 was built more recently Truckee became more accessible, although the population didn't grow much.

We walk down the main street, slowly looking into the windows of the shops. *I've never spent time in a place like this. The shops we walk past sell things I don't think I would ever buy. A little ceramic something-or-other with the name Truckee painted on it. Probably to remember I bought it here. But why would I care?* Another shop has linens and lace in the window. It seems to me Ophelia just places an order on Amazon and it appears. *If I was going to buy lace here, I'd have to take it home with me. How would I carry it? I'm not going to buy linen or sheets here, but I can see people who live her might. So another store I'm not about to go into.* The next is a restaurant, looking in the décor doesn't tell me much. *What kind of food do they serve here? Why would I want to eat here rather than home? I remember a report about people who had tried to recreate a place they had been to so people would be reminded of some place they may have been, or could have a sense of what it was like some place they have never been.*

Sanders doesn't seem interested in stopping so we continue our stroll down the main street of Truckee. "Where are the trails?"

"Not far. We need to summons an auton to take us out, which Sanders does. As he is doing so he looks at me and asks, "You don't have a phone?"

"I do, but it's home," I try to explain. I still haven't told him about being kidnapped, afraid he would either take advantage of my situation or possibly call those who took me in the first place. *I don't really know anything about him, but I do know I'm not going back to Stash or Rocketman or Aces. I'm going home. I just need to figure out how to get there.*

HAPPINESS

"I don't know anyone who deliberately leaves their phone at home. How do you get anywhere if you can't summons an auton? How do you talk with your friends or family? Don't they worry about you?"

"I'm sure they do, but it's all right. I'm sure they're used to me being on the road without it. I don't do this often as I've said. Spent almost my entire life in a cocoon."

"So this is a big adventure for you," Sanders notes. "But I don't understand why your parents would let you travel by yourself when they have kept you sequestered."

"I'm a college student. I'll soon be on my own in my own place."

"Are they going to buy you a cocoon of your own, or are they going to let you live in the wild, so to speak?"

Now I've had a chance to see a little of the wild, I'm not so sure I want to live in a cocoon. I'm sure Ophelia and Jason haven't thought about it either, expecting me to continue living with them. "We haven't had the last discussion about where I'm going to live yet," is my response. *Not very strong, but at least better than saying I don't know, which is actually more accurate.*

"I'd be happy to have you stay with me if you would consider it," Sanders offers. "It seems to me tech types can work anywhere they can get wi-fi."

"Very generous of you," I begin cautiously. *The last thing I want to do is have him ditch me here in Truckee, which is even further from home than Roseville was.* "Especially since you've only known me a few hours. I may be a slob and I note you keep a very neat house. I may stay out and party all night. You like to go to bed early. I just don't know how compatible our lifestyles would be. But let's continue talking. We may find there is some middle ground suitable to both of us."

Sanders smiles and gives me a sideways look. "You would actually consider it?"

"I find you fascinating. The way you look at things is just so different than anything I've known previously. So yes, I absolutely would consider it. I just don't have enough information now to know if it would be a good situation or not. What I can say is I can't move in today or even soon. I have obligations back in San Francisco I have to fulfill. Have to finish school. But I think of you as a friend I will want to keep and maybe at some point it would make sense."

"You sure your parents aren't diplomats? You said no, very diplomatically," Sanders responds with a sorrowful tone to his voice.

"I didn't say no, I said not now."

Sanders and I walk on in silence. As it grows so too does my perception of his insecurity. He wants me to say I'll stay, I'll be someone with whom he can share all the knowledge, all the experiences, all the opinions he has formed over the many decades of loneliness, in his house by himself. After our long conversations I'm starting to understand why in just a few hours I have become important to him. He's not ready to have someone else reject him as apparently so many have before me.

"Here's the auton," he nods to the approaching vehicle. We stop and wait for it to come to us, homing in on the beacon on his phone. When it has come to a complete stop he barely needs to reach to open the door for me. I precede him into the vehicle and take a seat in the back. He joins me. "I'm sorry."

"For what?" I'm surprised by his comment.

"Asking too much, too soon," comes a response more regretful than sorrowful. *Like he has realized by my silence I can't say more. I can't take back the facts of my life. I cannot simply step outside myself and be what he would like me to be. And worse, I can't explain all this to him.*

"Sanders, you are a very special person. I hardly know you, and yet I can plainly see you are. I've spent essentially my entire life protected from the very things you contemplate, you revel in, the things

236

you enjoy, the sensory perceptions you've come to seek out. I've barely been able to record any of them other than virtually. I need time and opportunity to catch up, even if only a little. To grow as a person into my own person. Not one shaped entirely by my parents, but also not by any one other person, but many people. Please understand I need an opportunity to discover myself."

Sanders doesn't react to my request, but continues considering where we have come to in such a short time. "I've not done this in a long time, you know. Ask someone to live with me. It was impulsive and if you ask anyone they will tell you impulsive is about as opposite my nature as anything you might imagine. So please don't consider this typical of what I am."

"How far is the trail head?" I change the subject so hopefully we can get back to a more social discussion.

"Maybe twenty minutes. Not far."

"If the trail is only about three miles we should be there well before sunset. What would you like to do until then? Are there other trails to explore, other things a babe in the woods would enjoy?"

At the use of the term, he smiles and looks at me again. "I was once, you know. A babe in these woods. I wouldn't let anyone show me the way. I had to discover it for myself. Maybe because I took over the company when I was so young. Everyone wanted to tell me what I had to do, what I needed to do and what I should do. None of them were playing with their money, with the lives of their employees, with the future of Roseville and the railroad family. Is that what you're saying to me? You need to find your own way?"

I nod, "Sounds about right. Only Jason isn't going anywhere. I don't have to worry about taking over the company. Being cocooned makes it more difficult for something bad to happen to him as happened to your parents. What's the last thing you remember about them?"

Sanders looks out the window as he responds, "I remember

making them angry."

"And you regret having done so to this day?"

"I do."

"Do you think they would be proud of what you have accomplished? How you have made decisions benefitting all those groups you mentioned?"

"My mother more than my father. He was never satisfied with himself or me. Nothing I did was as good as he thought I could do it. Mother used to tell me it was just his way of making sure I understood my responsibilities. But he was always wanting me to do more, be more, produce more. I tried, and I have tried, but it drains me so. I have to come out here. Be my own person for an hour or a day or only a minute if a minute's all I can get."

"So you do understand what I'm saying?" I ask just to confirm what I'm hearing.

"I do… but I'm coming to the conclusion my life will end some day and just before it does I'll look back and ask, what difference did I make? Could someone else have done better? Contributed more?"

Chapter Forty-Two: Rocketman

"You think it's her?" I ask Stash as we watch the couple walk down the street towards the arriving auton. *He is short, now I see him closer, so maybe she isn't as tall as I thought. From the back I can't tell if it is her or not.*

"Can't tell," he responds as if he's still trying to figure it out. "But if I don't hustle back for the auton they'll drive away and we'll never know."

"We'll stay here and watch which way they go," I respond and glance at Aces who shrugs at me, so apparently he doesn't know if it's her or not either. "Should have tried to get closer when they got off the train," I call after Stash. He doesn't respond as he's jogging back to the auton which is several blocks away. We'll be lucky if we can keep the auton in sight.

But Stash is quicker than I expect. We catch a break as the auton they drove off in stayed on the main street and just now has turned off. Stash comes to a quick stop with the door opening. We jump in and Stash takes off even before the door closes. "Which way?"

I point to the street ahead, "To the right, five blocks down."

Stash drives like a madman. Rolling through stop signs and nearly flooring it between. When we get to the corner where they turned I just catch the other auton turning to the left about four blocks down. Stash can see it so I don't need to tell him.

"Where do you think they're going?" I ask. "This isn't the direction of Tahoe."

"No idea," Stash responds. "Never been here. Apparently you have?"

"No," I respond, "Just looked at the map. Tahoe is south. We're going northeast."

"For now. They may be going to one of the resorts or something local."

I nod, "Makes sense, but the question is how do we get close enough to see her clearly without being seen? If it is her we can't afford for her to call a cop or something."

Stash continues to close the distance, but I put my hand on his shoulder, "Not too close. We don't want them to notice us. Need to stay far enough back, but close enough so we don't lose them."

"You want to drive?" Stash gestures to the steering wheel.

"I'd do better than you are."

Stash pulls over to the curb and opens his door. I grab his shoulder and pull him back. "You got the wheel."

"Then don't give me any more shit about my driving," he glares at me as he pulls the door shut and re-engages the auton manual drive.

I look up and don't see the other auton. "Where the fuck?"

Stash notices it's gone as well. "You look down the left side and I'll look this way," as he floors the auton to catch up. "Damn, where did it go? What is there around here anyway?"

I shake my head looking down the street as we come to it. "Nothing here. Did they pull into a driveway? Aces look out the back."

We drive on in silence, but I'm hoping no police see how erratic we're driving and stop us because then there's no chance we'll find the auton and the mystery woman. Another block, "Nothing this side, did you see it Aces?"

No response from Aces and a "Damn," under his breath from Stash. So we still haven't seen them.

"Do we go back?" I ask. "See if they went down a side street and we were just too late to see them turn again?"

Stash continues to look to his left, "No use. If they did, we'll never find them."

We come to the next street and I look down. "Nothing," I report, but then I notice an auton down several blocks entering the intersection. "Hold on... may be them, down about... four blocks running parallel."

Stash nods, floors the auton, speeding to the next intersection, turns right and repeats his high-speed maneuvers. "There," I point to an auton as it starts through the intersection now three blocks ahead of us.

We speed through the next block. Then two more before turning left. We see the auton on the road ahead of us, apparently leaving town. "Didn't know Truckee had this many streets," I admit feeling a little better we haven't lost the auton. We're about two blocks behind. I look into the rear window of the vehicle ahead to make sure it's the same couple. It appears to be, although a bit far to be sure. I won't be able to settle down until we get close enough to be sure we aren't following someone else. Then the question will be how do find out if it is her?

"What do you think? Is it the same auton?" I ask to see if either Stash or Aces has a better idea than I do.

Neither answers, which tells me we may be on a fool's errand here. Stash thinks it may be her, but I think he's probably clinging more to hope than any real evidence. But one good thing about following an auton, when in autonomous mode it only travels the speed limit. Makes it relatively easy to follow. "How much is a ticket to Buenos Aires?" I ask Stash.

He looks at me, knowing what I'm asking even though Aces doesn't and I don't want him to. "Haven't looked recently. But when Geraldo invited me down it wasn't bad. I could afford it. You want to come along when I go visit?"

"Wouldn't want to upset anything you've got going on with him," I respond since I think he's only saying this to throw Aces off.

"Really don't have anything lined up other than do the normal partying. The women are incredible, but if you don't speak Spanish, it could be a problem since few of them are bilingual."

"I speak the language of love…"

Stash starts coughing. I glance around. Aces is looking out the side window totally bored and apparently not listening, or if he is he's doing his best to ignore us.

"The invitation is there, once we cash out," Stash responds and again I think this is for Aces' benefit. If it's not, it's probably wishful thinking.

"I'll think about it, if you're sure it wouldn't be cramping your style."

"You sure you'd be okay spending time with me when we're on vacation?" Stash sounds wary.

"I'm thinking of setting up my own shop afterwards. Maybe you'd want to come work with me. Think we could take some work from Modor, just not the cocoon client. Don't think I want to get anywhere near them when this is all over."

Stash glances at me like I'm crazy. "You'd want me to come work with you?"

"You're offering me to come on vacation with you. Thought it's the least I could do."

"I don't even like you," Stash admits. "Why would I want to work with you one day longer than I need to?"

"The only reason you don't like me is because I act like I'm your supervisor at times," I point out. "Anyway, if you came to work for my firm I would be your supervisor. Then maybe you wouldn't care."

Stash laughs as he shakes his head.

"What? You don't believe me?"

"No, I actually understand your logic, but I have to admit I have no interest in working with you when this is all over. I think I'd rather have a daily root canal than spend one more day with you."

"So the invitation to come to Buenos Aires is withdrawn?" I ask realizing he's telling the truth about his feelings about me. I shouldn't be surprised because I have looked down at him, thinking he's weak and only here because he's supposed to keep the girl entertained.

"Probably better you find someplace where you're less likely to get into trouble, like maybe Costa Rica. All jungles and volcanos. You know? A place where you could hide from yourself and anyone else who's looking for you like every cop in this whole country."

He certainly isn't pulling any punches. I glance over my shoulder at Aces who seems to have fallen asleep, or is doing a good job of making us think he is. I decide to change the direction of the discussion. "Think you could get a little closer? I'd like to be sure we're not wasting our time."

Stash looks at me again, but then I see a slight nod. The auton speeds up a little. Not like his earlier madman driving, but we creep closer. We're only about a block behind when Stash notes for both of us, "I'm sure," and he slows down again.

"Sure which way?" I ask since he wasn't clear.

"It's the couple from the train, I'm sure."

"Sounds to me like you're still not sure if it's the girl."

"I'm going by hair color," Stash admits. "About all I can see."

"So what's the plan when they get wherever they're going? How do we get close enough without spooking her?"

"Have to assume they're going to a hotel," Stash offers. "We can drive past the auton when they get out and see if we can get a look at her, hopefully close enough to be sure."

"And then what?" I respond daring to consider the next step.

"We can't plan the next one," Stash responds.

"Why?"

I notice Aces has stirred in the backseat. He sits up and looks out the windshield, touches me on the shoulder. He points to a sign along the side of the highway.

Stash reads it, "Tahoe National Forest."

I look at him and respond, "Doesn't look like they're going camping."

Chapter Forty-Three:
Ophelia Braveheart

I'm looking at a map of Roseville, California, along with a history of the city and the highways through the area on the active wall. Trying to make sense of the video clip Peter showed me. *Why Roseville? There's nothing there worth taking such a chance. Bailing out of a moving vehicle on an interstate highway. Doing so was just crazy. Whoever did it must have been desperate. Does desperate describe Jaz? I hope not.*

Is she really this close or did they take her half way around the world? I have no idea and neither does Peter from what he said. Jason isn't even thinking about it. He's immersed in solving the problem the kidnappers gave him. A problem, he said himself, he never considered. So this must be just consuming him entirely. Tossed a live grenade and told to figure out how to disarm it before it explodes in your hands. No sense updating him, particularly since the news isn't particularly encouraging. Peter was trying to lower my expectations about ever seeing Jaz again. At least alive. I absolutely refuse to believe it will happen. No one would deliberately harm her. We've not done anything to warrant such treatment. Have we?

I see Peter appear in a window on my active wall. He appears to be in an auton travelling somewhere. He said he was coming back here, so where is he? "Peter. Do you have news?"

Peter shakes his head, "Sorry, O. But I wanted to tell you I did go up to Roseville and talked to the Chief of Police and a few others she pointed me to."

"But no news," I respond totally exhausted, both mentally and physically.

"It was worthwhile because I learned a few things. Some may be helpful as we continue our search."

"I thought you didn't think it was going to be… worthwhile." I press him since he must have changed his mind for some reason.

"I got to thinking about your reaction when I said I wasn't coming. Came to the realization I owed it to you to check it out since we had no better leads to pursue at the moment."

"So you've come to the conclusion it wasn't Jaz in the video?" I have to know the answer, but based on his first response I'm pretty sure I do.

"No evidence it ever happened, if you go into town. No one taken to the morgue, no one at the emergency room for trauma or even bruises. No one even reported the incident to the police, so the passengers of the auton must not have seen what happened."

"Jaz didn't wander in to the police department to report her abduction," I press him since he hasn't mentioned it.

"The Chief was aware of her situation. She would have been all over it if your daughter had. So, no."

"The Chief of Police in Roseville is a woman?" I'm surprised, but instantly wonder why I am.

"Very competent woman. You would like her," *Peter responds in a tone I don't recognize. I wonder why. Something there, but I have no idea what. But then again, we've been divorced a long time. Maybe he's changed in all these years.*

I decide to let it go, "So what's next?"

"I'm following up on a suggestion,"

"By whom?" *I'm surprised at how Peter is handling this. He has no evidence Jaz was even there. Yet he's spending time running down suggestions. Why?*

"The County Coroner," Peter responds. "Yes I talked with her…"

"Is everyone in Roseville a woman, or is it you only talk to the officials who are?" I hit him with another slam. *I just can't help myself.*

"No, as a matter of fact I did talk to a number of men. They just didn't seem to have better insights. Or maybe it's the women were more sympathetic to my search for a young woman."

I suddenly feel the tension in my shoulders. I need to relax if only for an instant. I exhale and empty out my lungs as I drop my shoulders. I try to loosen up my neck. Peter evidently notices.

"I wish I could hold you, if even for just this moment."

My head whips up. I look at him. Is this the Peter Tate I once loved and now hate? He's never once said anything supportive to me since the divorce or the year before it. "It's over, Peter."

"I'm not trying to get you back in bed. But regardless of what you think, I do care about you, care for you… as a friend since you'll not permit anything else now."

"Is this some existential angst on your part? Trying to make up for all your past sins?"

"Maybe for the first time I'm getting a glimpse of what my life might have been like had I been a little smarter when I was younger."

"An expression of regret?" *I can't believe what he's saying, but then again I'm sure a lot has happened to him in the years since we were together. I can't imagine, since everything I've read about him makes it seem he literally walked into the valley of death on more than one occasion and came out not only alive, but having resolved some major brewing international crisis. But as Jason has said to me, I don't know how many times, don't believe everything you read.*

"Maybe I came to the realization somewhere along the way Jazmin could have been my daughter if I'd only been kinder to you."

"Kinder?" I can't believe the term he would choose to describe his totally despicable behavior.

"I know you'd prefer faithful, but no one has ever accused me of being capable of being faithful."

"Even now when you can see what might have been?" I push since he started this whole discussion.

"Ask me in another five years," Peter responds with a twinkle in his eye I've seen many times before.

"Do you expect to be on your deathbed then?" I suggest to see if he will clarify.

"Not in the least. But maybe five more years of rejections and divorce settlements and coming away from each one with an overwhelming feeling of emptiness… "

"Still talking about your bank account… as you're coming up on your fifth settlement?" I interject to sidetrack his attempt at introspection.

Peter shrugs, "Maybe even a total rogue like me might get religion."

"Rogue? Do you actually see yourself as a rogue?" I still have trouble with his word choice as it undercuts the impression he's trying to convey.

"What word would you use?" Peter comes back at me, just like he used to.

"If you give me a second I can probably remember at least fifty I used at one time or another. Rogue was never one."

"Somehow I'm afraid if I agree to let you walk down memory lane I'm not likely to enjoy the stroll with you."

"Nor will I. Better to let the past remain in the past. But I do need what you've learned, so tell me. You were saying something about

248

talking to men. Now I have to admit you surprised me. If for no other reason I'd like to know what insights they may have shared."

"You've reminded me you wanted to know about the insight I got from the coroner."

"Since it hasn't changed anything I can wait. What did the men tell you?" I push to see how much he may have changed.

"You sure you want to go down this road?"

"You raised it," I point out resolutely.

"The men in Roseville. Okay, I talked to the druggist. Everyone in a small town at one time or another goes to the drug store and they usually gossip. So I figured if the druggist happened to be a woman I might get a tip about something. But unfortunately Pharmacist Stephen Ginsburg is one of those old-time pharmacists. He owns the drug store. It's not a chain like almost every other one you go into. He does know everyone in town. He knows what ails every one of them. But he refuses to listen to gossip. Says it's none of his business. And when it comes to what ails whom, well it's protected information under HIPA. Said it was a Federal law and he wasn't about to go to a federal penitentiary just to help some out of town detective, even if I am famous. Exactly what he said, honest. So he couldn't tell me anything."

"I take it you had to tell him you're famous? If he doesn't listen to gossip I would assume he doesn't watch the evening news," I respond.

"He does, but only Fox News, which I don't regard as news." Peter responds. "Asked if a young woman he'd never seen before had come in looking to buy aspirin or anything. He said no. So much for the pharmacist."

"Who else?"

"The ticket agent at the bus station. His badge said Mr. Holmes. Figured he had to be my man, but his first name wasn't Sherlock. It was Larry who was very hairy. Long beard, almost totally gray and you can imagine the rest. Confirmed he didn't sell a ticket to Jazmin after I showed him the picture."

"And?"

"Tried the train station since an Amtrak comes into Sacramento from there. Unfortunately the Amtrak station is so small they don't even have a ticket seller. So not a woman, but also not a man."

"Okay. I'm impressed. You seem to have tried to do a thorough investigation of Roseville, even though we had no strong indication she's ever been there. And the coroner?"

"Coroner asked me if Jazmin had been traveling through this way where would she have been going." Peter informs me. "You know I'd been so focused on whether she was there I hadn't considered where they may have been taking her. So I went back to the video. If she had been in Stockton she likely would have been going east. Bailing from the auton there like this person did, likely Roseville wasn't the destination. So I had to ask myself, what was it?"

"Did the coroner have an insight there?"

"She did. Asked me about the house I'd visited in Stockton. I described it to her. She said between Roseville and Reno it's nearly all national forest. So if they were going east she would expect they had a similar place either around Truckee or Lake Tahoe. But based on my description, Truckee made more sense since it was remote and there isn't going to be much in the way of law enforcement even if someone got wind they were there with the girl."

Chapter Forty-Four: Jazmin Braveheart

"Look, there's a sign," I point out to Sanders as our auton takes us to the trailhead. "What's the difference between a national forest and a national park?"

Sanders' eyes seem to sparkle as they have before when he was explaining something to me he knows and loves dearly.

"National Parks are for tourists," he begins as if he is letting me in on a big secret. "Everyone goes there, drives to the designated lookout points to see the famous feature of the park. It's like going to the Louvre in Paris and looking at the Mona Lisa. When you come into the museum they hand you a brochure telling you exactly how to get to it. Once you're there, you have to stand back in a crowd and look at it through a glass window. The museum channel's people so the true art lovers aren't overcome by all the tourists."

"I've never been to a national park or the Louvre," I admit, which I hope makes him feel even more like a tour guide for me.

"A national forest is for people who enjoy wandering through the splendor of nature."

"I thought the air was bad for you... pandemics and disease, and air pollution giving you respiratory illnesses, to say nothing of polluted waters and garbage strewn everywhere. Especially plastic bags and bottles and all kinds of bad things for you. Things which either shorten your life or kill you right away."

"People want you to think things are bad. Scare you to make sure they get what they want."

"Which is?" *I'm not sure what he wants me to think at this moment.*

"To stop polluting nature. The viruses you referenced? I'm not a scientist, but I think they're Mother Nature's way of thinning the herd. Paying us back for not taking better care of the incredibly beautiful and life sustaining world she has permitted us to inhabit. I'm an unashamed naturist."

"Naturist? I thought the term was naturalist?"

"Don't know. In my way of thinking a naturist is someone who cares about nature and takes care of it, preserves as much as possible, wants to see it remain a resource for all life species. But I think of a naturalist as someone who only wants you use and be in a natural setting, as opposed to a man-made artificial anything. Do you see the difference?"

"So I wouldn't be either living in a cocoon," I realize, not sure how he will take my observation.

"I'm trying to make you see what it's like out here, help you to understand the importance of being a naturist. Whether you want to become a naturalist is up to you. I'm not going to tell anyone how they should live, but as a naturist I'll not encourage you to use up natural resources to sustain your artificial world."

"I thought everything man makes comes from natural resources."

Sanders shows me his semi-smile I've seen when he thinks he has an important revelation I'd not considered. "What about your precious software? Does it consume natural resources?"

"Not the code itself, but the code has to be stored. You select the representations of the program and store them in a memory device so they can be recalled by another device and both are most assuredly made from natural resources. So I would have to say even software uses up natural resources."

"Then you know how I feel about everyone, because everyone uses natural resources."

"But you own a railroad…"

"I'm one of many owners of a railroad, I just own more shares than most."

"Okay, as one of many owners of a railroad, you must use all kinds of natural resources, indirectly."

"Do you understand my ambivalence about my life? I want to preserve and protect the resources consumed by the company feeding, clothing and enabling my lifestyle."

"Same for all of us, whether we live in a teepee in the plains and ride horses to hunt buffalo, or simply grow vegetables in a garden outside our cave which we heat through burning wood?"

"It is," Sanders admits. "But isn't it a matter of scale? I mean growing vegetables and heating your cave has a lot less of a negative impact on Mother Nature than living in a cocoon. A place powered by a generation plant some miles away. The electricity is brought to you over miles of cables hung from transmission towers. The house is heated by natural gas extracted from underground wells and piped miles underground. The house is built out of concrete, steel, and wood and glass, all of which are manufactured and transported to your location. A house filled with furniture made of similar materials, electronics filled with an array of minerals refined and manufactured into components to entertain you and monitor your health, wealth and state of being as you consume foods grown somewhere else in the world. Even those foods are shipped to processing plants and shipped again to stores and shipped again to your house. There you or someone transforms them into something edible. Afterwards you send waste back to Mother Nature as your gift to her."

"If you feel this way, why don't you sell everything and move to a cave?" I have to ask.

"I'd have to rely on myself for everything. Do you have any idea what that would entail? Of course not, you've grown up in a cocoon. You don't even make your bed now do you?"

"Make my bed?" I'm not sure I know what he's talking about.

"When you get up, do you go back and straighten out the covers? Make it look neat like it does when you go to bed at night? Do you change the sheets so they're clean for you to sleep on?"

"Why would I?"

"Most people do, but you're different. In your cocooned life, you have very little responsibility for yourself. Everything is done for you. Do you prepare your own food?"

I shake my head.

"Wash your clothes? Clean the house, cut your hair, grow plants, feed cats? Do you do anything other than consume the goods and services others bring to you?"

"Of course I do," I protest. "I study and research, exercise, write code and brainstorm products and approaches with Jason. I talk with friends…"

"On your active wall, but you never meet them, play sports or wander in the woods…"

"I am today," I beam at him, showing I'm actually changing what he finds unacceptable as a naturist.

"Are you sure you want to sully your reputation? Your parents and friends may not approve."

I suddenly wonder what Jason and Ophelia would think about me being out here in the woods, with a man I barely know, who clearly has some extreme views of the world they take for granted. But Ophelia keeps telling me I need to broaden my horizons. *Go wide and not so deep on everything. Question everything, learn what I can about it, and balance things against each other to see the relative merits. Exactly what I'm doing coming out here, walking in the woods, listening to the wildlife and the real wind as it blows my hair? I'm coming out to see a spectacular sunset because it may be the only time I'll ever pass this way.*

The auton turns off the main road. We are now driving along a two-lane road with trees as far as I can see on both sides. No houses, no signs of civilization as we drive deeper and deeper into the Tahoe National Forest. "How many times have you hiked out here?" suddenly occurs to me.

"I try to get up here at least once a week. I've been coming up here for decades because it's so peaceful, it recharges me, gives me a few hours in the sun and fresh air and allows me to just absorb the energy of nature."

"So a lot of times, but you said you've never hiked this particular trail? Why not?"

"I usually hike one trail. It's just the right distance, it fits into the time I have given the train schedule, and it's like an old friend, do you know what I mean? Everything is familiar so I don't get overwhelmed trying to take it all in. I look and see new animals I've not seen before, new flowers and trees coming up as seedlings. I get to experience what's new here rather than it all being new and not seeing ninety-nine percent."

"So it's convenient."

"For the most part," Sanders laughs with me which is nice. *I don't know why I feel so comfortable around him, maybe it's the contrast with Stash and his friends. At least I don't have to worry about them tracking me down. Could be why I feel comfortable with Sanders. Because I don't feel like I have to be looking for a way to outwit him so I can find a way to escape. Getting away is all behind me now.*

"I've only heard good things about this trail," Sanders interrupts my thoughts. "My ex-wife has been hiking it recently."

"Ex-wife? I didn't know you'd ever been married. Do you have any kids?"

Sanders shows me a wistful smile now as if remembering something he longs for now. "No kids, we were barely married long enough."

"What happened? If I'm not being too intrusive."

Sanders looks out the window for a moment and then back at me. His eyes are moist. "I actually met her up here hiking on my trail. She'd just arrived in Roseville and was getting settled. She twisted an ankle because she wasn't used to hiking, had kept on hiking and doing so only made it worse by the time I came upon her. So I walked out with her, letting her lean on me to keep the weight off. We just had such a great conversation when we got down I offered her a lift back to the train and we sat together all the way back to Roseville."

"Three hours," I note.

"Yes, although the time just flew by. We talked about all kinds of things. Just like you she had been so focused on her career she'd hardly ever spent any time out hiking or biking or skiing or any of those other '-ings'. So I took her to the hospital for an x-ray and made a date to take her for a hike when she was up to it. A month later we were married. That was the other time I was impulsive. It was the best thing I ever did."

"Why didn't it work out for you?"

"Her career got in the way," Sanders sounds regretful, "I wanted to travel and hike and do all the things I've become accustomed to doing. Her job kept her out late and often working seven days a week. So I started traveling without her. And when I was here she couldn't come hiking with me because she had to be at the police station. She's the chief, and her career meant more to her than I did."

Police! Holy shit. I can't let him talk to her about me. I'm only safe as long as I don't call home or talk to the police. If I do, Stash and the others will find me. I heard Stash say Modor has all communications with the cocoon tapped. They'll know exactly where I am and come looking for me.

Chapter Forty-Five: Stash

The auton stops ahead. I slow down because we don't want to be too close when they get out. Close enough for us to see them without them really seeing us. *How do we keep the balance? I don't know. But if we come in slow enough, hopefully we can pull up and see them when they emerge. We seem to be at a trail head. More than one, actually. Several pickup trucks are here, all the same dark green color. Why would they all congregate here? A hiking club or something? Then I see the National Forrest Service sign on the trucks. They could torpedo the plan if they show up at the wrong time.*

The man and woman emerge from the auton. She glances back at us as we approach. *I don't think it's her, although it's only a sidewise glance. The man looks at us directly, but I've never seen him before. Short guy, but stocky. Wearing hiking boots. Both of them are. But now we're closer I see it could be her. I'm still looking only at a profile of her face, which I don't remember really looking at when we had her at the various houses. She takes a face mask from the guy, who also puts one on, so no chance now to be sure. The clothes could be the same, but clearly not the shoes. Who is this guy? Why are they out here? None of this makes any sense.*

"Pull over there, by the other trail head," Rocketman nods to his left, away from them and turns away so they won't see his face. *Also means he's not able to get a good look at her. I don't know what Aces is doing, maybe he's getting a better vantage point.*

I steer away and glance out quickly when we're as close as we're going to get. She's looking the other way, so no chance to be sure. "I'm gonna say it's her, but I still might be wrong," I tell the others. I see Aces look although Rocketman doesn't for some reason. *With his hospital mask on I'm surprised he would think she would recognize him. Most people wear them so why is he not wanting to look?*

"I know the dude," Rocketman finally explains. "I've been to his place. Lives in Roseville. He's some big deal. Money, influence, you name it, although you wouldn't guess it from the place where he lives. Nothing special. Don't want him to see me because we didn't part on happy terms."

"Happy terms? What are happy terms?" I inquire wondering what he did this time.

"He caught me in his den. Sent me away, probably correctly thinking I was looking for where he kept his valuables."

"He wouldn't be able to recognize you with the mask," I point out.

"The glasses he's wearing?" I can't see them now as he's walking away from us, "They're C-through lenses. Augmented reality. They build a composite of what you look like from the bone structure of what is visible."

"I've heard they're not always accurate," I respond dismissing his paranoia.

"The cheap ones you or I can buy aren't, but he's got law enforcement grade lenses. They're unbelievable. Anyway, he filed a complaint against me with Modor, so he'll remember me."

"His complaint why Modor decided you would be perfect for this little side venture?" I decide to ask, not having heard the story before.

"She blackmailed me. I didn't want to have anything to do with kidnapping. This's bigger than I've ever worked. More time in prison if you get caught, and I'm not about to go in, even for a day, if I can do anything about it."

"Then what was the deal with the guy? Why you doing any of this?"

"Why are you doing this?" Rocketman pushes back on my questioning, but we both turn around as Aces gets out and follows the couple into the woods. I watch Aces to make sure he's staying out of sight.

"I quit Modor's company," I respond as I look at him, wondering what those glasses the guy is wearing would show me I can't see. "She wanted to know why. I told her I'd come to the conclusion I was never going to be able to get ahead working as a tech for her when I'm a systems engineer. I needed to go work somewhere I could use the training and experience I had from before."

"What did you do before?"

"I worked for a defense contractor, building surveillance systems for military and national intelligence applications."

"Didn't know. Why are you here if you had a big job with a defense contractor?" *Rocketman asks a legitimate question. One I'd probably ask.*

"Defense contracting is up and down, mostly down in times like these where pandemics and natural disasters are the focus of governments. When the first pandemic strain came through, the company laid off over half of their employees because the government spent most of the defense acquisition budget bailing out the economy. I didn't have the time in so many others had, so I was out the door. No one was hiring then. I was lucky to get any job."

Rocketman glances up the trail the couple and Aces took. "Hope Aces stays out of sight. I would have told him to wait, but probably better than one of us is following them, particularly if you think it's her."

"I said it could be her, not sure it is…" I clarify.

Rocketman sits quietly thinking about something he's not sharing, and then he glances at me and asks, "So if you quit, why are you doing this?"

"Modor," I respond honestly. "She offered more money than I could fathom. Said she would stake me if I wanted to set up my own company since I had contacts in the defense and intelligence communities from my last job."

"Explains…" Rocketman doesn't finish the thought.

"Explains what?" I can't help but ask.

"Why me," Rocketman almost sounds bitter. "Why I was the one who was designated to make the hand-off rather than you."

"Meaning?"

"Meaning at the hand-off I'm likely to get caught. She didn't want you to do the hand-off because you have no record. I don't either so I'm likely to get a light sentence. Aces, on the other hand… he did big time. No way was he going to do the hand off, but if it was a termination. Well… he's been there. No compunction putting her down and making sure no one ever finds the body."

I'm alarmed by what he's suggesting, but then also recognize Modor may have actually been trying to uphold her end of the bargain. To protect me as much as possible if I helped her get whatever she's expecting from this whole deal. She never said what it was. I'm probably better off not knowing. *Would make me even more problematic to her.*

"Good old Modor," Rocketman reflects on something he's not sharing.

"Have you ever actually been in the same place with her?" I ask, wondering if his experience is the same as mine.

"Just virtually."

"You sure it's her and not an avatar?" I ask the question I'd often wondered.

"Avatar?"

"I think she's a dude, personally. Something about the way she… I don't know what it is, but there's something about the way she comes at you. Do you know what I'm saying? It's almost too direct. Women aren't direct in the way they handle guys. It's always oblique, I think. Always leaving an escape route if you get upset. Always letting the guy think he's in charge somehow, even if we aren't."

Rocketman considers my observation. "Hadn't thought about it." He continues to mull my comment, all the time watching the trail even though it's likely to be hours before they return. "But I think I know what you're saying. So you think Modor's a dude?"

"I also don't think she's in California."

"Hold on now," Rocketman's not about to accept speculation on my part. "The business is here. She's got to be here somewhere. I mean someone has to be doing all the schmoozing to get the accounts. Getting business is her. At least I think it's her."

"Just because we've never seen anyone else, doesn't mean they don't exist," I point out. "She could have people here doing the selling just as she has people here doing the service. Doesn't mean she's here if she's hired them the same way she hired us."

Rocketman seems unsettled by this whole discussion. He finally opens the auton door and steps outside, looking around, but constantly coming back to the trail head of interest. "What do you think Aces is doing?"

"Probably taking a nap waiting for them trip over him when they return," I suggest sarcastically.

"I don't like the fact he's out there," Rocketman shakes his head.

"Not to worry. Someone needed to go along, if for no other reason than to alert us by text when they are coming back so we're not out here hanging out like we are at the moment."

Rocketman looks around but then seems to get what I'm saying. "Yeah. I get it. Damn. It better be her."

"You buy your tickets yet?" I push him back to reality rather than wishful thinking.

"Did you?" he seems genuinely surprised by my question.

"Flight 713 SFO to Buenos Aires three days from now. Doesn't make any difference to me which way this goes. I'm on the flight and from there I'll figure things out."

"I didn't think you were serious," Rocketman sounds surprised. "When did you buy your tickets?"

"A month ago," I confirm and watch his eyes grow.

"How could you figure out how this was going to take so long ago?"

"I don't care how this goes down. Either way I'm out of here in three days. I'll have all the money in my account or I won't. Doesn't matter because I'm out of here. Away from anything resulting from Modor's little project. Do you even know what this is all about?"

Rocketman shakes his head considering the actions I'd taken. Didn't think he did. "Cutting your losses."

"Neither of us have any idea what this is all about. No idea if we'll ever get paid or put in jail. I may be many things, but one thing I'm not is going to be sitting here watching the whole thing go to shit like it has and have to just wait for the cops to come arrest me."

"Explains why you never worried about the girl seeing your face." Rocketman realizes.

I simply shrug.

Chapter Forty-Six: Jason Braveheart

I sit in my lab at the cocoon, resting my forehead in my left palm. Too much Red Bull. The headache just pounds, threatening to split my skull, or so it seems. I was never able to keep going like so many I've worked with in the past. All those new grads used to staying up all night and studying for exams. I'd been able to stay up once. But it was a long time ago. Jaz doesn't seem to have my limitations. She probably got her resilience from her mother. The knock on the door is surprising. Ophelia is the only one here and she never comes in. This is my sanctuary as the media room is hers the one place we can be sure the other won't disturb us.

Ophelia opens the door cautiously since I've not responded to her. She peeks in, glances around at the walls and realizes I'm off line at the moment. The team is working a particularly hard problem and I wanted to give them time to just sit back and think it through since our tinkering and tinkering wasn't getting us to a workable solution. We either needed Jaz to guide us or to step back and give our minds the freedom to consider. "What?"

"I knew you weren't coming out until you have a working prototype. I wanted to see how you're doing. Do you need anything? Food maybe? Sex if you're horny. You always seem to get some of your best ideas after sex."

She's right. Some of my best products... "Have you eaten?"

Ophelia shakes her head. Didn't think she would. Never has in all the years we've been together. She always waits for me. Always wants to share my feelings of euphoria when I've come up with an elegant approach to solving a particularly hard problem. But it's been a while. The team solves those problems now. I only give them high level guidance. Maybe it has something to do with the new tools they use. The logic is light years ahead of what I used. Not sure I could use them the way they do. And Jaz... she just seems to be on another planet when it comes to how proficient she is. Why? Is there some kind of generational accelerator? An ability to pick up on the state of the art and take it to another level for every new generation? Might explain why kids seem to understand things people who grew up in more rudimentary states of the art struggle with. Might explain why I'm better off letting the team take the lead, give them the parameters of the problem and standing back. It took me a long time to accept I might be a limitation. A long time to realize I'm the problem and not the solution to the issue we are trying to solve. But now the team is working much faster.

"How about a quinoa burger, with lettuce, tomato and garlic flavored olive oil?" O asks. She knows it's one of my favorites.

"And a protein shake with kale, spinach and goji berries?" I add, to get a more complete meal nutritionally, which we have been focused on for so many years now. I can't even remember when we gave up all the foods we used to love, to eat healthy.

"Goji berries are out," O informs me. "Back to plain old blueberries sourced locally. All the fruit we used to import? Not shipping it in anymore. All the focus on local has killed the imports."

We're still adjusting to how the world economy has become a local economy. The local berries are good, but we seldom see the big berries we used to get. "I like blueberries," I let her know so she won't feel bad.

"You able to break long enough we can eat together?" O asks sounding as if she doesn't expect I am.

I nod and in a moment she's gone.

I look at the code once more now having focused on something other than the hard problem we've been working for even a moment. Suddenly I see a path forward, or at least a possible path forward. I send a quick note to the team and am just finishing up when the door opens again.

Ophelia peeks in as I come over and open the door for her. She enters carrying the two burgers and shakes on a tray I recognize. A friend made the tray in his woodworking shop from wine crates I shipped from Chile with bottles of wine we'd purchased. I'd love to have a glass of wine, but don't think it would help me deliver a final solution. The clock is ticking for Jaz.

O puts the tray down and sits down across from where I'd been working. I take my seat, but turn towards her. She points to the burger, but I take a sip of the shake first.

"Are you close?" O asks before taking a bite of her burger.

"Getting there," I respond although I'm not as confident as I'm trying to sound.

"What do you think will happen if you give them what they've asked for?" O asks.

I've been afraid she would ask me this question at some point. "It will work out."

O puts her burger down, finishes chewing and swallows. This was clearly not the answer she was expecting, or maybe hoping for, not sure. She looks at me curiously. "Don't bullshit me Jason. What's going to happen? I know just enough about what they want to know this isn't going to be a good thing."

I can't tell her what I expect to happen. I have to say what will make her relax, although likely not possible. "The only thing I can say is I'm focused on making sure whatever happens, Jaz comes home."

"How can you be sure?" she pushes me, although I've tried to explain it to her before.

"Jaz has to be on her way or I don't release the code."

"Damn it, Jason," Ophelia isn't happy. "What the fuck does that mean? On her way."

"I'm still working it," I tell her. "I have an idea, but it's not bullet-proof. You just have to work with me and trust I'm not going to do anything to jeopardize Jaz."

O shakes her head, "Not good enough. I can't just accept your 'trust me' solution. It's not a solution. So tell me, what are you doing to ensure our daughter is coming home?"

"I'm not going to give them the code until I know Jaz is on her way home."

"Chicken or egg?" O observes.

"You're afraid about who releases first knowing the other won't release until the other has?" I decide to put the conundrum on the table.

"Exactly," O responds.

"If they don't release Jaz, they don't get the code," I respond emphatically.

"But what happens if they won't release Jaz until they have the code and then don't release her?" Ophelia pushes the question we've all been asking since the beginning.

"We send in the Marines," is all I can think of to say to her. "The reality is we have to trust they will release her because if they don't the police will be fully engaged in hunting them down. If they release her then the pressure is off and it becomes a secondary investigation. One where they might get away with it."

"I want you to let me release the code," O informs me.

"I don't know," I respond without really thinking it through. "But let me take a look at what it would take."

I was hoping the latter qualification would appease her, but no, "You don't release anything unless I'm satisfied." O informs me. And there is no question in her voice about what she means and expects. For the first time I realize how difficult the hand over is going to be. Neither side trusting the other to live up to the implicit bargain. But at the same time needing to have one side make a concession in order for Jaz to come home. *I'm going to have to spend more time thinking this through since O has made her case. What I was thinking isn't going to work. So what now?*

"I'm good," I respond.

"Peter has to agree."

"Does he have to?" I respond thinking about her ex-husband who hasn't brought anything to the table as far as I can see. *But then I've been sequestered back here for the last several days. Maybe he has added some value she hasn't told me about yet.*

"I'm the last one to sing his praises after what happened between us. But somehow, I think he might just be able to help us not make a stupid decision."

I have to give her something since none of us have been in this situation before. Reportedly her ex-husband has been very successful in getting good resolutions in similar kinds of circumstances. *But then again, all I've heard about him from my very sketchy associates is he's more smoke and mirrors than actual substance. Although I have to admit it's probably the case for most people in an isolated virtual world. One where you can't get close to the subject or those who would do you harm. Everything is about what you can see and not what you can touch.*

"Jaz is the priority," I inform her so there is no doubt in her mind about how I'm looking at the situation.

"What happens after you give them your solution?" O asks. I'm surprised it has taken her this long.

"The world changes, not for the better as you or I would see it. But for those who have the tool, they'll think this is the path to nirvana." I respond having been facing this dilemma for many days

267

now. *I could never have created this tool for either side of the political divide. I can only assume which side these people are on. And have to further assume they see it as the pathway to heaven on earth for them and their close associates. But for the rest of us? Not likely a heaven on earth, or even a heaven. But simply another exploitation of all of us.*

Ophelia rises, walks toward the door. "Is this how the world as we know it ends? Cast upon the horns of a dilemma, we can only regain what is most important to us by throwing the world most important to everyone else to the winds of radical self-service?"

"What they've asked for will certainly upend the balance we've known in our lifetimes. But the balance was never permanent or even the usual state of affairs."

Chapter Forty-Seven: Jazmin Braveheart

Sanders insists I wear a surgical mask, even though we are going to be away from people on a hiking trail near the Nevada border. "Not so much to protect you, but so anyone we meet on the way won't be concerned. Everyone wears one when they're out. Everyone knows it just keeps you from infecting anyone you'll meet."

I put the mask on as he does. *The few times Jason and Ophelia have taken me out, I've had to wear one, but somehow out on a hiking trail, in the woods far from cities and towns and houses and large crowds of people I didn't expect this. But I understand. The trees and animals must be laughing at us. Afraid plants and animals might be dangerous to our health, even though we rely upon them to survive since they feed us. The plants and animals would probably be just as happy if we disappeared from the planet. We cut down the plants and eat them or build homes or burn trees from the forests. If we let the trees alone, they would help clean up the atmosphere. If we let the animals alone, they would prosper and multiply. Reestablish the great herds once roaming the US plains when we came and began to hunt them.*

But my knowledge of all of these issues is second hand. Delivered by my active wall, whether a school lesson or net search to satisfy my curiosity.

"Open your senses," Sanders recommends. I see him taking deep breaths of air, his eyes are wide as he looks around, his head tilted back as if accepting the sun on his face and the wind in his hair. I see he is welcoming the change from city life to natural life.

As we walk along I listen for the sounds of animals. I've imagined what it sounds like in a forest, but having never been here, I have to assume my imaginings are not entirely correct. A Disney world is only representative of the real world. I get a sense from the Disney experience, but I don't really understand the nuances, the subtleties, the shades of color found in the wild. Finally, here I am. Walking along a path I have no idea where it will take me other than a reported fantastic sunset. A path through the woods I hope will introduce me to so much I have not experienced because I've been cocooned in a virtual world of Jason and Ophelia's making. And it's all right. I have no reason to question what they hoped for to succeed. But I also have the opportunity to decide whether their world is the one I want for myself going forward. Stash made me question certain things, but Sanders is showing me happiness is not dependent on being safe. It's much more about living the life you want and are comfortable with.

Why is someone other than your parents able to show you how to be happy? It would seem your parents would have it all figured out. They've been down this path before you. Learned from their mistakes. Successfully negotiated the romantic landscape, because if they hadn't I wouldn't be here. So why aren't they the final authority when it comes to what I am to become? I don't know, but all I can put together here is just at the time when I'm beginning to question the world as it is, is also the time when I'm forming relationships beyond the home. When friends, who are also questioning their world encounter mine and ask, is mine any more relevant than their own? The more we talk, the more we realize the answer is no.

"What's new to you?" I ask Sanders as we slowly hike along the trail.

"I'm just overwhelmed by all I'm seeing, hearing, smelling and feeling. But probably the one thing I'm dealing with as we hike along is knowing my ex-wife has been this way many times. This is as familiar to her as the trails I hike are to me. So I'm kind of trying to see everything as she would see it, more so than just taking it all in. How about you?"

"It's so overwhelming. Just everything overloading my senses. But what I didn't expect is the smell of the pine trees." I respond, trying to sort through all of the perceptions I'm having.

Sanders seems to inhale and acknowledge the smell. A barely

perceptible head nod to closed eyes. "One I've come to assume. Thanks for taking me back there."

I see a deer darting through the trees quite some distance from us. It stops and stands very still, watching us as we make our way along the trail. *I would assume the deer is used to hikers by now. It must feel safe from hunters who are not allowed to kill animals in these areas of the national forest. A safe haven for wild animals who can't possibly understand how the world of humans work. But somehow they know they are safe, if only based on experience.*

"I see it too. Magnificent animal." Sanders notes. "Have you ever seen one up close? Growing up in a cocoon, of course you haven't. I have on several of my hikes. They come down, curious, but also wary of us."

"I should be? Wary in the woods?" I ask to see how he will take my observation.

"One should always be wary," he responds as if he's thinking of something he has chosen not to discuss with me.

We walk on in silence for a distance. The trees seem to be getting denser. I note it is becoming darker as we walk. Seems the tree canopy has blocked out more and more of the sun. *Probably's normal, although having never been out here, I don't know for sure. But it's interesting how the trees seem to grow close enough together to create an artificial twi-light.* "How do the seedlings get enough light to grow?" I ask innocently.

"Indirect light is enough," Sanders responds, "Like so many things in life. You don't need the spotlight on something for it to become important. Sometimes the things growing in the shadows are actually more important than those things everyone focuses on. Seen the scenario time after time. So I seldom pay attention to what everyone else is. I look for the things growing on their own, becoming important without the spotlight. The forest is the same way. These seedlings are going to be the forest of the future. When the big trees fall from rot, or age or fire or whatever, the seedlings are growing there all the time, ready to stand up and absorb the direct sunlight. Ready to be the primary tree in any particular area of the forest. You always have to be looking at who or what is coming along. Those who are holding their own at the moment? Their time is coming. You can only stand at the top of the forest for just so long and then something will cut you down and the seedlings there toiling in the shadows are ready to take their place."

"Sounds downright Darwinian," I note for him with a smile.

"Darwin got it right in so many ways, even though he was simplistic in so many others."

"Why don't you write your own theory of nature from the view of a naturist?" I suggest.

"Sanders Rose on nature? Do you really think anyone would be interested?" he sounds skeptical.

"Think about it, someone named Rose talking about nature. It just makes so much sense."

"I'm not much for writing," Sanders responds as his way of dismissing the idea.

"I could ghost write it for you," I offer earnestly.

"Why would you want to?" Sanders seems skeptical.

"You've graciously agreed to show me your conception of nature and explained why it's so important to all of us. Helping write your book would be the least I could do to share what you've shared with me," I try to explain.

"But you have software to go write. A book on nature just doesn't seem to fit, at least not to me."

"I'm not as limited in my interests as you would seem to think, based on your comment. I want to know about all kinds of things. Software is what I do to help my family make a living. Is it the only thing I care about? Not hardly. At some point it may be my primary focus, but at the moment, it's only one of several interests."

Sanders looks at me through his sun-sensitive sunglasses. The lenses have darkened which seems strange given I would expect them to lighten in the darkening woods. "What do you want to know about what you're looking at?"

"Any idea how old these trees are?" comes to mind as I look up.

"Hundreds of years. Would have to cut one down and count the rings to be sure. But I'm confident they're in the hundreds."

"Mostly pine trees?" which is what I'm looking at.

"This is a pine forest," Sanders responds.

"I was recently at a place where the trees were different. Curious smell, almost like they were covered Spanish moss, but I know there aren't any like them here. I think they were Eucalyptus/"

"Probably. There's a lot of them in northern California.

"Why aren't there Eucalyptus trees here?" I wonder aloud.

"The Eucalyptus were planted in areas where there weren't trees in the late 1800s when they were building the railroad. You see them along the tracks everywhere. But this forest predates the railroad. Predates men moving into this area of the country."

"Where is this ridge where we're going to look at the sunset?" I ask not seeing anything resembling what he's described."

Sanders looks around, removes his phone and locates us on the trail map. "Says we're still a mile or so from it. You still comfortable going the distance and then hiking back down? We can turn back now if you'd rather."

"I'm good. Besides I should easily be able to hike further than you since I'm so much younger."

"Hiking requires stamina and strength," Sanders responds knowingly. "I actually am concerned about both for you since you've spent most of your life cocooned. I walk miles nearly every day. How far do you walk?"

"Don't know, but I keep to a rigid vegan diet and hour of exercise every morning so I should be fit," I dismiss his concern, but have to admit my legs are getting a little tired.

We come to a fork in the trail. The sign points to the west trail and east trail. "Which way?"

Sanders looks at me, "Think about it. We're going to watch a sunset. Would you go east or west to watch a sunset?"

I have to think about his question for a long moment before it occurs to me what he's asking. "West trail."

"Why?"

"Because the sun sets in the west, so if we want to watch it, we probably need to be looking west, thus the west trail."

Sanders smiles, "You'll make a fine naturist when you finally admit it's important to take care of Mother Nature so she will take care of us."

We follow the west trail.

Chapter Forty-Eight: Peter Tate

Truckee is a small town, about the same size as Roseville with less than 20,000 residents. But unlike Roseville, most aren't in the town. Rather they live in the countryside around the town. Parked under the tree canopy of the National Forest and surrounding tree stands. *I didn't realize it was such a long drive. Didn't look this far on the map.* I call up Sheriff Thompson Dale who I've never met. But then again, I've never been in Truckee or even in this area of the State of California, even though San Francisco isn't far away. I grew up, fell in love with O and thought I was going to spend the rest of my life in San Fran. *At least I thought so at the time. Strange how life takes you so far from where you expect to be.*

"Sheriff Dale," comes the answer to my call. Apparently the Sheriff is not in his office as all I'm getting is his voice.

"Sheriff, Chief Rose over in Roseville suggested I check in with you. My name is Peter Tate," but before I can even say why I'm calling he cuts me off.

"Just got off the phone with her so I know why you're calling," the tone is presumptive, as if he's already formed an opinion of me and from the tone I don't think it's favorable. "Look Tate, I don't want you doing a whole big social media expose on my town. If it were a more favorable topic I might not mind quite so much, but a kidnapping isn't the kind of thing to bring out anyone we might want to come visit with us. Am I making myself clear?"

"Perfectly Sheriff," I try to placate him as much as possible, without making it sound like I am. "What Chief Rose probably didn't convey is this is a personal matter. I'm not intending to do anything with this case other than solve it."

"What do you mean personal matter?" The Sheriff sounds

suspicious. Apparently he thinks anyone who has sought recognition can only work one way and doesn't have a personal life. Or at least not one they would be above exploiting.

"The missing girl is the daughter of my ex-wife," I admit since it's better not to seem disingenuous when he already has a negative impression of me.

"Which one?" the Sheriff comes right back, "Don't you have like a harem or something?"

I laugh, although it may not sound genuine to him so I move on, "No. Just four pissed off women that I couldn't keep their favorite plaything in my pants."

The Sheriff snorts, "Not an expression you hear every day."

"Maybe not, but it pretty much sums up a big part of my life."

"You make it sound like being a big deal isn't all fancy parties and private audiences with important people like the Governor or the President."

Apparently he's taken the time to research me after the Chief's call, although he said he just hung up with her. Must have been doing the search as they talked. "I take it my reputation precedes me to Truckee."

"When Chief Rose mentioned your name, I knew instantly who you are. Seen you more than once on the newsfeeds. Don't you have like a private jet or something?"

"Had to sell it for alimony."

"Which wife?" the Sheriff takes another swipe.

"Number three. The judge thought she needed child support. Of course I disagreed."

"Didn't know you had kids, must have missed something," the Sheriff admits, surprisingly.

"I don't, but she was so young the judge thought she should be getting child support rather than alimony."

"Sounds like you just make friends everywhere you go," *the Sheriff sounds pleased with himself because he can feel superior to my wastrel life. I'm fine as long as he works with me rather than trying to undercut everything I may need to do here.*

"My mother would probably still like me if she could," I toss out there for him to grab hold of.

"She pass on?" the Sheriff guesses sounding regretful.

"Probably wishes she had," I decide to leave things there. "So Sheriff. Since I'm sure Chief Rose sent you the picture of Jazmin Braveheart, any chance you or someone in Truckee may have seen her?"

"Chief Rose told me if she made the assumption Miss Braveheart had come this way, had survived the moving auton escape, had found someone to offer assistance, and for some mysterious reason had chosen not to seek help from the local police, she might have come here. Or she may have just been brought here by her kidnappers. Chief Rose said you hadn't been able to figure out which it might be, or whether she was even in this part of the state, or the country."

"Sounds to me like you're a good listener," I try to compliment him, sort of.

"The bulletin on her came through and was filed with all the others, so we were looking for her just like all the others. And until I got the call from Chief Rose, we'd seen just about as much of Jazmin Braveheart as we had all the others. So the answer to your question is no. We've not seen her or had any indication she is either here or been through here."

"I would assume you have your share of bed and breakfast places and vacation rentals."

"We do, and they all follow the sanitary code requirements to get

277

the health department certifications. I follow up on those personally because the last news story we need up here is an outbreak of the next worst virus coming along." *Wow was he defensive. Must mean they had cases here at one time. Probably during the first outbreak before anyone was really following the procedures.*

"I would assume Chief Rose told you why we think Jazmin Braveheart may have come here or at least in this direction?"

"The video…" his response answers my question even if he doesn't realize it does.

"Did she tell you we suspect she may have been held at a short-term rental three-bedroom house near Stockton for a few days?"

"I don't recall if she did."

"Remote area nearly a half hour from town," I try to draw the picture for him. "No neighbors to observe their movements. Up a long dirt road. Sound like any properties around Truckee?"

"Sounds like more than half the homes around here."

"And they all file the health department disclosures which might enable you to see if we have any names we might recognize on the rental agreement?"

Silence greets my request, but then he finally answers, "There may be a few who miss them from time-to-time, although as soon as we figure out what they've done we fine them and do random checks. Like I said, we don't want any virus outbreaks up here."

"So if you were to do a check for me, you may or might not be able to tell if someone was holding a young woman against her will."

"We've had a few instances of reported violence against women in some of the rentals. They're the worst because at most of the B&Bs there's someone around. But the rentals? Since they have to prepay, most of them show up, retrieve a key from a hiding place and no one even sees them. Gone before the maid comes to clean up before the next party comes in."

"Murders?" I push.

"Not recently," is all the confirmation the Sheriff wants to give.

"Okay, Sheriff Dale. I'm sure you run a tight ship, you keep everything in hand and the people there appreciate how you do it. I think Chief Rose said you've been Sheriff for how many decades?"

"Going on three," he responds proudly.

"Means the people are satisfied. I will be too if you can help me find out whether Jazmin Braveheart is in your town, was there, passed through or enable me to believe she was never there."

"My deputies are already checking out the rental angle, you said you have some names you want us to look at?"

"I'm sending the names we have, although they don't track with the pictures we have and am sending too. I have a possible on one of the men from a driver's license record, although it's only a possible because the body cam photo resembles the DMV picture, but the software isn't confirming a positive match. It's possible the guy had surgery and changed his appearance for some reason."

"I'll give the photos to my deputies. But the one thing you're going to find out about Truckee is we're spread out all over. Someone could easily disappear here by going camping off the beaten path in the National Forest, or staying at one of the more remote cabins. Not the three-bedroom house you described in Stockton, but if I were a kidnapper, there's a whole host of places out here nobody but the owners ever visit."

"Chief Rose mentioned what you described as the reason they may have been bringing her up this way," I note in full realization this is not going to be easy. "Real hard to find."

"My deputies are good, Mr. Tate," he tries to reassure me, so apparently the hostility has been overcome. "We've all lived here for enough years. If something out of the ordinary happens we're all over it."

I glance at the clock on the auton. "Looks like I'll be there in about fifteen minutes. What would you recommend I do not to duplicate what your team is working?"

"I'd suggest you get a room and something to eat. It's getting late. Not much you can do until morning," the Sheriff seems to be responding to a text message as his line of thought is interrupted. "We'll work through the night. See what we come up with. Then I can meet you for breakfast. Let you know where we are. I assure you this has our highest priority because we know if she either was or is here, we don't have much time to catch whoever has her."

"One final question, Sheriff. If she escaped her abductors, what would cause her to come up here rather than go home?"

"Young girl?" the Sheriff is thinking quickly, "Hell, it's impossible to know. Most people come here to visit the lake, but stay up Truckee because it's cheaper. Others come here to hike or camp. Some people come up here because they just want to explore the small California towns and have some peace and quiet. None of those make any sense to me for a girl who escaped her captors. What do you think?"

Chapter Forty-Nine: Jazmin Braveheart

"The air smells different here," I look around but don't see anything to explain what I'm smelling. Sanders stops and inhales, nods. "Smoke from a fire. I don't think there are any close by. Nothing to be concerned about."

"Fire?" I respond, "You mean like a campfire?"

"Could be, but smells more like a brush fire. We have controlled burns and wildfires in the forest. Happens every summer when the undergrowth gets dry from the draught. It's Mother Nature's way of clearing out the dead growth and making way for the new. Just like people retire from companies to make way for the new people who are joining."

I've never thought about people retiring to make way for younger people. The way it's been explained to me before is people work a certain number of years, earn enough to live off savings and payments from former employers and the government. When they have enough income and savings they go do the things they never could when they were working. *Nothing about making way for new people. At Jason's firm, we hire people for jobs we get or for skill sets we need on our ongoing work. We just don't have any older people working there so I guess I never thought there might be a link as Sanders has described.*

"I've never smelled fire before," I want him to know, but don't want to sound like I'm totally deprived or something, having never smelled a fire.

"You really don't smell the fire, you feel the heat or smell the smoke. Like smoked meats. The smoke gives the meat both a particular smell and flavor."

"I wouldn't know since I'm vegan," and I've never really thought about meats… at least not to eat.

Sanders nods to himself, probably thinking I'll never be a naturist. I've never experienced nature in all the years I've been growing up, so how could I possibly suddenly begin to appreciate it. "We may encounter campers on the way out. It will be dark and if they've set a campfire we'll be able to see it even at quite a distance. It's so dark here light can be seen from a long way away."

"It will be completely dark before we get back to the trailhead?" I suddenly realize, not completely comfortable with the realization.

Sanders glances at me, "I told you it would if we stay to watch the sunset. Will be totally dark probably before we even begin the return leg, which will likely take less than an hour. Not much to see in the dark."

Now I'm feeling not so comfortable, but only because I don't like the idea of being totally in the dark after being taken from my cocoon in the dark. *Sanders knows this area even though he admits he's not hiked this trail before and usually doesn't hike after dark. The more I think about it…*

Sanders stops to look at something, but at first I don't see what. He apparently notices and points to a massive redwood tree off to our right. "How old do you think it is?"

I shrug, still uneasy about the thought of a dark trail.

"Easily over a thousand years based on its size. The oldest ones anyone's found have been well over two thousand years. Most of these here are likely five hundred or more. Have you ever seen anything so old before?"

"Rocks. Aren't they millions of years old in some cases?

"You should go to the Grand Canyon. You can see the evolution of the planet just looking down at all the layers. Some of the rocks exposed there are estimated to be nearly two billion years old. If you stop and think about how long Mother Nature's history is versus our history... our earliest ancestors only showed up less than two million years ago, and those most like us about 150,000 years ago. So in comparison to mother nature, we're mere day trippers."

"I don't know what you just said, day trippers?" I'm confused by the term he used.

"Day trippers?" Sanders smiles at me with a knowing smile. "Someone who's only here for a very short time. Someone who visits a place for just a day rather than staying a lifetime, for example."

"You're saying Mother Nature lives here and we're just visiting?"

"What do you think?" Sanders starts walking again. I glance back at the thousand-year-old tree once more, knowing I've never seen first-hand anything so old and then follow along.

I hear an unfamiliar sound as we hike, "What's the sound?"

Sanders cocks his head and glances around. "I hear birds, the wind in the trees, some animals trying to make their way from one place to another without being spotted by predators."

"It's the louder sound," I finally determine where it's coming from. "Over there," I point to my left.

"A stream. Sounds like it's dammed up and you're hearing the water falling over rocks. If it was just flowing within its banks you likely wouldn't hear anything."

"Can we take a look?" I'd like to see what he's describing.

Sanders nods and together we follow the sound of water falling over rocks. It doesn't take but a few minutes and we're looking at a mass of rocks, branches and mud nearly closing off the water flowing and falling over exposed rocks. "What is it?" I'm totally mystified. It doesn't look like something Mother Nature would have caused to happen.

"Beaver dam," Sanders responds in instant recognition.

"You have beavers here?" I had no idea.

"Last time I looked I think there were somewhere around three hundred different species of wildlife in these woods. Over a thousand different species of plants too. So if you want to go around and keep a notebook of the different kinds you see, we could spend a long time looking and recording."

"Since someone counted them, I assume someone did," I realize.

"People have been exploring and cataloging things about this area since the 1850s which was just before the railroad came through."

"So how did they get here?" I'm still trying to reconcile the history lesson Sanders has been imparting to me in installments.

"Earliest settlers came over the mountains by wagon train from the east, although some went all the way to the coast and over time moved back this way when the gold rush was over. After the gold petered out all people had to look forward to was farming or lumbering in these parts. We needed a lot of lumber just for the rail ties."

"It all comes back to the railroad for you, doesn't it?" I want to see if he hears himself.

"Of course. In my family every lesson was somehow tied back to the family and the importance of what we did in the development of the region. Without the Transcontinental Railroad, it would have taken much longer for Sacramento and San Francisco to develop. They would have been much smaller communities. Roseville probably wouldn't exist, other than, maybe, a farming community of a few hundred people. So yes. It all comes back to the railroad for me, and it should for you too."

"For me, history pretty much began in the 1950s with the invention of the integrated circuit," I admit. "It's the foundation for the transition from the printing press to stored electrons as the repository of all human knowledge."

"We do live in very different worlds," Sanders notes more to himself than me. "I look back to see how we got here as a framework to understand what is happening today. You look forward to how you can transform today into tomorrow."

I hear what he's saying and realize I spend all my time with people like me, which has not given me an appreciation of the many more people like Sanders. *Who was it? Stash maybe? Who said there aren't many cocoons? Not many people who live like I have. The vast majority are people like Sanders, who are happy putting life into historical context. Who take the transformations people like Jason have made in technology in stride. Not understanding them. Not caring. Simply accepting someone was able to create something new making their life easier, or more convenient or more sustainable. I am like Jason in so many ways. I'm only happy when I'm in the shop with him working on some new algorithm, or some new device no one else has been able to create. But do I need to be locked away in a cocoon to be able to create? I'll bet Jason and Ophelia wouldn't want to come out hiking like this. If they wanted to they would. But they have defined the world as poisoned, polluted and virus prone. They see it as something to be avoided, cancelled out and sealed away from our daily lives. Maybe there's more to life than just the act of creating. Maybe life should be a balance between understanding the past, enjoying Mother Nature in the present and creating the future. I don't know, but I have a lot to think about.*

The brown furry beaver comes out of his house and looks around. "Look!" I point to the creature as he turns toward us. I've apparently startled him. At first he draws back into his house and watches us. When we don't move or make any further sounds, he decides it's safe and comes out, again looks around and in a moment swims away carried by the current downstream.

Sanders touches my arm and points to our left. I see a small reddish-brown animal looking something like a dog, but I'm not sure. "What...?"

"A Sierra Red Fox," Sanders whispers so it won't run away. "This is the only place where you'll find them."

We watch the fox until it stealthily moves away apparently looking for its next meal or another Sierra Red Fox to mate with.

"We should move along if we want to be at the look-out in time for the sunset," Sanders suggests.

I am immersed in the sounds of the forest. The birds, so many different calls I am now hearing and I see different colors darting amongst the trees, winging from one perch to another. I hear the wind attempting to make its way through the dense tree stand, feel it on my face. Smell what I can only imagine is the moist earthiness, a smell I've never perceived before in my cocooned life. This is the real world. The one here before we came to settle. The real world going back billions of years. I am discovering there is so much more to life than I ever imagined. So much I don't understand. I will have to find more friends like Sanders who will show me the world they live in.

I notice the path ahead seems to be getting lighter. As we keep walking it is apparent there is a break ahead. A place where the trees thin out and more light is coming in. "Is...?"

Sanders nods and keeps walking.

It takes only a few more minutes for us to reach the breakout where a ridge drops away. We see the forest ahead of us. This is the end of the trail. This is the look-out where we will watch the sunset. It seems I am able to see for miles and miles. All trees, all green, like a blanket laid upon the land by Mother Nature. Then I see a white or grayish white plume in the distance. "Smoke?" I point as I ask.

Chapter Fifty: Stash

I'm napping in the auton when I hear the door open. I get my eyes open just quick enough to see Rocketman also starting like he'd been asleep too. I turn around. Aces is standing in the doorway. He doesn't get in but looks back to the trail head. "Is it her?" I ask, but Aces doesn't answer.

"If he's been following them all this time it's her," Rocketman answers for him.

"Time to take our places then," I respond, excited and amazed as I get up and exit the auton. We decided earlier we would form a triangle around the trail head so we could head her off in any direction if she makes a run for it. I'm walking towards a spot to the left of the trail head and slightly into the trees. Rocketman walks over to a point directly across the parking area from the trail entrance. Aces moves to the right but about equal to the parking lot entrance to the trail and walks about thirty feet away so he won't be noticed until they come out into the opening.

We don't have to wait long. I hear her voice first, "How long before the auton gets here to pick us up?"

Yes, it clearly is her voice.

"Shouldn't be long," the guy with her responds. "We should be back in Roseville by one or so."

It isn't more than a couple minutes before they emerge from the trail and can be seen under the light marking this trail head. I start walking up from behind them as Rocketman steps forward and crosses the lot.

"Hello, Jazmin," Rocketman greets them as he approaches. I watch as she grabs the arm of the guy with her, although I instantly know he's not going to give us any trouble. Three of us against just him.

The guy observes, "He knows you."

The girl nods and holds even tighter.

"What do you want?" the guy asks Rocketman, not yet realizing Aces and I are closing in on them. But before Rocketman answers we make our presence known. They both look around realizing there is no escape.

"She needs to come with us," Rocketman responds calmly, but with a clear threat apparent.

"She's with me," the guy responds clearly unsure what this is all about.

Rocketman frowns, but then seems to realize something and nods, "Probably better you come along too. Just so you won't be able to notify the authorities."

The girl turns around, sees me standing there and looks me in the eye, "You need to help me." But before I can respond, Aces grabs her. Roughly pushes her along towards the waiting auton. The guy looks around wide-eyed, but follows Aces and the girl. I take his cell phone and put it in my pocket.

Once we are all in the auton, Aces inputs the address. A moment later the door closes. We are moving down the long lonely road back to Truckee. But we're not going there. Nothing is said, apparently the guy is waiting until he can talk with the girl alone to find out who we are and why we are taking them somewhere. Rocketman's comment made it clear we aren't returning them to the train or her to her family.

Before we get to the main highway back into town, the auton makes a turn. Takes us back into the forest on a deserted barely two-lane road. It clearly doesn't get much use. I quickly am lost and have no idea where we are or are going. It takes about a half hour before we turn up a dirt road, and follow it through a dense growth of trees. I can't even see moon light at this point it is so dark.

A light on the first floor of the two-story log cabin appearing house marks it for us as we approach. If there had been no light we probably would have driven past it and not even seen it. I realize just how remote this place is. *Probably even the neighbors may not be aware this place exists, although this is California and people seem to know more than you would think about their neighbors.* The auton stops directly in front of the door. The girl looks around, wide-eyed, while the guy seems more focused on something he is thinking, probably what this is all about. The door to the auton opens automatically. Aces jumps out first. Then I remember, he's already been here and must have the key. He opens the door. Rocketman goes in to look around as the girl and guy slowly follow, clearly trying to see as much as possible, which isn't much in this darkness. The trees are right up next to the house and there is very little clearing around it.

Once inside I realize this house is completely modern. Apparently even has electricity from the grid as I don't hear a generator or anything. Didn't see any electric lines coming in and thought this might be a kerosene lamp kind of survivalist camp. *Nope. Modor got us a place with all the conveniences.*

The girl keeps her head down, although I catch her glancing around as if she were looking for the trap door to return her to the parallel universe from which she came. I feel sorry for her, apparently having thought she'd gotten away. It was only dumb luck on our part we found her. *What were the odds? Had to be like winning the lottery. Everything tells you it won't happen but for someone it does. Why me? No idea, but maybe it's an indication maybe my luck has changed and I'll get my new life in Buenos Aires. More likely it's an indication I've used up all my luck and this is as good as it's gonna get. Wish I knew the answer so I'd know whether to actually buy a ticket.*

The guy whispers something to her. She shakes her head in response. *Probably wants to know if we're likely to hurt them. Think Aces settled the question with his rough treatment of her back at the trail head. I don't know why he was so rough other than maybe he was trying to convince them not to resist. But he's has a different look in his eyes since he came out of the woods. I almost get the impression something happened to him either in there or some other time he was in the woods some other place. He just seems edgier than I've seen him. Almost as if he's spoiling for a fight. An opportunity to hurt someone, likely because he can't hurt whoever or whatever hurt him in the past. But what do I know? I've read books making me think about how other people think, but I doubt Aces does. Never seen him read anything unrelated to work. Rocketman either. Why don't people read anymore? Why don't people try to understand how other's think and feel? But then, what good does it do me? I'm not exactly getting rich because I'm empathic. In fact, if I were I wouldn't even get what Modor owes me.*

The girl turns to me, "Is there anything to eat, or should I ask is there anything I can eat?"

Aces turns around, races towards her, thrusts his hand up under her chin, pushing her across the room and into the wall, lifting her up off the floor. The guy and I both react at the same time while Rocketman just watches. The guy gets to him first, tries to pull Aces' arm down, but Aces punches him in the face with his other hand. When I reach him only seconds later, I hit him on the back of the head and scream in his ear, "Put her down. You won't get a dime if you kill her."

Aces' wild eyes look at me through his ski mask. After a very long moment he apparently comes to the conclusion I'm right. He lets her down, slowly. When his hand comes out from under her chin she sinks to the floor... hard. I get between them as the guy goes to the girl to see if she's alright.

Aces just looks at the girl as if seething inside about something he's not about to discuss. I wonder what the deal is about wanting to eat, but realize it may have something to do with her comment about something she can eat. Why would what she can eat set him off? Her calling attention to the fact she's got it made in life even though she's done nothing to deserve it. And Aces is just fucked, no matter what he does. It's the only thing I can think of. I gently push him back, he looks up at me. His eyes are now hard, as if just filled with hatred. I look back at Rocketman wondering if he has any better idea of what's going on with Aces. I gesture to see if he gets my point and Rocketman shrugs with a grimace.

Aces finally stands back and walks away, going over to the family room where he pulls out his cell phone. He appears to try to scroll for something, but shakes his head and puts his phone away. Makes me think there must not be any cell coverage out here. *So we're off line. Good thing we have a dedicated auton or we'd be stranded out here until Modor sends a car for us.*

I turn to look at the girl who seems to be trying to swallow… unsuccessfully.

"Just relax," the guy says to her. "He didn't do any permanent damage."

I remember Rocketman said he knows this guy, but I ask, "How did you end up in the middle of all this?"

"What is 'all this'?" he asks. From his point of view it's probably a reasonable question.

"She hasn't told you?" I seek to confirm before I say anything.

The guy shakes his head, "Said she's been traveling."

I don't know how to say this so I try: "She's being held until we are notified she can be released to her parents," is the best I can do without being specific.

"Held… like against her will. She recognized you, so you were holding her before?"

I don't respond but wait for him to tell me how he got here. I watch as he thinks the whole situation through. He finally glances out a window and responds, "Where do you want her to sleep? It's getting late."

"She can have the bedroom, but you're out here with us," I inform him.

The guy helps the girl up. She goes in. He closes the door behind her, then goes over to the family room and lies down on the couch. Aces has his head back and would appear to be asleep although somehow I doubt he is. Rocketman is chewing on a long carrot so I go over to him and quietly say, "Probably time for some sleep. I'm gonna leave the light on over the sink. You okay?"

Rocketman shrugs and heads off to the other bedroom. Only one comfortable chair left so I know where my head's about to lie. I think about locking the door but realize it doesn't make any sense since either of them could unlock it from inside. Besides we're so far out in the middle of nowhere, they wouldn't get very far even if they were to try to escape again.

Chapter Fifty-One: Jazmin Braveheart

Asleep, I'm not sure but it seems someone is getting into bed with me. Is this just a dream or is it actually happening? I need to shake off sleep so I know. Then I feel someone climbing on me like Stash did. This is no dream! Someone is pinning my arms to my sides so I can't resist. Can't push him away. "Get off me! No! No!" He's grabbing at my pants and pulling them down. I feel the full weight of his body pressing me down into the mattress. The hot sweaty breath in my face and nose. I feel the mask over his face. This is Aces. Shit.

He's feeling for my vagina, but having trouble because I'm bucking and squirming and doing everything I can think of to get him off me. I spit in his eyes, hoping he will try to wipe it away, but no reaction from him. He's getting closer to his objective. I try to force him off by rocking and rolling, but I suddenly feel his finger penetrate. It's like an electric shock causing all my muscles to spasm in response, an uncontrolled jerk and I momentarily can't resist him pushing further inside.

"Stop him! Somebody stop him!" I scream as loud as I can but I can't expect anyone will care. My hope crashes as I feel his finger retract, knowing what is coming next. How do I stop him? I can't. There's nothing I can do, but I'll never just let him do this to me. I buck and try to roll, try bringing my knees together and up under him so he can't do what he intends. I bite at his mask, but he pulls just far enough away so I can't grab hold of his mask or his nose or anything. "No! Get off me!"

Then something hits my face. Hits it again. I'm dazed. What just happened? I stop my resistance, not because I want to, but because I don't know what just happened to me. It takes a few seconds for me to regain a presence of mind, and even longer for me to resume bucking and resisting this weight upon me, pinning me to the bed, keeping me from pushing him away. And then a third blow practically knocks me

293

out. I'm clinging to consciousness by a thread.

Aces is feeling for my vagina again. This is the point where he wins. Nothing I can do to keep him out now. In a moment I expect to feel the pain of his entry, his penetration and his self-satisfaction at my expense. What can I do? I never expected to be in this situation. Ophelia never gave me advice about what a woman can do to protect herself, maybe because she was never here. But I am. "Stop! Don't do this! Please…"

Something pulls Aces weight up for a moment. I feel him swinging at something or someone I can't see, but then I realize I have my eyes closed. I blink them open and see Stash standing over the ski-masked face over me. Stash has pulled Aces' up with an arm under his neck. Aces punches but Stash is holding him tight enough and far enough behind him the punch has no force. The pull isn't working. It's distracted Aces, but he's still pinning me down. Stash moves his forearm up under Aces' chin to choke as he stands behind him and pulls back. Now Aces is the one who is kicking and flailing his arms in an attempt to get hold of Stash somehow.

A strong tug by Stash and push by Aces sends them both over backwards, off the bed and onto the floor. Now Aces is on his back on top of Stash, but Stash is still holding him tightly, preventing him from turning over. I think Stash is still choking him. I hear Aces gasping for breath.

Stash yells at me, "Get out of here. Go to the kitchen. Now!"

I climb out of bed and gingerly walk around them. Aces tries to grab me. I leap away from him but Aces grabs my left ankle. I turn around and stomp on his hand with my right foot just as Stash pulls him back again. Aces lets go and I quickly jump away from his grasping hand.

When I'm out of the room, I look back. Stash tries to roll over on top, but Aces gets loose, turns over atop of Stash and punches him in the face.

Chapter Fifty-Two: Ophelia Braveheart

"What do you mean this is harder than you thought?" I question Jason, who looks exhausted, but I don't care. *He's got to finish today. Give it to whoever has Jaz, bring her home to me today.* We're in his lab where I never go. He's been reviewing the test results, ignoring me until he couldn't any longer.

"We're close," Jason tries to take the sting out of his sentence of Jaz to another day away from home, away from us, away from the safety our home ensures… at least it did until she was taken from us. "Some parts are working flawlessly, but others…"

"What's it going to take? To get it fully functioning?" I assumed all he had to do was hand over the code and hardware. Then we'd get Jaz. But Jason corrects my assumption.

"They… have to see it work… before Jaz comes home. I have three… teams working. Each on different… approaches to the problem," Jason responds as if he's exhausted and unable to think clearly or answer more thoughtfully. "One of them… will figure it out."

"Which one is Charly on?" Charly Fuller is his brightest data scientist, at least in my opinion. If she's building the model I'm expecting it to work the first time.

"Primary. But her model… didn't work," Jason is trying to put this all into context for me. "So. She's starting over. Taking… different approach. She may be last… with functioning solution."

Not what I want to hear. But then I realize, "You've never given me the details of how this whole hand-over is going to work."

Jason looks like this is a question he was hoping I'd not ask. He finally nods, "Okay. They have a lab… somewhere. Hardware was sent. When software is finished… I upload to website. When operational… they send an auton… pick me up. Take me there. If followed or tracked… they walk. We never see Jaz."

"So you're supposed to demo the system and either way they have what they want," I summarize.

Jason nods with exhaustion. "I have to demonstrate it… Full functionality... One update, if needed… If it works… they release Jaz. Blindfold me… so no idea where lab is."

"There's got to be a thousand ways to track you. Find out where they're taking you."

"Probably take BART," Jason dispels my optimism.

"Bay Area Rapid Transit. So underground and maybe even under the bay," I summarize.

"So even eyes in the skies… they won't find me," Jason sounds totally spent.

If Jason, who is a security systems expert is pessimistic, then he has walked through all the likely scenarios. He's tried to find a way not to turn over a finished product. But now he's saying he's decided he has to. "And what about our nation once these people have it?"

Jason shakes his head. He seems to try to push his exhaustion aside to answer my question. "An artificially intelligent… voter pattern recognition… algorithm set. They can… test any message, any action, any candidate for likelihood… of election. Test it against… every registered voter's… expressed interests… and voting record."

I'm horrified by what he's just said. I had an inkling but didn't expect this much power in the tool. The ability to target proven messaging to the individual voter for an unlimited number of candidates? The ability to test out candidates, find out who will be successful without going through all the primaries. Who knows what kind of candidates they will field, what kind of likely actions they would take once in office?

"The only thing... sure of... field extreme positions. Pass... extreme legislation..." Jason concludes.

Jason looks at me. I see only the exhaustion. He's not thinking clearly now. He's barely thinking. I ask, "Why don't you get some sleep? Charly has her team well in hand, I'm sure. And the others? If they come up with something first? All good."

He closes his eyes. I see how much trouble he is having reopening them. I come across the room and kiss him on his forehead. "I'll come wake you if anyone has an update needing your attention." I take his hand and pull gently so he will follow me. He does even without opening his eyes. He follows me to the bedroom, where I lead him to the bed, sit him down and take off his shoes so he can sleep. He never opens his eyes or says a word.

I go back to the lab so I can monitor the teams working the various alternatives. Then I dial up Detective Stebbins.

I see his image come up on the active wall screen. "Mrs. Braveheart. I take it you're just checking to see if we have any new information on your daughter?"

"I am."

"We have investigated over one-hundred and twenty-seven reports from people who thought they may have seen her. None have proven to be her."

"So you are continuing to eliminate false positives," I state the logical argument rather than the mathematical.

"One way of looking at it, but I prefer to think we are much closer. Maybe the next report will be her. We will continue to investigate any report we believe could hold any possibility."

"But are there reports you aren't investigating?"

"There are," the detective acknowledges. "We use triage to work through the information we are getting. If the identified person is male rather than female, if the person is apparently with a family at an outing or family gathering, we don't require a visit. You would be amazed at how many sixteen-year-old slight-built young dark-haired women there are. Just in northern California the number is huge."

"It sounds to me you have given up trying to find my daughter."

"No," Detective Stebbins responds immediately. "We are following procedure. The procedure we have developed has been shown to lead to the quickest recovery of missing persons."

"It sounds to me you're waiting for my husband to finish this new system they are demanding and you are hoping to capture them after they've returned Jaz to us."

"No," Detective Stebbins responds. "We are doing everything we can to find her right now, this minute. There is usually something the abductor does which leads us to them. It may be as part of the communications to get their ransom, it may be at the time of the ransom hand over. It may be something they do while holding the person. Someone observes unusual behavior, observes the missing person, observes a family member or friend talking about the event in such a way the observer reports them. There are lots of ways cases like this break."

I'm still not expecting anything to come from Detective Stebbins. Peter's investigation just seems so tenuous I have no hope he will find her. Then I ask the question I probably shouldn't, "Have you accessed satellite imagery?"

"Only available to FBI on domestic cases," he responds immediately.

"How do you know she's still in California?" I push.

"We have no evidence to say she's not so I can't bring FBI in, at least until we have some indication they've moved her interstate."

"Jason has the imagery," I confess. "We gave it to Peter Tate. You can get it from him."

"Why didn't you provide it to me at the same time?" Detective Stebbins demands to know.

"Because it's inconclusive," I inform him, feeling even more exhausted myself.

"If it's inconclusive why did you ask?"

"I wanted to see if you're really doing everything you could. You just confirmed you aren't."

"Mrs. Braveheart. I realize how emotionally draining this for you and your husband. Your daughter may be traumatized by these events. I'm painfully aware of the possibility. I'm in touch with Mr. Tate. I know what he's doing in Roseville and now Truckee. But I also know the evidence she was or is there is no better than any of the other reports we've investigated. I sincerely hope he finds her. Brings her home because in the end bringing her home is all that matters. In the mean time we have literally thousands of police officials looking for her. They have talked with tens of thousands of people looking for clues or indications your daughter may have been in any given location. I know you don't want to hear what you think are excuses, and I'm not giving you excuses, I'm telling you how we find missing persons. We are following the playbook. It will eventually lead us to her."

"Bullshit, detective," is all I can think of to say. "Call me when you find my daughter," and I hang up.

Almost instantly thereafter I see the anorexic dark features of Charly up on the active wall screen, "Oh, hi Ophelia. Is Jason where I can talk with him?"

"He's asleep, first sleep in I don't know how many days," I respond.

Charly nods. I see the exhaustion on her face as well. "Not sure how to respond to this. We got an inquiry from the FBI. They want to know how we got access to a particular database."

"The FBI?" I must be standing there with my mouth open because

Charly looks at me sidewise, "Why would they be concerned about a public database?"

Charly frowns, "Because it's not public. It was necessary to get the results we need. We knew of its existence because we built and maintain it for a certain customer. We didn't think they would notice..."

Chapter Fifty-Three: Jazmin Braveheart

All I can feel is how much my face hurts and throat aches and my vagina is unbelievably sore where he pushed his finger in. It's like nothing I've ever experienced, never having been sick even one day of my life. I've been pumped so full of all the right foods, vitamins and minerals I've never experienced sickness or real aches or pains. Never exercised hard enough to pull a muscle since my exercise routines build up slowly to get to optimal strength. But now everything hurts and I'm having trouble even thinking.

I hear the bedroom door whipped open as it bangs off the wall. Aces comes charging out of the bedroom, straight at me. "No! Get away from me!" I move to put the kitchen table between him and me, but he comes right over the top of it. I duck into the dining room just off the kitchen, try to stay around the other side of the dining room table, but again he comes across the top.

I flee down the short hallway to the family room, but stop short as I look out the window and see a rapidly growing red and yellowish glow through the trees, not so far away. *What I'm seeing can't be good.* Sanders is up on his feet looking out as well.

Aces piles into me from behind, taking me down on the floor. He's on top of me. I don't know what to think, whether anyone will try to help me or just let me burn up as the wildfires consumes this place. But Stash comes flying out of the bedroom. He gets Aces in a choke hold "It's over!" Stash yells at him, although Aces swings wildly trying to get hold of Stash to break the choke hold. I don't know if they both see the approaching fire or what, but I hear Stash say, "Shit, what's that?" Aces apparently sees it and stops trying to grab Stash, who lets go and stands back.

Now Rocketman comes up beside Aces, but he's looking out the window too.

"It's not a controlled burn," Sanders explains to everyone.

"What do you mean?" Rocketman asks.

"The Forest Service burns sections of the forest every year. But only where the underbrush has grown up and dried out so much it sets the conditions for a wildfire," Sanders explains. "Doing a controlled burn they can keep it from getting out of control and preserve the trees they want. But it's always well contained and enables new growth to start. What you're seeing is a wildfire coming straight at us. From the look of it we don't have a lot of time to get out of here."

Aces gets up off me and Sanders helps me up. The fire is closer than my first observation of it before Aces took me down. I look at Stash who seems bewildered.

Rocketman shrugs, "Hey I came here in the dark and didn't see shit."

Aces isn't talking but also isn't paying attention to me now. He may be agreeing with Sanders. Aces turns and heads for the door. Rocketman and Stash are after him, probably to make sure he doesn't leave without us.

We all pile into the auton. Stash gets behind the wheel. "Take us to Truckee, but avoid the fires."

The vehicle doesn't move.

"It doesn't understand your command about the fires," I tell Stash. "It will take us the shortest route regardless, unless you drive."

Stash looks around at me, apparently judging whether I know what I'm talking about.

"We better go," Sanders reminds Stash. "We don't have much time."

"Wait," Rocketman stops Stash. "How do we know the fire is coming here? It might be going in some other direction. How do we know this isn't just an attempt to get us out where people will see her? Call the police on us?"

Sanders shakes his head, "You want to die here, be my guest. But the rest of us are leaving before this place burns to the ground with or without you in it. From what I saw coming here, there's only one way in and out. If we don't get out now, we likely won't."

"How do you know so much?" Rocketman pushes back.

"I hike this forest every week. Have for a couple decades. I've watched the Forest Service do their controlled burns, seen what happens when it's controlled. I've been here when wildfires have blown through, but have always been lucky enough to survive them. I can tell you right now, this isn't one you want to mess with. The heat and winds are up and the drought's been particularly bad for the last several years. There's no way they're going to put this one out quickly. Not even a possibility."

Rocketman's resolution seems to be wavering, wondering if he stays if he will get out. Rocketman looks to Aces, apparently wanting his thoughts. But Aces is just glaring at me. He doesn't even acknowledge Rocketman. Next Rocketman looks to Stash, who seems unable to make a decision. Rocketman finally just says to Stash, "Fuck it. Do what you want."

Stash immediately turns and starts the auton, much to everyone's surprise. We head down the long dark drive, past the towering tree trunks hiding this house from the road. As we get to the two-lane road we'd taken to get here, Stash asks, "Do we go towards the fire or what happens if we go the other way?" He head nods in the opposite direction.

Rocketman pulls out his phone and almost instantly realizes, "We don't have service out here."

"So no maps." Stash confirms.

Stash stops the auton and looks around toward Sanders, "You know this area, what do you think?"

Sanders considers, shaking his head. "I don't know this particular road. You did a good job of getting even me lost. From what I know about the area, there are a lot of roads going nowhere, meaning they don't connect to another. Given how remote this is, I'd have to say it's more likely there's no place to go that way."

Rocketman isn't buying Sanders' expertise. "Unless we go right and get to a place where we're past where the fire comes through. Then we can just wait it out and come back if this place is still standing,"

"You're asking me to think I know more than I do," Stash responds and turns left, back the way we came in. We're now heading directly towards the fire. We can see it has gotten a lot closer.

"It's moving fast," Sanders whispers to me, but everyone in the auton hears him. "Even faster than I estimated. This is going to be bad."

"What are you saying?" Stash asks over his shoulder.

"I'd drive faster if I were you," Sanders responds with fear now evident in his voice.

Stash glances up at Sanders in the rearview mirror. But then I feel the auton accelerate.

It isn't long before I see the actual trees on fire, the bright orange, red and yellow flames engulfing one and jumping to the next. It seems to almost be alive as the winds drive the flames forward almost directly towards our fast moving auton. We are coming together at an incredible speed.

"The fire's going to jump the road just up ahead," Sanders informs us, shaking his head.

"What do I do?" Stash asks, sounding like he's afraid to do anything.

I study the flames as does Sanders. I'm not sure what he's looking at, but I'm trying to judge the speed at which the flames are coming at us. All I can tell for sure is they seem to be moving faster than we are, not a good thing. *Don't think we can outrun them.* The flames start up on the other side of the highway and it now looks like we are driving toward a tunnel of flames.

"All you can do is drive into it," Sanders finally pronounces, although I can tell he wishes there was another possibility.

"What? You've got to be shitting me," Stash shakes his head which turns side-to-side taking the whole fire in.

Rocketman seems glued wide-eyed to the windshield.

Aces still stares at me, ignoring the potential death sentence Sanders has just given us. I don't look at Aces, but just hope he's not going to take advantage of Stash being occupied trying to get us out of here to finish what he tried to start in the bedroom. My face is still numb, I still can't hardly swallow, and I feel like I need to go pee, but I'm not about to give him the satisfaction of knowing he hurt me.

I get up and stand behind Stash just as a precaution. We drive into the tunnel of flames. We are in the midst of the fire with everything on both sides of the road ablaze. The air conditioning is quickly overwhelmed. The temperature in the auton immediately starts rising.

"Turn up the fan, blow the air through," I point to the button on the screen next to Stash. "Moving air is cooler."

Stash complies and keeps the car moving as fast as possible, but then another vehicle comes out of a side road right in front of us. We nearly crash into it, but somehow Stash avoids the collision. Only now we are behind a slower moving vehicle. I look up the road the car came out of, I see a smallish two-story log house totally ablaze with the front door open. It collapses into the fire having burned its structure out from beneath the roof.

"Can't you pass it?" Rocketman sounds impatient, probably because we are engulfed in flames. In only a moment the vehicle ahead of us comes to a stop. "Holy shit. What now?"

Stash tries to look around the vehicle ahead of us, "Looks like trees down across the road."

"We can't go over them," Sanders informs everyone.

I look around and see two more houses set back a ways on my right fully engaged in the flames.

"What do we do?" Stash asks anyone willing to answer. "We're in an inferno."

I'm desperately looking around, realizing we won't get out of here if we don't find another way. I'm just beginning to think we need to turn around and go back when I spot what looks like a road, "What's that?" I point to my left.

"Power line," Sanders identifies it. "They clear cut a right of way around the power line. Flames have jumped it already so not even a break is slowing this down. Would be rough, but likely a way out."

Stash doesn't wait for further instructions, but starts backing up, "Where?"

"Right there," I point it out to him.

"Transmission line," Stash notes, "It has a bigger right of way because the towers are higher."

Stash backs up and maneuvers onto the power line right-of-way. Sanders was right, this is much rougher than the road. The auton rocks back and forth as we crawl over rocks and uneven ground, but we are able to keep moving. We are surrounded by fire and the heat continues to rise in our auton. I feel the sweat drop into my eyes. Trees fully aflame drop into the right-of-way right before us, but the cleared area is wide enough we can drive around them. The progress remains slow. At least Aces hasn't made a move on me. Rocketman hasn't said a word, probably holding his breath and wondering what will happen if or when we get past the fire. I'm already trying to figure out some means of escaping once we are clear, but so far no plan has come to me.

HAPPINESS

I feel a bump as a wheel drops into a hole. The auton suddenly comes to a stop. Stash tries to drive the auton out of the hole, but the tire spins and spins without gaining traction.

"We're not going any further," Sanders announces. Everyone just looks at him, disbelieving.

Chapter Fifty-Four: Peter Tate

Sheriff Dale was kind enough to pick me up at the Amtrak station and drop me at my hotel. It gave us a few minutes to talk. The Sheriff said he wasn't going to be able to spend much time working my missing person right now because a wild fire had started north of the city since we talked. During wildfires it's all hands on-deck. I asked if I could ride along. Another pair of hands I'd said, not having been out in an actual wild fire before. I quickly regret making the offer.

The Sheriff drives over to the area of the fire and is going house-to-house to get people to leave their homes before the fire comes through. He is able to identify the expected route of the fire on the laptop in his car.

"The damn wind has picked up at just the wrong time," he says as we leave a home where the owner and his family were fast asleep, not even aware of the oncoming danger.

"You ever find people out here who have no means of getting out?" I ask looking at the old beat up Ford station wagon this family owns.

"Usually everyone has a truck. But occasionally we find someone who can't get a vehicle started. In those situations we take them out, if possible."

"Why wouldn't you be able to get them out?"

"More of them than fit in the car I'm driving," the Sheriff responds, glancing around as we head to the next house about a half mile away according to the map on his lap top.

"Is anyone working those houses east of us?" I point out houses identified on his map now very close to the rapidly-advancing raging inferno.

"Yes, my deputies. All the fire crews are cutting fire breaks. Try to stop it from advancing by starving it of trees or underbrush."

"Or houses," I note seeing the markings for homes already in the area showing where the fire rushes across more and more land.

"We don't talk about the houses," Sheriff Dale responds with clear regret.

We soon find the next house, I go to the door while Sheriff Dale checks in with his deputies. I knock realizing it's probably 2:00 am. I knock again, this time a man, likely early thirties, long hair and beard comes to the door wearing just a pair of blue jeans and tattoos on his left arm. He looks at me sleepily. "What?"

"Wildfire coming this way. You need to gather your family and head west as quickly as possible," I repeat what I'd heard the Sheriff say.

"Who are you?"

"I'm in town helping the Sheriff. He's in the car if you want to talk with him."

The man peers out, sees it's a Sheriff's car, and sees the Sheriff sitting behind the wheel talking. "I'll take your word for it. How much time I got?"

"Winds are strong tonight. Probably not more than thirty minutes.

I hear a woman's voice calling from inside, "What is it Jerome?"

"Got a fire coming our way," the man she called Jerome responds, "We need to head out of here, so get dressed and bring the bank information, we may need it."

"Good luck," I nod to the man named Jerome and walk back to the car.

As I get in Sheriff Dale remarks, "Buckle up, need to go check out a report."

I don't question his advice as I assume he's planning to drive faster than normal conditions would permit. It only takes a few moments to confirm my assumption.

It takes another twenty minutes to reach his destination, a transmission line where it comes out of the fire. Didn't realize we were going to get this close. The fire continues to rage southeast and the power line emerges from the flames in a southwesterly direction. As we pull up under the power lines and look back towards the fire I see several people making their way on foot, coming out of the inferno.

"Looks like there's more of them than we have room for," I note.

"Deputy will be here in a couple minutes with another car."

We sit and wait for the people on foot to come over to where we are, but notice they stop.

"What do you think?" I ask the Sheriff.

"Only one reason folks don't want to talk to a Sheriff," he gets out of his side.

I do the same and follow along. I now see there are five of them. One looks to be a woman all dressed in black. *What has the fire flushed out?* I wonder.

They apparently realize they have no choice but to talk with us and wait for us to reach them. "Would have been easier if you had come to us," Sheriff Dale begins as we slow our approach. We are about seventy-five feet from them. One, who has a ski mask on, moves quickly to grab the girl, but she breaks free and sprints away from him directly towards us. The guy with the ski mask chases after her, but the Sheriff draws his service revolver and yells, "Stop where you are, I'm armed."

The guy with the ski mask apparently realizes he's not going to catch her and stops, raising his hands into the air. Two of the three who stayed where they were raise theirs as well. One does not. *Curious.*

As the girl gets close she calls out in a hoarse voice, "I'm Jazmin Braveheart."

"You're safe now," I respond as the Sheriff keeps walking towards the others with his gun drawn.

I turn around as I hear an auton door close. A deputy has arrived and is walking out towards us. I turn back towards Jazmin, "Do you know who I am?"

Jazmin looks at me but doesn't answer.

For the first time I notice a bad welt on her face just below her right eye. Notice red marks on her throat. "Are you okay?"

"Think so," she kind of croaks in comparison to the more emphatic effort to tell us who she is.

I look at the wildfire continuing to rage just a very short distance from us, lighting up the nighttime sky and blowing sparks in every direction.

I hear the Sheriff say, "Sanders, what the hell are you doing mixed up in all this?"

Chapter Fifty-Five: Jazmin Braveheart

When I arrived home I told Jason and Ophelia I didn't want to talk about any of it until I had enough time to put it all into perspective although they listened as I gave the detective my statement. Had to as the detective wouldn't let me come home until I did. It's been a week now. I'm back on my diet, although I lost nearly ten pounds. Even I thought it was too much. I haven't gained much back but at least I'm not losing more. Maybe Ophelia will let me get the breast augmentation I was talking with Phoebe about when this all started. It seems so long ago, but I remember thinking I hardly recognized myself in the simulation. I hardly recognize myself now but not in a good way.

It was nice meeting Ophelia's first husband. She never talked about him before, but now she's been willing to answer my questions about him. And to think he could have been my father if Ophelia hadn't gotten sick of him. Guess he was very different back then. Something I have to remember. People change. Stash seemed to, catching me by surprise. I've changed. From what I learned having changed is probably a good thing. As I think about the last days, I'll never be what I was. Aces' attempt to rape me alone has changed me more than anything. I never want to feel that helpless ever again.

Sanders and I speak every day. He even agreed to come here to meet Jason and Ophelia. No, it's nothing like what you're thinking. Sanders is a mentor for me. I want Jason and Ophelia to meet my other mentor, someone who is going to continue educating me on the world they are unfamiliar with, but he knows so well.

Speaking of Ophelia, she knocks and enters my room, "Not on with Phoebe?" she asks.

I shake my head, which she takes in her hands and inspects my face, "The welt is nearly gone. Do you want to talk about it yet?"

I shake my head.

"The UK police took Grendele's Modor into custody today," Ophelia informs me. She was aware from my statement to the detective, but I've not mentioned her to Jason or Ophelia, not mentioned the attempted rape, not mentioned so much that happened to me. The detective said I'll probably be called to testify when my case goes to court, but he had no idea when it will happen. I just don't want to go back through it. At least not yet.

"Ironic she never figured out the reason Jason couldn't get the algorithms working is because I developed the original base system," I reflect having heard the ransom demand from Jason.

Ophelia gives me a hug. "I'm just so relieved and happy you're home."

"You know I learned something important over the last few days," I try not to be too blunt about this discussion I've wanted to have, but haven't found the right opening.

"What?" Ophelia seems curious about why I'm raising this.

"Happiness isn't situation specific," I lay on her. "I discovered people can be happy despite their circumstances. Poor people who are happy even though they have to deal with many unseen viruses and pollution of the air and water and congestion of traffic and poor quality of food and sanitary conditions and even homelessness. And I met people who have always been wealthy, but live relatively simply and have reconnected to nature. I guess what's important is not how you live, but what you do with the life you have."

"What are you trying to tell me?" Ophelia seems suspicious I've been indoctrinated by aliens.

"What I'm trying to say is I now have an appreciation for many things I'd not had just living here. I want to experience life, not virtually, but in person. I want to learn to enjoy and recognize smells as simple as pine trees or dirt, or fire or flowers. I can't when I spend my whole life in a cocoon."

"You've had your experience," Ophelia pushes back. "And we almost lost you because of it."

"There's so much more to the world than electrons. I know you and Jason make your living from them and it's likely how I'll make mine. But living to me now entails experiencing the world and putting it into historical, natural and technological context. I think, and I may be wrong, but I think I need a balance you and Jason have never sought. A deeper understanding of the world we live in. And a commitment to make the world better not just from algorithms. To me, doing and being more is happiness. What will make me happy. At least for now."

The End

About the Author

dhtreichler is a futurist, technologist and strategist who toured the global garden spots as a defense contractor executive for fifteen years. His assignments covered intelligence, training and battlefield systems integrating state of the art technology to keep Americans safe. His novels grew out of a need to deeply understand how our world is changing, developing scenarios and then populating them with people who must confront how increasingly sophisticated technology is transforming our lives and how men and women establish relationships in a mediated world.

Keep up with all of dhtreichler's latest work and essays at www.dhtreichler.com and www.GlobalVinoSnob.com.

Also by dhtreichler

Courage

TRUTH

A Cat's Redemption

CHOICES

HOPE

Emergence

Barely Human

The Ghost in the Machine: a novel

World Without Work

The Great American Cat Novel

My Life as a Frog

Life After

Lucifer

The Tragic Flaw

Succession

The End Game

I Believe in You

Rik's

The Illustrated Bearmas Reader – Ralph's Ordeals

The First Bearmas

Made in the USA
Columbia, SC
30 August 2020